Whistle in the Dark

Lisa Caretti

Eloquent Books
New York, New York

Eloquent Books
An imprint of AEG Publishing Group
845 Third Avenue, 6th Floor – 6016
New York, NY 10022
http://www.eloquentbooks.com

ISBN: 978-1-60693-743-3, 1-60693-743-X

Printed in the United States of America

Book Design: Bruce Salender

The wise man in the storm prays God, not for safety from danger, but for deliverance from fear.

—Ralph Waldo Emerson, *Journals*, 1833

Dedication

I dedicate this book to Richard, Maggie and Joey. Though you do not know this, you were my inspiration.

Acknowledgments

All my appreciation and gratitude to:

My sister Laura and my brother-in-Law Tim, for your continuous support, guidance and endless encouragement.

My dear friend Slim (Sharon Shea) who would eagerly wait in anticipation each morning for a new chapter to be emailed over. Thank you for falling in love with the story from the first page, you kept me going.

My mother, thank you for your editing and proofreading talents.

My editor Kathleen Marusak, who was a joy to work with. Many thanks for all your hard work and patience.

Betsey Backe, for your professional contributions, helpful suggestions and inspiration.

And last of all, to my husband Joe for having absolute belief in me without actually having read the book.

Chapter One

Dena whipped her car into the driveway, jumped out and ran up the brick path to her recently painted red front door then fumbled to get the right key in the lock.

Finally getting the old door unlocked, she dashed through her spacious colonial house to the newer addition that sat in back. With lots of windows to allow the sun to come in while offering a breathtaking view of the landscape's trees and flowers, it resembled more a sunroom than a psychologist's office.

Dena hated to be late for anything. Hair appointments, lunch dates or even church. She was always on time. In fact, she usually arrived at least fifteen minutes early, just to be safe. That was one of the reasons her patients came to her. She never had to worry about getting caught in traffic or bad weather. She was never late to their appointments; she simply had to run down the stairs.

That is why it brought her great distress to realize *she* of all people was going to be late. To her, it was unthinkable that she would be late to visit the new home of her oldest and dearest friends. However, after ten minutes into her trip, she discovered that the directions and, of course, Marcy's not yet published phone number, had been left behind in her office. Dena recalled taking down those directions while chatting with Marcy and, in her excitement to see her friend, forgot to grab them.

Dena tossed her purse and keys on the desk and frantically began her search. After a few minutes of scattering papers around, she became aware on some level that she was hearing voices. She tilted her head to the side as she tried to concentrate on their source. Male voices. Perhaps someone was out back working on the power lines, she thought as she looked out the window behind her desk. Her backyard appeared peaceful and inviting and its only occupant was a blue jay in the birdfeeder. She most likely left the radio on in the kitchen and made a mental note to check it on her way out.

She continued her search for the missing directions when abruptly her hand stopped by the answering machine. The "in use" light was on, and she realized that the voices seemed to be coming from her phone. Wondering if perhaps she had hit the play button by mistake, she leaned towards the machine to take a closer look.

The delicate hairs on the back of her neck stood on end and a deep shiver traveled down her spine. Something was wrong here. This was a conversation, not a recording. Her purse must have hit the speaker phone button when she threw it on the desk. Two things then quickly became clear: someone was talking about her and that someone was in her house.

"Yeah, that's the info I got," the deep voice said. *"The doctor's here alone every morning until her first appointment comes at 10:00. But, like I said, she's not here. The house is empty."*

A crisp, professional voice replied, *"Well, our client will be very disappointed. Today was definitely the day to take care of this."*

Though the words made no sense, she felt fear and knew she had to get out. Hastily grabbing her car keys, her hand hit a stapler on the desk and sent it flying into the metal wastepaper basket. Its landing made a thunderous crashing noise that gave Dena's heart a start.

"Wait..." the deep voice said, *"I think she's here. I'll call you back."*

He's coming for me. Run! Get out now! Dena's mind screamed.

She ran through the hall towards the front door, aware someone was pounding down the stairs just behind her. She tripped over a rug by the front door and stumbled, knocking over a coat rack on her way down. Pulling herself to her feet she pushed the coat rack behind her, just as his hand made contact with her hair, snapping her head painfully back. His face was so close behind her that she could smell his sour breath. She gave the heavy oak coat tree a hard thrust backwards; one of its branches made contact with what she thought was his eye.

"Bitch!" he yelled, his hands automatically going to his face.

She made a break for it, afraid that at any moment a hand would grab her and tackle her down or shoot her in the back.

She ran to her car and was unbelievably grateful she was still clutching her keys and that this one time, she did not lock her car door. She willed her hands to stop shaking so she could get the key in the ignition, and after several attempts, they finally obeyed.

She felt him getting closer, but she refused to look. Instead, she used all her concentration to perform the simple task of putting the car in reverse, backing out of her driveway and getting the hell out of there as fast as possible.

She used the drive to the police station to calm herself, using the techniques she taught and knew well. Now you get to practice what you preach, she told herself. Besides, this is not the first time you have been terrified. Hell, you should be a real pro at this by now.

She only hoped this encounter with the police would be more positive than her last.

Chapter Two

Dena sat in the busy police station and watched the flurry of activity buzz around her as she waited for an officer to take her statement. The smell of burnt coffee and stale cigarette smoke permeated the musty air and did nothing to help her already nauseous stomach. She glanced down at her watch and decided she had about one more minute before she would either vomit right here on the ugly worn-out tile or make a dash for the front door.

"Ms. Davis," said a too thin, tired looking female officer who approached her. "If you will follow me to the desk over there, I can take your statement now."

"I'm Detective Thatcher," she said with a solemn and unpleasant look on her face, her hand pointing to the chair to indicate Dena should have a seat. "Let's hear it."

Good thing she's not a doctor with that bedside manner, Dena thought. She thought of all the victims before her that had to sit in front of Detective Thatcher and share their personal tragedy and she felt deeply sorry for them. She ran though her story, noticing for the first time her voice was hoarse, like she had been screaming.

"So, Ms., ah, Davis," officer Thatcher said. "You said you overheard some men talking on the phone, could it have just been that your lines crossed with someone else and you were hearing their conversation, or a message on your answering machine that was playing back?"

Officer Thatcher sat on the edge of the desk as she stared down at Dena. At thirty-one years old, she had mastered how to look tough. Years of sun worship gave her the leathery hard appearance of someone older and more experienced.

Dena stared back at the hardened detective and clearly understood what the woman was saying. She thought Dena either fabricated the entire tale or must be on something. Not again, she thought. This cannot be happening to me again. I am not that stupid scared little girl anymore that no one believes. I am a successful psychologist with a sound reputation and practice. "No officer...Thatcher, I did not happen to overhear a party line. I told you, I hit the speaker phone button by mistake and I could hear their conversation." Dena's voice still remained calm; she was always the cool professional, in full control.

"The man in the house must have heard me; he came running down the stairs. He pulled my hair, for God's sake! I did not imagine that."

Just then the detective's partner made his way over to them. Detective Begley, who had been quietly filling out the report forms two desks over, finally spoke up.

"I am Detective Begley, Ms." He put his hand out to shake, which she took gratefully.

"I understand you've had quite a scare today. Trust me, we do want to get to the bottom of this."

With quite a few more years on the force than his partner, Bob Begley knew how to get information from victims as well as suspects while keeping them from becoming hysterical. But this one was a cool customer. She seemed so calm and relaxed, as if she were here to help them in some way. "However, we did send a cruiser to your house and they came up with nothing. No one was there."

"What did you expect to find, detective?" Dena gave them both a thoughtful look. "That they would stay and have lunch?"

"No, but we did expect to find perhaps a broken lock, some sign of forced entry. Any sign that someone other than you had been there," Officer Begley replied gently.

"Officers, I heard two men talking and I am sure one of them was *IN MY HOUSE!*" This time she did start to show her anger. "They were discussing their disappointment that I was not there as planned." Dena could see she was not getting anywhere with this and let her voice drop. "And that their client wanted it taken care of today."

Officer Thatcher glanced at her watch; the mention of lunch reminded her she had a date. "OK, who would want to hurt you?" she asked as she reached over the desk to grab hold of the report from her partner. "Do you have many enemies in your line of work?" Scanning the sheet to see what this lady did for a living, she found nothing. "What *do* you do for a living, Ms. Davis?"

"Actually, it is Dr. Davis, Officer Thatcher. I am a psychologist who specializes in grief therapy and trauma. My office is in my home and I hold my first appointment at 10:00 am, so I am always home in the morning." Dena could see at least she had their attention now. "This morning was different. I took the morning off to visit a friend in her new home. That is why I went back to the house. I had left the directions on my desk."

"How about an ex-husband or boyfriend? Or perhaps a friend pulling a prank on you? Perhaps one of your patients?" offered Detective Thatcher.

"No. There is no one who wants to hurt me. And my patients are victims who have been wounded physically and emotionally, they are not interested in stupid pranks. As for my friends, none of them would find this even remotely funny." She turned and looked directly at the male officer.

"What is the next step, Detective Begley?"

"Well, we have your report here, Ms., ur, Dr. Davis. And to be honest, since nothing was missing or even vandalized, there is nothing we can do. Heck, even if your house was tossed, there isn't much we could do except see if the things missing show up later."

"What about the phone conversation I overheard? Doesn't that bother you?" Dena noticed her hands were clenched in fists, an old habit making its way back. She took in a deep, cleansing breath and willed herself to be calm. "I can tell you, *detectives,* it sure bothers me."

Officer Thatcher, taking another quick peek at her watch, stood up from her perch on the desk, signifying that she was finished. "OK, well, we have everything we need. If you have any other problems give us a call. We do understand your concern, but try to see it from our point of view. Nothing was missing or even moved in your home and you really didn't see anyone either. So basically, we got nothing."

So this is it, thought Dena. I am on my own. "OK, I'll be sure to call you if I have any other unwelcome guests."

"You do that," replied Thatcher as she hurried out of the room.

"Thank you for at least pretending I am not a nut case, Officer Begley. I'll get out of your hair now." She knew she was not crazy. She did hear voices and she certainly had a scuffle with someone at her front door. And though she couldn't explain it, she knew he would be back.

Begley came over to her and sat in the chair next to her, a serious, concerned look on his face. "I know someone who can help you, who can do the digging we can't. You ought to look him up."

Dena looked down at the white business card in her hand. In bold black letters, it simply read: "Nick O'Neal, Private Investigator."

Chapter Three

Becoming a private investigator had not been Nick O'Neal's first career choice, not even his second. But opening his agency gave him the opportunity to pursue his one true passion: writing.

Being a private eye was a lot more exciting on TV than it was in real life. Most investigative work these days was done by tapping computer keys rather than pounding the pavement, and since he had Edward to handle the technical side of things, he got to manage the more exciting tasks. Like surveillance work. He had once written the entire outline for a murder mystery while keeping tabs on a wealthy, cheating husband for his client.

She happily cleaned her ex-husband's clock in court and he got his first bestseller.

His company handled just about anything that needed investigating, from missing persons to simple background checks. They had even helped solve a couple murders along the way and developed a good rapport with the police department. They always had plenty of work and the office hummed with activity.

He finished wrapping up some paperwork on an old case while waiting for his next appointment to arrive. A lady had called and sounded desperate, pleading with his secretary to be seen today. He had been on his way out the door and headed for the gym when his assistant Margaret convinced him to stay, reminding him of the files and mail that cluttered his desk.

He agreed to stay only because she was right about the paperwork. He did indeed have a stack of mail that had been pushed off to the furthest possible corner of his desk without actually falling on the floor. He also had in his possession four or five files to sign off on that billing was anxiously waiting for him to hand over.

A frantic phone call from anyone who needed to be seen right away was either from a woman who was sure her husband was cheating on her or someone convinced that their neighbor was a terrorist.

The intercom buzzed and his feisty but loyal secretary announced that his client had arrived. He didn't bother to correct her that she was not a client yet or that he had only promised to give her ten minutes before shipping her off to someone else. "A Dena Davis to see you, Nick."

"OK, thanks Margaret. Send her in."

Nick caught his breath when his next appointment walked in and was secretly glad he had stuck around. She was not what he had been expecting, but then it is so hard to tell over the phone. Even though he did not speak to her directly, a mental picture had formed in his mind anyway. He guessed it was the writer in him. He watched a striking woman with long, straight sandy brown hair highlighted with streaks of gold walk towards him and hold out her hand to greet him.

"Dena Davis. Thanks for seeing me on such short notice."

Her hands were cold and trembling. He was a little surprised since she gave off such a calm, together appearance. Upon closer inspection, he wondered why he thought she was striking. In fact, he noticed that she seemed to downplay her looks. She wore little or no make-up or jewelry that he could see and her clothes were professional and appeared to be expensive.

"No problem. Nick O'Neal, and please, have a seat," he said as he walked around his desk.

"O'Neal? You don't look Irish. Too tan, plus I was expecting you to have red hair." Dena flushed a little at her comment. She hadn't actually meant to say that out loud.

Nick laughed. "My mom is a full blooded Italian. Dark skin and hair. I take after her. I got the blue eyes from my dad." He volunteered because people always asked. A tall, rather large and good-looking man of forty, he was accustomed to female interest. "What can I do for you today, Ms., or is it Mrs. Davis?"

"Please call me Dena." She took in a deep breath before beginning. Dena felt a moment of embarrassment that he too would think she was not all together there. She had learned a long time ago not to care what other people thought about her, but having this extremely handsome man stare at her was making her feel self conscious. "I just came from the police station and a Detective Begley gave me your card. He said you might be able to help me."

"What is it you need help with?" God, he hoped it was not another cheating husband thing. He had already taken two calls on that today and it was only just after noon. He had Margaret direct those to his staff but sometimes she slipped him a few just to keep him on his toes.

He walked back around his desk and sat down, indicating with his hand she should do the same.

She spoke slowly and deliberately, as if it would give her some credibility. "Today, there was a man in my house. I believe he was there to kill me or harm me in some way. But, as you can see, he failed. And because I am not dead or injured, the police are unable to help me. Can you?"

Nick was silent, letting this roll around in his mind while clicking his ball point pen. If Begley referred her, he could see why Margaret gave him the call. Finally, he spoke.

"Maybe you should start at the beginning. Tell me everything."

Dena once again went through her story. He was extremely attentive, his ocean blue eyes never leaving hers. He was also difficult to read. When she finished, he said nothing and continued to play with the pen. She was just about to say something when he spoke.

"Well, that is some story." He noticed the flicker of anger in her eyes. "Relax, Ms. Davis, I didn't say I didn't believe you. It's just one of the more intriguing cases I've heard today. To have what sounds like a hired hit man coming right to your door...any ideas on whom that client the man referred to could be?" If what she was saying was even true, he wondered what she did to invite this kind of trouble.

"No." She shrugged her shoulders and looked exasperated. "I live a simple life. I have a job I love, a few good friends and a nice house in a good neighborhood. Average would about sum it up."

"Married?" Nick asked. "Any scorned exes, or maybe a few skeletons in your closet?" Though he asked for professional reasons, he found he was curious what the answer would be.

"No." She hesitated for a moment. "I am a widow and I haven't done much dating." At the mention of her late husband Paul, she looked down at her ring finger. Just last week she finally took her wedding ring off and put it away. She was wearing it more out of guilt anyhow. It was time, well meaning friends had told her. But time for what?

"I'm sorry." And he was. "I didn't mean to bring up a painful subject but I had to know. What do you do for a living? Get along with your co-workers okay?" He let it go that she didn't say anything about the bones in the closet comment. It was a standard question he asked and one that usually got an, "Oh no, not me," response or a look of absolute panic if they thought something ugly from their past could soon be paying them a visit.

She noticed he was not writing any of this down. Was he just satisfying his curiosity on a few things before he showed her the door? Though he said he did believe her.

"I am a psychologist and my practice is out of my home in Oak Park. My patients are victims of violent crimes and sometimes people who have witnessed a brutal crime and need someone to talk to. I never work with the criminals themselves, only those whom they have preyed upon. Does this mean you will take the case, Mr. O'Neal?"

"Yes, and please, it's just Nick. Because someone was in your home, and you sound pretty sure of that, I feel you do need help. But, you have to agree to my terms or forget it. I am an ex-cop who has been around the block a few times so you will just have to trust me." He didn't mention that he was also an author under another name with a few bestsellers under his belt. Or that he opened this business to provide fresh writing material as well as an income. The trouble people got themselves into; who could make this stuff up?

"Okay," she agreed, though she was wondering if she was really overreacting. Her gut said no.

"I will be staying with you for the next couple of days and keeping a low profile in case they are watching the house. I want them to think I'm your new boyfriend, so we have to look a little cozy when we are in public."

He wondered if she would object to that part. If he was honest with himself, he might admit that was one of the reasons he took this case. A fully qualified staff sat right outside his door that was more than capable of handling anything. These days, he primarily overviewed the cases, tied up loose ends and was available to help the others whenever needed.

He also knew it probably was not necessary to have a round-the-clock bodyguard, but this could be intriguing research for a future novel. He believed someone had been in her house. You did not imagine someone grabbing hold of your hair unless you were a nutcase, which of course he couldn't rule out. He would have Edward check her out right away.

But it was the client thing she overheard that really bothered him. One does not hire someone to break into a house, unless it is a mansion or museum. No, in neighborhoods like hers, the bad guys do their own work.

He watched her play that last part out in her head and then finally ask, "When do you start?"

"Now," he said as he threw some papers in his briefcase. "First, we're going to run by my place so I can pack a few things. We're taking your car so if someone is still watching you, they will know you are home."

Dena stood at the window taking in the incredible view of Lake Michigan. His apartment was a spacious loft in what looked like an extremely pricey piece of real estate. Private investigators must do better financially than she thought.

"Maybe I should have inquired about your fee first," she said as she looked around anxiously at the contemporary but comfortable living quarters that appeared to be professionally decorated. Either that or he had a real flair for interior design. Soft beige leather couches faced a large brick fireplace and a lovely framed painting of a Tuscany hillside hung above the mantel.

"Don't worry. I'm very reasonable," he said with a grin and caught the doubtful glance she cast his way. Probably trying to analyze him just like he did when deciding if someone was dishing out bullshit. He shrugged. "I've done well with some investments," he added, to help ease her curiosity.

His home was his retreat. He had wanted a comfortable place to crawl to after work where he could escape from the scum he dealt with during the day. When he was married, he never paid much attention to decorating or even where he lived. That was Leslie's thing. But now that he was on his own, he discovered he liked nice things and had hired a decorating firm. His comfortable domain was also the place where he would lock himself away from the rest of the world, sometimes for months, when working on a new book. Something he should be thinking about doing again soon, according to his agent.

"Okay. All set," Nick said as he held up a black leather duffel bag. "Let's head back to your place now. We'll stop and pick up an early dinner. Any good take-out places around your neighborhood?"

"Yeah...we have a few." Dena was a little blown away by all this. It was too much to take in at once. Just this morning she was on her way out to visit Marcy to have a quiet breakfast with her one really close girlfriend. Now, this man she barely knew was taking charge of her life and moving in with her. "I don't know how to feel about all this." Dena confessed.

"My interest is only to save your life. You will have to give up some control of it for a while, but it won't be forever. Come on, let's get going. We'll start working over dinner."

The drive to Oak Park went by quickly, perhaps because Nick was a fast but careful driver and had pulled off a few minor traffic violations along the way.

She had chosen this town for its peaceful beauty, away from the congestion of Chicago. It had been the birthplace of Hemingway, who once had referred to Oak Park as a place where the people had wide lawns and narrow minds. And since she was a huge Hemingway fan and felt compelled to agree with what he said, she decided to call this home and always felt a sense of tranquility whenever she returned from any absence. But this time, when they pulled into her driveway, her hands started to sweat.

"Stay in the car, I'll go look around," Nick said as he jumped out, taking the keys with him.

After a few minutes Nick returned to give her the "all clear." Everything was just as she had left it that morning. It was almost as if nothing had happened. Remains from her peaceful breakfast, before all the excitement, were left in the sink. An empty coffee cup was still on the counter and crumbs from her toast on a plate. Except something was off balance.

Something was different and it hit her as soon as she walked through the side door. It was nagging at the back of her mind, begging her to pay attention. The only problem was, for the life of her, she could not think of what was wrong.

Chapter Four

Over hot plates of steaming Szechaun Shrimp and spicy Lo Mein noodles, Nick started asking questions. Who were her friends, neighbors and former co-workers? She was being most cooperative, but still he felt she was holding back. He wanted her to trust him. It would certainly make his job a whole lot easier, but if he was honest with himself, he would admit he had more than business on his mind. He mentally scolded himself and made a promise to keep his thoughts strictly on work.

"Well, so far we haven't come up with anything," Nick said in between bites. "What about your patients?" She was easy to be with. Not just because of her looks, but the relaxed way she talked and listened to him.

For her line of work, he guessed it fit. The complete opposite of his ex. Every conversation had to be about her. She hated to hear about his work and barely tolerated hearing about his family. Born into a wealthy family where no one actually had to work, Leslie thought the idea of going off to work everyday was more of a novelty. At first, being married to a cop was such a thrill. Like having a really great party trick, she would take him around her circle for all her friends to meet. Then there was her parents' disapproval, which at first, he genuinely believed upset her. Well, it's obvious love makes you stupid as well as blind.

"I'm through with relationships," he once told his buddy Pete. "Staying for breakfast is too much of a commitment." And so far, his promise had not been very challenging. Most of his dates lately gave him a headache and more often than not, made him wish he would have stayed home with a cold beer and watched football.

"I am sure you know that I cannot discuss my patients with you."

"Even if one of them wants you dead?" he replied.

"It is not one of my patients," she said firmly. "These people put their trust in me to help them. In some cases, I am the only one they will talk to. Don't forget Nick, these are victims, not criminals," she said with conviction in her voice.

"I know that some of your patients are casualties of random violence and just happen to be in the wrong place and all that. However, most murders are committed by someone the victim knew. Perhaps someone you are treating now, or even in the past, has an angry spouse that does not like them talking to you or the advice you are giving them." Nick could tell she did not want to even consider this line of reasoning and she was trying to dismiss it. But these were the facts. Back when he was a cop some of the worst runs he had been called to were domestic disturbances. In so many cases, the same man that promised to love and cherish his wife had just beat her unconscious. It made him sick to arrive at the scene, and hear the husband say she fell down the stairs or worse, she had been asking for it.

One day he snapped. He was responding to several complaints from neighbors and so he knocked on the door. The man answered with blood on his face and hands and apologized for his thoughtless wife. He said he had to teach her some manners. Nick looked behind him to the woman who lay moaning on the floor. Her face was a swollen, bloody mess. She was naked and had bruises over most of her body, some weeks old as well as fresh ones. He took the guy by the collar and shook him until his head whipped around like a rag doll while shouting, "Just what exactly did she say when she ASKED FOR IT, you asshole?" Then Nick planted an almost lethal right hook under his jaw in a trained, professional way that would not leave a mark. His partner politely whistled and looked the other way. After that he knew he needed to consider other career options, this was not something he could stay in another twenty years.

Dena abruptly stood up and walked to the refrigerator. "I need a glass of wine, would you like one?" she asked as she pulled a chilled bottle of chardonnay out and reached for two wine glasses in one fluid movement.

"Yeah, thanks," Nick replied, noticing how exhausted she seemed. Not the good doctor's ordinary day for sure and the stress was starting to take a toll on her. But she still managed to look incredibly beautiful, one of those naturals, he guessed, who looked good no matter what. She had changed into navy sweat pants with a white T-shirt and pulled her long hair into a ponytail. She resembled more of a co-ed than a doctor.

Nick took a sip of wine while watching her intently. "Why don't we take a break for the night? We can start fresh in the morning." He could keep working the entire night without so much as a cup of coffee but could sense he would get more useful information out of her after some rest. There were still numerous questions he had to ask about her patients and chances were, that was where he would find the answers. Complete strangers simply don't hire hit men to break into your house and kill you. He also wanted to know a little about her late husband but could sense it was a tender subject. Still, tomorrow it would have to come up to rule out any possible connection.

Dena retreated to her bedroom with her glass of wine and headed straight for bed. She set the glass down carefully on the nightstand and adjusted her pillows so they were stacked high behind her back and then let herself sink into them. She visually took in all her familiar pictures and possessions, hoping the normalcy of her room would relax her. She closed her eyes to replay the day's events in her mind and to see if anything came to mind. Maybe it was a case of mistaken identity, she thought, because who could want her dead? Or was she just overreacting? Robberies take place everyday in all neighborhoods and most likely, she just interrupted one in progress. That had to be it. To her surprise, sleep was coming quickly and the events of the day started drifting slowly away.

A glimmer that something was off when she returned home today was the last conscious thought she had before she drifted off.

It came to her at 4:00 am.

She bolted out of bed and stood in the middle of the room, unaware that her clothes were drenched in perspiration.

Taking in fast shallow breaths of air while running her fingers through her hair, Dena tried to put the fragments of her dream together.

It really made no sense at all, but then again dreams seldom do.

She paced around the room, closing her eyes and allowing the nightmare to play out again in her mind. Like rewinding a movie, she waited until she could recall the beginning, than sat on the edge of the bed to watch the mental images replay.

"Paul! My God, what happened to you?" Dena cried out. *"Where have you been?"*

Paul began walking towards her, through the thick and misty jungle. She then noticed his clothes were torn and bloody, every inch of his body covered with wounds and dried blood.

"Please Dena," he begged *"I need your help. You're the only one who can help."* *He stopped walking with his hands outstretched.*

"What, Paul? Anything."

"You've got to remember. Try, for God's sake, Dena!" he sounded desperate and almost angry. *"You are running out of time."*

Frustrated, she said "I don't understand. What is it you

want me to remember? I want to help you, Paul!"

"No!" He yelled. "You have to help yourself."

The mist was getting thicker, and she reached out to touch his battered face when he disappeared into the fog.

Suddenly she was greeted with the overpowering smell of cologne, so strong she started to gag. Instantly she awoke.

A deep, penetrating chill ran down her spine and a prickly sensation covered her skin.

Not just any cologne. Paul's favorite scent made especially for him years ago by his sister, a chemist who worked for a fragrance manufacturer. She had surprised him one year for Christmas with his own unique scent and it would always bring on instant memories when she smelled it. That was why she threw it away after he died; she did not want the reminder and she couldn't very well give it away to someone else.

It was also what had greeted her yesterday when she returned home with Nick.

The next morning Dena felt she was in a daze as she made her way to the shower. She peeled off her sweats and threw them in the hamper and turned the faucet on high, letting the water get hot. Some of the tension began to melt away as she lathered up with a wonderful French milled soap that was her favorite. Ah, it's the little luxuries in life that bring such pleasure, and she always allowed herself a few. Actually, she allowed herself only two extravagances other than opulent bath products to indulge in. She had a passion for fine wine and excellent coffee.

She finished up her shower and with clean hair and smoothly shaved legs, she felt like a new woman. Well, maybe not a brand new woman, but one much improved anyway.

After slipping on a pair of well worn jeans, an oversized pale pink cotton sweater and some tan leather mules, she walked into the kitchen to start the coffee.

Dena looked up at the clock on the wall and wondered what time Nick would get up. The guest bedroom door was still closed, so she probably had some time to herself. Pulling open a cupboard door, she took out her French press. Yes, today was definitely justification for good coffee. The only problem with using a press was that it took longer and her need for caffeine was urgent, but she knew the end results would be worth the wait. After completing the task of putting the coffee together, she stood at the kitchen island and carefully went over the scattered pictures in her dream.

Many dreams are like a puzzle. Fit together the bits and pieces and you have a message from your subconscious. Sometimes it may be a deep, buried secret that desperately needs to surface; others are just hints about yourself, like you are concerned about money or afraid of failing.

Dena poured some coffee and cream into one of her favorite mugs and sat at the table that looked out into her yard, warming her hands on the steaming mug. Thoughts of a different, distant nightmare from her past tried to surface, but she pushed them aside. Instead, she did what she always did when inner turmoil tore at her heart; she focused on someone else's fears or grief.

A former patient came to mind whom she had treated early on in her career, before she started specializing.

Martha Levins had come to her to be treated for severe depression and mentioned one day a recurring dream that she had over the years. She dreamt she was locked in a small room or a closet and could not move or speak; the floor beneath her was wet and she knew without looking she was sitting on several coins that felt more like rocks. She was hungry, cold and extremely uncomfortable and she could not move to get herself out. And though she did not know why, she knew she was terrified.

After Martha underwent a series of several therapy and hypnosis sessions, clues began to surface about her past and finally, almost a year later, she was able to recall what had happened.

There was a small crack in the closet door that she was peering through and although she did not want to see these horrible images in front of her, little Martha could not pull her eyes away.

Just minutes before, her father had thrown her in the closet after she saw a car pull up in front of the house. "Keep quiet, Martha, don't make a sound no matter what," her father had warned. She promised she would not, for she loved to make her daddy happy. She bit her lip to keep from crying out when she saw two men kicking her daddy in the stomach and swinging a bat at his head. They were very mad at him and yelling the whole time. She sat there like a good girl, unaware of how hard her heart was pounding or that she had wet herself and she was oblivious to the fact that the blood from her swollen lip was ruining her new beautiful dress. She had no conscious thoughts, none that she would remember later anyway, as she sat quietly in that same position for nearly four hours until her mother found her.

No counseling sessions followed Martha's terror. Her mother thought it would be best if they never spoke of it again. And they didn't. They never discussed how he died and the exact date of his death was never remembered.

After Martha Levins relived that awful day, another memory rose to the surface. Her father had hidden money under the boards of the closet floor. It had been their little secret; she was not to tell anyone, even her mother. And she never did until now.

After she'd witnessed something so horrifying and traumatic as a small child, it was amazing Martha hadn't suffered from more severe psychosis.

Fortunately, Martha's sister still lived in that same house and when she came back for her follow up appointment, she informed Dena that she and her sister located the money. When they found the stash, almost a million dollars, they knew then that their father was involved in something unsavory and perhaps was caught stealing. The mafia crossed Dena's mind but she believed Martha would come to her own conclusions.

"Well," Dena thought, "It would be nice if I could make some sense out of my own dream, though I'm pretty sure it's not going to lead to a stashed away fortune."

With the feeling that someone was watching her, Dena

glanced up at the kitchen doorway and saw Nick standing in the frame with a thoughtful look on his face.

"I thought I smelled coffee, may I?" he made his way over to the coffee set up on the counter.

"Please, help yourself. The mugs are in the top cabinet to the right of the sink." It somehow felt intimate sharing a kitchen with someone at 6:30 in the morning, almost like they were living together. But they were not, Dena reminded herself. This man is here to help me and this is only a job for him.

Nick sat down across from her and stared out the window as a brilliant orange and yellow sun was just starting to make its entrance into a new day.

"Rough night?" Nick asked softly, his eyes still focused on the sunrise.

The simple question took her by surprise.

"What makes you say that?" Dena reluctantly asked. *God, please tell me I didn't cry out in my sleep.* Talking in her sleep, sleep walking and nightmares were a part of the past. She had worked through those problems and was finally no longer afraid to close her eyes at night.

"You just look like you could have used more sleep," Nick replied casually. OK, if she didn't want to talk about it that was fine with him, but she looked terrible. Dark blue smudges rested under eyes that were already puffy and red, like she had been crying. There was a dramatic change in her appearance since last night. The stress was starting to take its toll. But even with her bags and circles he could not help noticing that her eyes were beautiful, a unique hazel color with long dark lashes. They were captivating, and he had to force his own eyes to focus somewhere else. Unfortunately, his gaze landed on another part of her anatomy that had him guessing. What was she hiding under all those baggy shirts? Reluctantly, he dragged his eyes away from her body and forced them to look down at his coffee.

Besides, you are only a paid bodyguard to her and she is a widow, still in mourning. Not a winning combination.

"Well, I did toss and turn a bit last night," she said as she got up to refill her coffee and go through the process of making more. "How about some breakfast? I could scramble up a couple of eggs."

"That sounds great, thanks," Nick said as he ran a hand over the stubble on his chin, wishing he would have taken the time to shower and shave before joining Dena in the kitchen.

With her back to him as she cracked eggs in a bowl she said, "Why don't you go shower while I cook?"

Nick gave the back of her head a quizzical look as she read his mind. *She must be dammed good at her job.*

"Yeah, I think I'll do that," he said as he headed towards the door.

Fifteen minutes later Nick reappeared just as Dena was putting the plates on the table. Dressed in sporty looking khaki Chinos and a white Polo shirt that showed off his well built arms, he was ready to get down to business and start his day.

He dropped a manila folder on the table as he sat down across from Dena. "I think you should clear your schedule for the next couple of days. Do you have someone that can take over for you?"

Dena hesitated. She didn't like the idea of her patients being interrupted like this, but what else could she do? She had decided last night before climbing into bed that if nothing else happened in the next couple of days, she would thank Nick for his help and get her life back to normal. She was beginning to think she had overreacted and felt like a fool.

"Yes, I can call a former colleague of mine. But I need to call my patients first. They should hear this from me. Although I'm not sure what I will say to them."

"Tell them you have a family emergency and that you should be back to work in a few days. Tell the same to your colleague friend."

"You mean Brad?" Dena cried. "We are friends, I just can't tell him I have an emergency and leave it at that. He will be worried sick. Besides, he knows I don't have any family."

Nick looked at her with disbelief. "No family at all?" He thought for a second. "Why don't you make up an old aunt you want to visit?"

"I would never go to see anyone in my family, he knows this. He used to be my therapist."

Nick thought about this for a minute. He wondered why a therapist would need to see another therapist. Perhaps after listening in on others' deeply disturbed thoughts day after day, you may feel your own sanity slipping. Or maybe it was a just little grief therapy after her husband died.

"Then just tell him you are taking a vacation, you have been working too hard and think it would best to get away for a few days."

After a few moments of silence, Dena finally agreed. "That will work. He is always after me to take a vacation." She got up to get the coffee from the carafe she had filled earlier and instead set the carafe in front of Nick. "I'm going to go into my office and call him right now before his first appointment."

When she returned to the kitchen twenty minutes later, Nick was typing something on his laptop. "Did you get in touch with your colleague?"

"Yes. Brad will take over for me for the next two weeks. Hopefully, it will not be as long as that."

"All right then. Let's get back to work."

Turning to a fresh sheet on his legal pad, Nick was ready to start firing questions. He turned his head to say something just as Dena was leaning in front of him to refill his coffee, his face right at her neck. He could smell her perfume, something light, floral and wonderful. And for the life of him he could not remember what he was going to say.

Snap out of it, Nick, you're starting to act like an idiot.

"OK," Nick said a little too loud. "I am going to start asking you questions about everyone and everything that have any relationship to you. Just answer them, even if you are sure they have nothing to do with this. Sometimes a clue comes from an unlikely source, plus this will help eliminate several possibilities right from the start."

"I will answer all your questions, except of course those related to my former or current patients." She took their privacy and confidentiality very seriously.

Nick tried to hide his annoyance. "Let's start with your late husband, what was his name?"

"Paul. Paul Davis." Suddenly Dena realized just how hard this was going to be. He was going to be asking questions about her past. Personal questions that she could not answer. She knew her hands would start shaking and did some deep breathing to relax.

He could see this was painful for her, that she still was grieving, but he had to go on. "Tell me about him. What did he do for a living, the names of his friends, hobbies and so forth?"

"Paul's passion in life was flying planes. It was his hobby and really, his life. Since the day he became old enough to work, he held some type of job related to flying. He started D & D Aviation about 15 years ago with his long-time friend, Bob Denton, and two twin engine planes. At the time of his death they had three jets and three very nice airplanes. One of the jets was an air ambulance with a pilot on call to leave at a moment's notice and the other aircrafts were mainly used by wealthy people who wanted and could afford private transportation. Certain companies would also charter planes to fly their employees out to see important clients."

"So, you own half of this company now?" Nick interrupted. He suspected she let someone else handle the business end of things at D & D.

"No. Bob bought out my half when Paul died."

"Were there any problems with that? I mean, did you two agree on everything and did you receive a fair price?"

Dena shook her head. "No problems at all. I didn't care about the business. I let my lawyer handle everything. I don't even know how much it sold for. Doug took care of all the details and even invested the money from the sale."

"Doug is your lawyer?" Nick asked. A little red flag popped up in his head and waved madly. He was having a hard time believing she was that naive and trusting. An aviation company that specialized in executive travel had to be worth a pretty penny and she didn't even want to peek at the sale amount?

"Yes. Douglas Greenly is my lawyer. I have known him for years, actually, since I was a child. He has always been good to me. Nice to me." She smiled as if a fond thought played out in her mind.

Nick got the impression from her that he was an old man by now. Somehow, he liked that a little better. "How old is Mr. Greenly?" Perhaps he didn't have all his wits about him and missed something in the sale, like forgetting to hand over all the proceeds after the transaction.

"Doug is just a few years older than I." Dena gave him a funny look. "Why do you ask?"

"Just the way you said he was nice to you made me think he was older. I thought by now he must be elderly."

Dena gave a little laugh. "Doug was nice to me at a time when most people were not. I am sure he did an excellent job with the sale of the business," she concluded, deliberately changing the subject. She had surprised herself by revealing something she had never told a soul, except during therapy.

Nick was starting to get the feeling something was off. "Do you have the papers from the business here, including all the documents from the sale?"

"No," Dena replied. "I put all of Paul's things, including his files, in a storage center."

"Well," Nick said as he got up quickly, "let's go take a look there, shall we?"

Chapter Five

Aunt Ada's Attic storage center was a thirty-minute drive from Dena's house. As they got closer to the facility, Dena recognized the familiar logo of the old woman in a rocking chair next to an antique cedar chest. It gave the place a homey, trustworthy feeling.

They pulled up in front of the neon sign that flashed "office" and went inside. Behind the counter stood a man who could have been anywhere from in his late thirties to well into his fifties. He pried his eyes away from the cartoons he was watching just as he finished shoving what appeared to be an entire submarine sandwich into his mouth. He wore a shabby white T-shirt decorated with dried paint and holes, and worn out blue jeans. He also had the greasiest hair that Dena had ever seen. Aunt Ada was obviously not strict about the dress code. Dena approached the desk as the man wiped his hands on his shirt in an effort to clean them.

"My name is Dena Davis and I need to get into my storage unit please."

She held up the key to the center as she spoke.

"Yeah, fine," Greasy hair said, spraying bits of his lunch into the air. "Like I told ya yesterday over the phone, you don't need to check in first if you have your key. Just pull on up to your door and help yourself."

Nick looked at Dena and raised an eyebrow, and she shook her head no.

"Did you talk to someone yesterday about Ms. Davis's unit?" Nick asked.

"Yeah, I talked to her." He pointed to Dena. "She called yesterday to see if she needed to check in with the office before going to her locker. She called it a locker." He must have thought that was funny and gave a chuckle. "I said as long as you have the key, just help yourself. I remember it on account of we only had two other calls all day."

"What else did you tell her?" Nick asked with more patience than he felt.

"Nothing. Well...just the storage number, she said she forgot it." The man's face was starting to look as shiny as his hair. He could see Nick's jaw getting tighter and soon got the feeling he had done something wrong. "Hey, I didn't break any rules here, buddy. The lady called up for info and I gave it to her."

Nick dismissed the clerk with a nod and laid his hand on Dena's arm, guiding her to the door. "Any idea who that lady could be?" he asked once outside.

"None at all. I can't think of anyone who even knew I had a storage unit, nor can I imagine why anyone else would want to see what's inside." Dena ran her hands through her hair in frustration.

They got back inside the car and turned left on the driveway next to the building. The storage center was one story high with each unit having a steel garage door as the only entrance. Number 135 was at the very end on the left.

As they got out of the car and approached the door, both noticed at the same time the padlock had been cut.

Nick was experiencing mixed emotions. So far he had not come across any evidence of strife in Dena's life other than she was too trusting of her lawyer. Was this lady crazy and wasting his time when he had piles of work at the office waiting for him? Not to mention he needed to start his next book. Or was she really in trouble?

An inner voice was telling him to back away from this one and let her be someone else's headache. But he knew he couldn't walk away, because for some irrational reason he felt a need to protect this woman he had just met. And that thought scared him much more than what could be waiting on the other side of this door.

"Get back in the car for a minute," he said in a low authoritative voice while pulling out his gun. If Dena was about to protest, it was cut short when she saw what he had in his hand and she did as she was told.

Nick took the rest of the lock off and lifted up the garage door. He then jumped to the side and waited to see if he had surprised anyone. He was sure whoever broke in was long gone, but he'd rather be overly cautious than dead. One glance inside told him he was most likely alone, but to be safe he scouted around and behind every large box and file cabinet before waving Dena on in.

Dena stood with her hands on her hips in the doorway and took it all in. It was obvious someone had been here and was searching for something. Files were scattered about and boxes tipped over with the contents spilling out onto the ground. The unit itself was not large, about the same size as a single car garage with no windows. "I am not sure if I will even know if something is missing. Other than a few old former patient files that I had stored here, the rest belonged to Paul."

Nick glanced over at a very old but still in good condition Mahogany desk; it seemed out of place with all the metal cabinets and boxes. "Did this belong to your husband?" he asked as he went over to the desk.

"Yes, that was in his office. The desk had been in his family for years and his father had used it until he died." Dena opened the top drawer, expecting it to be empty but instead finding it full.

"Hmm," she said as she opened the rest of the drawers. "I rather thought the movers would empty out the drawers before moving it, but they are all stuffed." She rifled her way through boxes of paper clips, ink pens and a few manila folders. Her hand froze when it came upon a worn leather binder.

"This was Paul's personal planner. He took it everywhere he went, on every flight, and brought it home with him at night. I guess I assumed it was with him when he died." She quietly flipped through the pages of appointments listed over five years ago.

Nick spoke and brought her back to the present. "Why don't we pack up whatever we think could be important and bring it back to your house? That way we can take our time going over it." He bent over and picked up an empty box and looked at Dena for an answer.

Dena gave her head a slight nod and looked at her watch. "We should go through this then, I guess," she said, looking down at the planner in her hands as she gently placed it in the carton. Together they filled up four boxes with anything they thought could be useful. As they were headed out the door, Nick gave a glance over at Paul's old desk again.

"I am a little surprised that you wouldn't want to keep that at your house. Especially since it was a favorite of your husband's and I'm guessing a family heirloom." Curiosity getting the better of him, he wanted to know what made her tick. She seemed to be a contradiction, one minute genuinely grieving her lost husband, the next cold and reserved. Beautiful and yet plain. That was another thing that was bothering him. She almost went out of her way to look plain and unattractive, which was impossible, but why the camouflage?

"What, that old desk?" Dena asked, looking it over as if seeing it for the first time. "It never occurred to me to keep it. I'm not the sentimental type, but perhaps I should offer it to his sister."

"I'm not either, but wouldn't you have wanted to keep that in the family if it belonged to your father?"

Dena's blood ran cold and her eyes glazed over. "I would

never want anything that belonged to my father," she said firmly but quietly then walked out towards the car.

Nick let that comment go, certain that it wasn't a topic she wanted to pursue and he did not need to be a detective to figure that out. Hell, she could turn fire into ice with the look she just gave him.

Neither one said much on the ride back, which was fine with Dena. *What is it about this man that gets me to say more than I want?* Secrets that she had kept hidden for years were gently pried out of her one at a time. Things that she only revealed to Brad during her sessions were coming out and even then, she had kept a few locked away in some untouchable part of her mind. She was starting to feel she was taking a ride on an emotional roller coaster. Maybe she should cook something for dinner tonight; that would help her relax a little. Whenever things got crazy with work or she just felt wound too tight, she discovered that spending time in the kitchen preparing a meal worked wonders. By the time she was done dicing, slicing and sautéing, the tension eased its way out of her shoulders and many times she was able to ward off a headache.

"Let's stop at that market over there, I feel like cooking tonight," Dena said, breaking the silence.

Nick could not have been more surprised. But he was more than delighted. Somehow, she did not seem like the domestic type, or maybe he was just used to women who thought the kitchen was only to be utilized by the hired help. When he was married, if the housekeeper did not prepare a meal, they either went out, had carry out or had it delivered.

His mother did not count. She was your typical Italian mother and she made the kitchen everyone's favorite room. There was always laughter there and something wonderful on the stove.

He was not much of a cook himself, probably because when he was growing up, he could never get near the stove. His mother stood guard with a wooden spoon in her hand to ward off any vultures trying to sample her work before it made its way to the table.

"Do you have a problem with that?" Dena asked, referring to the odd look on his face.

"Uh, no. That sounds great, actually." His stomach growled in anticipation and he silently prayed that she really could cook.

They walked into Mario's Market and Dena grabbed a shopping cart and went to work. She selected things for tonight's dinner as well as a few things to keep on hand. As much as she loved to cook, she did not like to do it just for herself. It made her feel too lonely. So, even if this wasn't a social call for her guest, she was pleased to have the opportunity to practice her culinary skills.

She went down the aisles tossing in different pastas, fresh bread, wine and lots of fruits and vegetables. Nick was in tow behind her, watching in amazement the flurry of activity.

"You're not allergic to shellfish, are you?" Dena asked as they headed over to the meat counter.

Nick shook his head no, wondering what she was planning on cooking. Dena ordered shrimp, cheeses and a few other meats as well as lunch meats for sandwiches. He had been dying for a beer last night and told her he would be right back.

"Pick out some good beer Nick, please," Dena shouted after him. He faltered for a second and then went on his way. How did she do that? That's a neat trick; she must be lots of fun on a date.

As they stood in the check-out lane the cashier chatted on about how busy they were and she was sure it would storm later on in the day. Just look at those dark clouds rolling in! Dena automatically turned her head to the front of the store to look outside and instantly the smile left her face. Nick was engrossed in a Sports Illustrated he happily found near the checkout line when the worried cashier's voice broke his concentration.

"Miss? Are you okay?" The cashier asked with genuine concern in her voice.

Nick looked over at Dena and quickly grabbed her arm to support her. All color had drained from her face. Even her lips paled. Her breath was coming in short, choppy rasps and Nick was not sure if she saw something that frightened her or she was having some sort of seizure.

There was nothing outside the storefront that he could see except an exceptionally attractive woman reading a sale flyer that had been taped to the glass. Grabbing a wad of cash out of his pocket, Nick threw some bills at the chatty clerk. He hoisted up the bags with one hand and ushered Dena out the door with the other.

Once inside the car Nick noticed she looked a little better, but was still visibly shaken. "Are you all right, Dena?"

"She's gone now," she replied, staring at the storefront.

Confused, Nick followed her eyes. "Who's gone?"

"The woman standing in front of the store looking in at us. Didn't you see her?" She needed to know that this was not a trick of her imagination. But it must have been, for what she thought she saw was impossible.

"Yes, I saw her," Nick said patiently, wondering what possibly could be the connection to her almost fainting and a woman checking out the day's specials. "Did you know her, Dena?"

She turned to address him. With a defiant look on her face, she replied, "Yes, I did know her. She died with my husband in a plane crash."

Chapter Six

Nick was quiet on the way back to Dena's, replaying this new revelation in his mind a few thousand times. One thought that did occur to him was that the good doctor might be crazy and he was wasting his time. Perhaps she snapped after the death of her husband, and as a cry for help, made up that story of hearing someone in her house plotting her death. Or worse, she actually believed there was a man in her house. The only evidence he had seen that something was not right was the break-in at the storage unit. And hell, that could have been her as well or even that greasy manager poking around.

Dena was reasonably sure that Nick thought she was unbalanced. Not that she blamed him really, so far she had been unable to give him anything other than her word. She already had lived through the horrors of being the victim that no one believes and she was determined not to go through that again. If the police and Nick did not think the evidence was credible, then she would just handle it on her own. Once in the kitchen, she starting putting the groceries away, keeping out those she would need to make dinner. The familiar, reassuring task of cooking would relax her, and she needed to do something soon before a migraine took hold. Nick was sitting quietly at the kitchen table. She noticed he was scribbling notes in his file, probably, *"this lady is a nut, case closed."*

Not one to leave loose ends, Nick decided to get a little more information before running out the door. "Tell me about this woman," he asked without looking up.

Dena let out the breath she was holding when he finally spoke. She was beginning to think he'd silently gather up his belongings and make a bee-line for the door. "Well, her name was Bridgett Bonner. She worked for Paul for about two years as a nurse when he would fly patients to and from hospitals all around the U.S. She started off working part time at first, but as his business grew, he needed her to be ready at a moment's notice, so she quit her other job at the hospital and started full time with D & D Aviation." Dena was racking her brain for any other information that might be useful, but realized she knew very little about Bridgett Bonner.

"What about her age, family, where did she live? That kind of thing?" Nick asked.

"I don't know much about her personal life. Paul met her in a hospital when he drove one of his mechanics with a bad gash on his hand in for stitches. He was looking for a nurse and she seemed competent enough, he said. I think she had an apartment in Chicago with another girl. I believe her name was Suzie."

Nick knew that with a few phone calls he could find out anything he needed about the late Bridgett Bonner, from where she had liked to shop to her favorite brand of toothpaste. He needed to do some research and make use of the resources at the office so he decided to head over there before dinner. He did not for a minute think that Dena had seen this Bridgett today, but looking up a little information would be a nice touch to his report when he handed in his bill, maybe even as early as tonight. He also did not think much would turn up on Bridgett but he wanted to be sure.

"I am going to run to the office. I'll be back about seven,"

Nick said as he stuffed the papers in the manila folder. Even if this was about her dead husband, something should have happened before now. He'd been dead what, over two years now? Almost as an afterthought Nick asked, "Did anything strange happen right after your husband died? Homes are burglarized often during funerals, all the crooks need to do is check out the obituaries for a schedule of what houses to hit and what time to do it."

"We didn't have a regular funeral, just a private memorial service about a month after the accident. But no, nothing strange happened. My house was not broken into if that's what you mean." Dena had stopped dicing the onions and peppers and looked Nick in the eye, wondering if he would even come back for dinner. Not that it mattered; she was used to being alone.

Nick was halfway out the kitchen door when a thought came to him. "Just curious, why did you wait a month for the memorial service?"

"I was still clinging to the hope that he might be alive. Maybe they survived and swam to some deserted island. Their bodies were never found, nor was the plane. They just disappeared."

"What, like in the Bermuda Triangle?" Nick asked.

Dena looked a little surprised. "Yes, exactly like that. They had filed a flight plan to Bermuda."

"I suppose the authorities checked out the maintenance logs and records for their plane?" Nick asked, rubbing his chin absentmindedly.

"I'm sure they did. There was some kind of final report from the safety board, but without the plane, no one will ever know what actually happened," Dena said.

A few ideas were spinning around in Nick's head as he drove out of Oak Park and headed back to his office. The ugly gray sky that had been present all day was now turning an angry shade of black, promising one hell of a storm.

He had taken this case mainly because it intrigued him. Dena intrigued him. Though at the time he had told himself he was taking this on with the idea that she would make an interesting character in his next novel and he was after all, experiencing a period of writer's block.

Being nosy by nature is what makes you a good investigator. That and the strong belief that everyone is a liar, which they usually are, and if they are not lying to you at the moment, they will sooner or later if you give them enough time.

He originally thought she walked in on a burglary in progress and just let her imagination run into overtime. Then he started to suspect the doctor might be in need of professional help herself.

But now, a bell was starting to ring somewhere in the back of his head. *What if* there was more to these incidents than he originally thought? The break-in at the storage center. A nurse that is supposed to be dead turns up at a grocery store. And then there was that annoying little detail of the bodies never being found. And if by chance this did turn out to be something bona fide, he had the feeling that Dr. Davis would not appreciate his not mentioning he was an author. *But since Brent Crawfield is my pseudonym, I guess she really doesn't need to know the truth. So why do I feel like a shit?* Nick asked himself.

It wouldn't hurt to get background information on the late husband and his business, Nick thought as he reached for his cell phone.

"O'Neal Investigations," Margaret chirped professionally.

"Hey Margaret, how's tricks?" There was usually an easy, good natured banter between the two of them. The truth was that Nick would be lost without the ever efficient assistant and office manager.

A widow and a mother of three grown boys, Margaret's life now revolved around the office and giving Nick a hard time. She answered the phones, did the filing, handed out assignments to the staff of four investigators and even found the time to help with research for his novels. It makes a wonderful hobby, she had told him, and helping him with the books kept her busy. Margaret found having plenty to do also kept her from living a lonely life, something she decided long ago she would never do. But soon she discovered she had a real knack for research and loved watching his stories unfold.

"He lives and breathes!" Margaret practically yelled into the phone. "You leave here two days ago with a pretty lady and that's the last anyone hears from you. I didn't know if you were kidnapped or if you eloped."

Nick chuckled into the phone, shaking his head. "Now don't go getting your feathers all ruffled, Margaret, it was nothing that exciting. You know, I do have a cell phone for those times you wish to speak to me."

"Well then, you might want to try turning the thing on. You want your messages now?"

"Only the urgent ones. I am on my way in as we speak."

"OK boss. The detective from Georgia returned your call on that missing Trask woman. Said they had interviewed all her family and friends in Georgia at the time of her disappearance and he thinks she just plain ran off. The word is that the husband was, and I am sure still is, an overbearing, pompous ass, and the general consensus is that she left him. Anyway, he said you have his number and it's your dime if you want to chat more. The other messages can wait until you get here."

"Good enough. You calling it a day, Margaret?" It was almost 5:00 pm and he was sure she had been there since 7:00 am that morning. He didn't like her working such long hours, and sometimes had to gently tell her to leave. "I promise to check in with you personally tomorrow if I don't make it back to the office."

"I was on my way out the door when you called, but I can stay if you need me to."

"No, that's fine. Go have yourself a wonderful dinner, Margaret." After he hung up, his thoughts wandered back to Dena and her dead husband. Edward will have his work cut out for him tonight, Nick thought as he pulled into the parking lot of O'Neal Investigations.

One never knew if Edward ever left the office, or even his cubicle, for that matter. You could count on the fact that Edward Carr would be there morning and night, weekends included. He was a true computer genius. Top that off with the fact that he loved his job, and you had the perfect employee.

As Nick entered the dark office, he was greeted by the reassuring sound of computer keys clicking. He made his way over to Edward's cubicle and cleared his throat to get his attention. Waiting for him to look up, Nick glanced around his employee's work space, noticing for the first time his lack of personal items. Not one picture or even a favorite coffee mug adorned his work space. It was the same as the day he started working here three years ago. In fact, even Edward looked the same with his wire-rimmed glasses and white button-down oxford. Finally Nick realized he would actually have to speak if he wanted to get his attention because it was obvious Edward wasn't ever going to turn around.

"Hi, Edward. How's it going?" Nick asked.

"Fine, sir. Just fine," Edward replied, blinking several times, his eyes attempting to adjust after staring at the screen for so long.

Nick had given up asking him to call him by name instead of "sir" all the time. He ran a professional but relaxed office, and everyone called him Nick. Sometimes Margaret would call him "Nicky" when she was trying to irritate him, but otherwise it was a first name basis for all employees.

Knowing he was not one for small talk, Nick got right to the point. "I need some information on a dead man. The name is Paul Davis and he died in a plane crash about two years ago, along with a nurse that worked for him, a Bridgett Bonner. Davis owned a Lear jet company with a Robert Denton called D & D Aviation. Check out the nurse and partner, and while you're at it, the lawyer, Douglas Greenly. And you might as well see what you can find out about Davis's wife, Dr. Dena Davis. Are you able to start on this right away?"

"Of course," Edward replied, already turning around to face his computer and begin working. As Nick walked to his office he realized that Edward hadn't even taken so much as one note when he was talking to him. *Glad the guy is on our team,* thought Nick.

Nick spent the next twenty minutes clearing off his desk, returning phone calls, reading mail and putting his signature on a stack of letters Margaret had left for him.

Running through his e-mails he came across one from Clarissa Beacher, the sister of the missing Michaelene Trask, requesting her daily progress report. Since hiring him over two weeks ago, she had e-mailed daily for updates. Sometimes she would phone in, but preferred her reports in writing.

Unfortunately, there was not much more to say that she didn't already know. No sign of foul play, no body, no ransom requested and she had been married to a first class jerk. But, being a jerk didn't necessarily make the man a killer. However, the fact remained, Michalene Trask was missing and had been for two years. If she had not shown up by now she either really didn't want to be found or she was dead. Nick surmised it had to be the latter. If she was as close to her sister as she said she was, Michalene would have gotten in touch with her somehow by now.

Clarissa had another agency working for her in her home-town in Georgia with which Nick had kept in touch. After learning that Michalene had made frequent trips to Chicago, Clarissa hired Nick to find the connection and, hopefully, her sister. Nick sent her a reply with a Georgia cop's name and phone number along with the message he left and copied it to the other agency. At least it made him look like he was doing something constructive with his time. Just as he completed his e-mail he looked up to find Edward standing there, waiting to speak to him.

"What's up?" Nick asked. Surely he couldn't have found anything out this quickly.

"I have some information for you. I thought some of this might be beneficial for you to know now as opposed to waiting until my report is complete."

Nick gave a nod for Edward to continue and leaned back into his chair. In his hands were several computer printout sheets, which Nick knew would be for his benefit, not Edward's.

"First, her late husband, Paul Davis, started D & D Aviation in 1986 as a very small time operation and grew it into a large, successful business in a relatively short amount of time. He had some pretty important and powerful clients. Big time law firms, corporations such as Coldwater, General Motors and Trask Industries, to name a few. His business partner was a good friend, nothing shady on him as far as I could tell. Bridgett Bonner worked for Paul for two years but knew him for at least five years before that. She was known as a 'blonde bombshell,' and it was rumored the two were having an affair even before and after he married Dena..."

"Wait a minute," Nick interrupted. How in God's name he had gotten all this information in such a short time was beyond him. "Back up. Trask Industries, as in the company whose president and CEO is Haidyn Trask?"

"Yes, sir. His wife is your missing person's case, Michaelene Trask," he replied nonchalantly. All open and closed cases were listed on the office database to allow one to easily check for cross references. Stranger things had been known to happen and finding a connection between two cases had, at times, proved invaluable.

"Huh," was all Nick said, absently rubbing his chin. Well, you know what they say about a coincidence, he thought, no such thing.

"I will e-mail you all information as I find it, so you can have access to it immediately. You will be taking your laptop with you when you are not in the office?" he said more as a reminder than a question. Ever so efficient, Nick sometimes thought Edward should be the office manager. But his only true love was computers; people were not of interest to him and mostly, they got on his nerves. No, his real talent truly was in computers and he could find out almost anything. Being a former law enforcement officer, Nick was pretty sure some of Edward's methods were illegal. But hey, sometimes you have to break a few rules to catch the bad guys.

"One more thing, sir. There was nothing much on Dr. Davis, other than where she grew up, went to school. That kinda thing."

"I'm not surprised," Nick said under his breath, thinking what a goody two shoes she must have been growing up. From the way she dressed to the car she drove, she always took the straight and narrow path.

"However, I did find she has a sealed juvenile record, so that will take me a little longer to open. I'll let you know what I find out," he said as he turned and exited the office, leaving Nick with a stunned look on his face.

Chapter Seven

Dena set the stove on low to let the sauce simmer while she finished tidying up the kitchen. *A glass of wine and a hot bath are just what this day calls for*, she thought as she filled her glass with a chilled California Sauvignon Blanc. Tonight she decided to reach for the Waterford instead of her regular, everyday stemware. The exquisite piece of crystal, a gift from Marcy, never failed to bring her pleasure.

The thunder was still rolling outside, but at a distance now and its sound was more soothing than threatening. The rain kept up a slow, steady pace as it gently tapped against the windows.

She put on some of her favorite classical music; a mixture of Bach and Beethoven along with a few other great composers, which she had ordered off an infomercial late one night when she could not sleep. She used her insomnia to catch up on paperwork, pay bills and do a little light shopping on one of those home shopping channels. She did not consider herself a full fledged insomniac, but she could usually count on at least one or two nights a week without sleep.

Being a psychologist, she could usually figure out what had triggered the latest episode. A bad dream, something one of her patients said, or perhaps something as simple as a scent.

There were still certain smells that would make her knees instantly weak and send her spinning into a dark hole. Once at a dinner party with some colleagues, she had almost passed out when a man with a pipe in his hand turned around and blew smoke in her face. She had instantly turned white and felt her knees begin to turn to liquid. She quickly made some excuse and left the party, trying hard not to think about the man she once knew who used to smoke a pipe. She did not sleep for five days after that. This physician could not heal herself. Did not want to. Some places were too horrible for even a trained psychologist to go.

But she would not allow herself to think of anything dark or horrid now. In fact, she would not permit herself to think at all. She willfully shut down her mind and concentrated instead on the flickering glow of the lavender candles that framed the base of the tub while she enjoyed her blissful soak. She allowed her eyes to close and let the tension melt out of her. *Several more minutes of this and I will be asleep*, Dena thought as she started to drift.

It was then that she first became aware of a noise. Unable to identify it, she glanced at the window she had left open a few inches. The safety lock was in place, reassuring her it could not be opened any further. There it was again, that sound. It was as though someone were quietly trying to open the window. Common sense told her that was impossible since she was on the second floor, but she held her breath while trying to listen anyway.

Dena sat up in the tub, staring at the window while protectively using her arms to cover her breasts. All she could see out the window was the thick darkness that had settled in for the evening. The thought that someone might be watching her terrified her, but it also made her question her own sanity.

"Dena," a voice whispered.

"Oh God!" she whimpered as she struggled to get out of the

tub.

What happened next seemed to play out in slow motion, like a scene from a horrifying dream where you are trying to escape from danger and then suddenly find yourself running in water. Your brain screams for your legs to move faster, but they just can't get going.

The window suddenly shattered with brutal force, glass flying inward with such intensity it almost seemed like an explosion. As she tried to run for the door, her feet slid on the wet tile, sending her backwards onto a bed of broken glass. Her mind screamed for her to get up. Get up and get out of this bathroom or she would be trapped. She scrambled to get to her feet using the sink to help her stand. And with speed she didn't know she had, Dena ran out of the bathroom, through her bedroom and down the stairs. As she turned into the kitchen, two masculine hands roughly grabbed her and blocked her path.

Nick didn't know what scared him more, the scream or the sight of her. Probably a little of both. The vision of her standing naked before him, he knew, would be forever etched in his brain.

Shamefully, given the situation, the first things he noticed were her breasts. Where in the hell had she been hiding those? He forced his eyes back to her face so he could figure out what was wrong with her. Something had frightened the good doctor enough to have her run through the house naked.

"He's here! Upstairs, I was taking a bath..." Dena tried to give Nick an explanation.

"Stay here!" Nick ordered while running out of the room and pulling out his gun in one swift motion.

Nick found her bloody footprints in the hall and followed them into her bedroom and then into the bathroom. He saw the remains of her bath and the broken glass and got the basic idea of what had happened. It also explained the footprints. He stuck his head out the window to confirm there was a ladder and that whoever was here, was now long gone. It would be dusted for prints, though he was sure none could be used and the ladder most likely came from Dena's own garage or the house next door.

He used his cell phone to call 911 while he finished searching the house, sure he would come up empty. His best guess was that his headlights had alerted the intruder and he took off.

If there was an intruder. She could have staged it. The ladder, the window, she could have broken the glass, it was possible. But that just didn't make sense. His gut was telling him it was real. Two break-ins in two days was more than a coincidence. Someone either wanted something she had, or wanted her. He hadn't thought she was in danger and now he could kick himself for leaving her alone. He took the job and she was, after all, on his watch. He messed up.

Back in the kitchen, Dena was calm now as she sat at one of the dinette chairs and peered up at him with huge, glassy eyes. She was wrapped in an afghan she must have taken off the couch when she realized she was naked. Nick kneeled in front of her and asked how she was doing. Only then did he notice the blood seeping out the back of her wrap.

"Christ, Dena," Nick said, trying not to let the alarm he felt show. "You're hurt. I need to take a look at your back. Let's go over to the bathroom." He helped her up and remembering the bloody footprints, started to lift her in his arms.

"I can walk. My feet are fine." She sounded convincing, but he was doubtful, given the mess he just saw. Still, he guided her to the guest bath down the hall. He had her sit on the toilet lid, her back facing him. Gently, he pulled her only covering down to her waist and held back a curse.

"You need a doctor, Dena." This was more than a job for a few Band-Aids. Her back was covered with a dozen or more cuts, most of them full of glass. She was also losing a fair amount of blood. "Wait right here," Nick said as he rushed out of the bathroom in search of something to put on her. He returned momentarily with a pair of gray sweat pants and a fresh blanket to wrap around her.

Dena began to feel a little woozy and as Nick was helping her up, she saw his face begin to swim in and out of focus. She cursed herself for feeling so weak. She certainly had been through worse pain in her life, but perhaps combined with being frightened out of her mind, it was all too much.

"I don't feel so good," Dena stated weakly. She hated to admit she was going to have a hard time getting out of the house and into the car.

"Really?" Nick with a small grin. He wanted to just sweep her up in his arms and carry her to the car instead of walking at this snail's pace, but somehow he thought she would object.

This is awfully nice of him to help me like this, Dena thought. *Maybe he is one of the good guys. If there is such a thing. I guess I should thank him; this can't be much fun for him.* She stopped, turned and lifted her head to address him. "I just want to say..." were the only words she could get out before her head fell back and her body dropped.

Nick saw it coming, saw her eyes start to roll backwards and was ready to catch her. "OK," he said as he scooped her up into his strong arms, "we're outta here."

Three hours and twenty stitches later they returned to her house.

Nick had made a few calls while at the hospital and had the window boarded up along with the mess cleaned up as soon as the police were finished with the scene. As a favor to Nick, an officer came to the hospital to take her statement.

Dena felt emotionally and physically drained. Her entire body hurt and she did not know what to do with herself. She needed to sleep, desperately wanted to stop thinking, but wasn't sure she could.

Nick gave her a glass of water with one hand, and two of the prescribed pain killers with the other, without saying a word. She gratefully took them and let him guide her quietly upstairs to her bedroom. She winced as she took each agonizing step. The small cuts on the soles of her feet were burning but relatively minor compared to her back.

Once in her room, he stood her before the bed and slowly pushed her sweatpants down her long, shapely legs and gently helped each foot out while she leaned against him. He damn near stopped breathing when he was reminded she wasn't wearing panties but he pretended he did this sort of thing everyday as he sat her back on the bed. Her eyelids looked like they were suddenly getting too heavy for her to keep open and he suspected she would be fast asleep before he made it out of the room. He covered her up and turned out the light. He was halfway out the door when he stopped, went back in and then on impulse, bent over and kissed her. On the lips. He continued for several heart pounding seconds until he heard her moan.

Back downstairs, Nick forced himself to get back to work. He flopped down on the couch and folded his hands behind his head. Forget about Dena's sanity, it was his own he was concerned about now. He had meant to just plant a nice kiss on her forehead and instead had to force himself to leave her room. Since when did he fantasize about attacking helpless women? And besides, she was a client.

He had to look at Dena differently now that things were obviously becoming more dangerous and were not just the elaborate handiwork of a crazy woman. What could Dena know that would put her life in danger?

An officer that Nick knew from his police days had shut the stove off and stuck the pan in the fridge. He thought about it now as his stomach growled; maybe he would heat up whatever it was and eat while he worked. But first he had to check his messages on both his cell and office phone, and started dialing while booting up his laptop. No urgent calls on either line, but he did have an e-mail from Edward.

"The lawyer, Douglas Greenly, you had me check out came back clean, but interesting. His financial status has greatly improved in the last few years; however, I am still trying to track where it is coming from. Also, still working on the details of that sealed file on Dena. I did find out she spent time in a juvenile detention center, it appears, for murder. I will let you know the details as I get them."

"Murder?" Nick said out loud. He never saw that one coming. If he were a gambling man, he would have thought the only possible crime Dena could have committed was shoplifting penny candy. But it would have been more believable in his mind if a friend had been the one stealing and she had been there by mistake.

He picked up his pen and began another rapid session of clicking while his mind processed the information he had received. He had two files open in his head now: one was labeled future novel and the other, his client file, Dr. Dena Davis. He hoped Edward would hurry and break into that file. It seemed that even the firewall set up by the government was no match for him. He knew he should not be encouraging an employee to commit a felony, but he had to know.

His bullshit detector was usually foolproof and he knew if someone was pulling his chain even before they opened their mouth. But this time, with Dena, he wasn't sure of anything.

This entire case just kept taking wild and unexpected turns. It was like driving down a dangerously curvy road on a foggy night, unsure where you are headed because you cannot make out the path in front of you.

A potentially crazy client, or at least he had thought that, and some questionable characters, both dead and alive. He knew he didn't like the lawyer from the get go, but that could be due to how he felt about lawyers in general. Nick let what little he knew about Dena marinate in his brain as he played with his pen, clicking away while trying to sort it all out.

He had a feeling that the doctor's good friend and legal council, Doug Greenly, somehow took advantage of her husband's death to become a rich man. He probably just saw it as an excellent business opportunity, too good to pass up.

The question was, did Greenly have anything to do with what was going on now or was he merely an opportunist?

Nick stopped playing with his pen as a thought occurred to him. If Greenly did have something to do with what was now happening to his client, and she wasn't a nut, then that meant he might have had something to do with her husband's death.

He knew that was really a stretch, but hey, the motive was there. He got paid to always assume the worst, and in most cases, he was right.

It sounded like a good idea to stop in and say hi to Dena's

Lisa Caretti

childhood friend and lawyer.

Chapter Eight

Nick wanted to just leave a note for Dena and surprise Greenly at his office the next morning, but with everything that had happened, he did not want her left alone. For any amount of time. At least until he figured out what was what, she either came with him, or he would have to get someone there to watch her.

He was feeling strangely protective of her and that annoyed him. He knew several people that were more than capable of doing the job of watching her, a few already on his payroll. They would be just as qualified to have a chat with a scumbag lawyer as he would. In fact, he thought of someone who would actually enjoy the job.

Hank Morelli, a retired detective that Nick used to work with on the force, started at O'Neal Investigations the day he opened his doors for business. Hank hated not being busy and could only play so much golf. Either he had to find something to do or Joanna, his wife of forty years, would divorce him.

He thrived on digging up information and solving cases. Like a dog with a bone, he was consumed with a job from start to finish. He was also an incredibly intelligent man with a photographic memory, often remembering names, addresses and sometimes even driver's license numbers from cases he handled more than a year ago. His brilliance would almost always catch the suspect off guard because Hank looked so ordinary, even a little frumpy. Except when he smiled.

"Hank," Nick said into the phone. "Didn't wake you, did I?"

"No, no. What's up Nick?" Hank said as he put down his cup of coffee and took his bifocals off, resting them on his morning newspaper.

"I need you to take a look at someone. Douglas Greenly, a lawyer in the Chicago area. Maybe pay him a visit. I want to see how he handled the sale of Dr. Davis's half of a company called D & D Aviation, his financial records and anything else you can dig up. Edward can take care of the computer end for you. There's a chance he could have had something to do with the death of her late husband, Paul Davis, who was part owner of D & D. I really have no proof of anything, just a gut feeling about him. Why don't you see what you can come up with?"

"Sure thing, Nick. I'll call you as soon as I have something," Hank said as he put the phone back on the receiver and folded up his newspaper, eager to get to work.

* * *

"I'd like a moment of Mr. Greenly's time, please ma'am," Hank Morelli said to the secretary. Even though he was smiling, he still came across as, well, terrifying.

Hank Morelli undeniably had a way of getting information out of people who might otherwise be reluctant to talk, or getting them to do something they really did not want to do. He never needed to partner up and play good cop, bad cop with a suspect. He had his own unique way of getting people to divulge all their secrets.

"Do you have an appointment, sir?" the young receptionist asked, hoping to sound professional. She was new to the job and trying her best to lose her small town Southern accent, with which she couldn't get people to take her seriously.

"Well now, I don't believe I do. But, I think if you tell your boss that a private investigator is here to discuss the welfare of Dr. Davis, he will agree to see me. Go ahead and give him a ring, miss," Hank said smiling, and pointed to the phone.

The smile had almost a hypnotic effect and sent a chill down her spine. The receptionist did as she was told, repeating word-for-word into the phone what the man who was staring a hole through her had said. "He will be able to see you briefly right now," she said, the phone still in her hand. "You may go right in, sir."

Douglas Greenly was seated behind his immaculate desk and rose to greet the detective as he entered his office. He wore an impeccably tailored grey Armani suit and a quizzical look in his eyes.

Everything about him was well organized, compulsively neat and had that expensive, professionally pulled together look.

Hank took his time as he glanced around the room, seemingly unaware of the impatient man in front of him.

"Nice office," he finally said.

This large, rumpled detective certainly did not fit into the morning agenda, but Doug's curiosity got the better of him when he told his dim-witted secretary to let him in. He glanced at his Rolex, more to make a show of how busy he was than to check the time, before offering him a seat.

"What can I do for you, detective?" He put on his best, rather nonchalant appearance, when in fact he was anything but. And the last thing he wanted to do was to talk about Dena. Hell, he had spent more than half of his life talking or thinking about that woman.

"Actually, I am a private investigator. Hank Morelli," he said, holding out his business card. "I wanted to chat a minute or two with you about an acquaintance of yours, a Dr. Dena Davis? I know you are a busy man, Mr. Greenly, so I won't take up too much of your time." With this, Hank pulled out his notebook.

"A private investigator? Who in the hell hired you?"

"I work for a firm that Dr. Davis hired herself. She has been having some trouble lately and I am just trying to get a little background information on her past. Your name came up a few times so I thought I would come and pay you a friendly visit." To prove he was indeed friendly, he gave the lawyer a smile.

Douglas Greenly practically spit out his sip of coffee when he caught the detective's hideous grin. He wanted nothing more than to wrap this up and get him out of his office.

"What kind of information would you like to know? I am a good friend of Dr. Davis and very fond of her. I won't be giving away any secrets about her, Mr. Morelli," said Greenly smugly as he needlessly adjusted his tie.

"Well, now that you confirmed you do know secrets about her, does she know yours as well?" Patiently, Hank waited, not saying anything. Silence can be a powerful tool, leaving the other person to start talking to either fill the void or calm their own nervousness. Often, they say things that they never intended to and later regret.

He also found it interesting that the doctor's long time friend hadn't asked what kind of trouble she was having that she would need to hire a private eye.

"You were taking me literally, Mr. Morelli, when I referred to giving away secrets. I only meant I would not discuss anything that Dr. Davis would want to stay private. If there is something she wanted you to know, she would have already told you herself. As for myself, I don't have any secrets from Dena...Dr. Davis." He then proceeded to pick an imaginary piece of lint off his suit coat.

"So, she knows then that you are now half owner of D & D Aviation? I thought that since you have your shares listed under an alias, you might be hiding that from her."

Greenly's face paled visibly. He took a second to collect himself before replying. "Yes, well, I do own half of the business now and you are correct in assuming that Dena does not know. I did use a different name, but not to deceive her. Quite the opposite. I did not want to cause her any more pain as I know she wanted no further association with the business." Greenly said this with a smug look, pleased with his own answer.

"So, lying to her was really for her own benefit?" Morelli said, seemingly fascinated.

"I never lied to her," Greenly snapped back. "I just never told her. She did not want to keep her share of the business even though I strongly advised her to do so. It was such an excellent business opportunity, the company was doing extremely well and I knew it would keep growing at a fast rate. When she would not take it, I bought the shares myself. Nothing immoral or illegal about that."

"How long have you known her?" Hank inquired.

"Since we were kids. We grew up together in a small town in the South and eventually both moved here to build our careers. I see her both professionally and socially," Greenly replied, hoping this would wrap up their little session so he could get back to work. He made another show of looking at his watch and tapping his fingers on his desk.

Morelli made no move to hurry, resting back in his chair and opening up his notebook and for some reason, enjoying Greenly's irritation. "Let me just write down a few things so when I give my report to my boss, I won't get confused. Oh, one more thing, did you and Dr. Davis ever have a romantic relationship?"

Panic flashed in his eyes, but Greenly was quick to recover. Confused my ass, he thought. He can save his shabby, dumb detective routine for some other sap. "No, of course not. We have always been just good friends. Now, if you will excuse me, Mr. Morelli, I really need to get back to work."

"I think I got what I needed, Mr. Greenly," Morelli said, shoving his notebook in his pocket. "Thank you for your time." With that he strolled out of the office, humming one of his favorite tunes from the musical Showboat. So, the lawyer's got the hots for the doctor. Now that's something to think about.

And somehow, he doubted the feeling was mutual.

Chapter Nine

Dena awoke slowly the next morning after a much needed, drug induced sleep. She would have preferred not to wake at all, at least not this early, but her back was on fire. The pain pulled her out of her deep slumber. She made her way slowly into the kitchen for coffee, hesitant in taking each step to avoid hurting her tender feet. Lucky for her they weren't as bad as her back. She stopped short when she saw Nick at the table, already hard at work. She had forgotten for a moment he was here.

He wore a white T-shirt and red flannel pajama bottoms, and it looked like he just got up. However, judging from the amount of work on the table, it was obvious he had been at it for quite a while. He was talking on his cell phone, his laptop was up and running and he was writing something on a yellow legal notebook.

Dena suddenly felt a flash of embarrassment as she remembered the events of last night. More precisely, she recalled the part where she stood naked in front of him while screaming. She surprised herself by admitting she was not upset by that, in fact it pleased her. She could feel her face turn scarlet just as Nick looked up. A smile spread over his face when he saw her and he quickly ended his phone call.

"How do you feel?" Nick asked with concern in his voice. She had given him quite a scare last night, and he was glad to see her up and moving around so well.

"Like I fell down on a bunch of broken glass," she said, moving stiffly across the room to pour a cup of coffee. "So, what do we do today?"

"We start going over names, one at a time. I've looked at the list of names you gave me, and though I'm not positive, I don't think it's one of them. It just doesn't feel right. I think if someone's trying to hurt you, it's more personal than that. So, have a seat and let's get to work."

"That just doesn't make any sense. None of my friends would try to hurt or scare me." This was all such a mess. She wanted her life back, to have things normal again. That's all she ever wanted, a peaceful, normal life, and she had worked hard to achieve it. Now, even that was being taken from her.

"You're right, this person is not your friend," Nick said, flipping over the pages on his legal pad.

Her brain was still fogged with drugs, so she was a little slow this morning. It took her a few seconds to realize something he said.

"You said *if* someone was trying to hurt me. You still don't quite believe me, do you?"

He sat back in his chair and sighed. "It's against my nature to believe anyone or anything without solid proof to back it up. So far we have none, but I am checking each angle, every possibility."

At least he was honest. He didn't really believe her, but he was not dismissing her as a lunatic. But the fact that he still doubted her, stung.

"So, let's begin with your lawyer."

"Doug?" Dena said, her eyes wide with surprise. "What about him?"

"How close are you and what kind of legal matters has he

handled for you? Tell me anything and everything about him."

"Doug is a good friend, I've known him forever. We grew up in the same town together, a little place called Elmhurst, Georgia. He was always kind to me and I never forgot that. He handles all my legal matters, always has. I trust him completely," Dena said, her mind fondly drifting back in time to her childhood and that young man who came to her defense. He was responsible for some of the few happy childhood memories she had. He later told her he became a lawyer to ensure she would never be treated unfairly again, so if she ever needed him, he could actually do something to protect her.

Nick pinched the bridge of his nose, trying to choose his words carefully before he spoke. She obviously could not be opened-minded when it came to Greenly. And who knows, he could be wrong about the guy. After all, she was a psychologist. She should be a decent judge of character. The sound of his cell phone going off interrupted his train of thought.

"Yes?" Nick said into the phone on the first ring.

"Hey, Nick, it's Hank. Got a bunch of information on Greenly, but I need a little time to separate the sheep from the goats, so to speak. But I have a couple of things I can give you now. First, the guy owns half of D & D, under the name of Mark Hartford. It was a great investment and his client didn't want it, so he bought it but never mentioned this fact to the doctor. He wanted to save her from any additional pain. He's a real thoughtful guy."

"Yeah, sounds like it. What was your general impression of the guy?"

"Anal retentive, neat freak and a bit of a show off. He's hiding something, all right. And by the way, he's in love with the doc."

"That is interesting. Thanks, Hank, let me know if you come up with anything else."

"Oh, I will. I'm just skimming the pond here," Hank chuckled as he hung up.

Nick looked over at Dena who had been watching him throughout the conversation. "That was one of my investigators. He did a little research on Greenly for me." Nick wasn't going to waste time beating around the bush. "Were you aware that Greenly owns half of D & D, under the name of Mark Hartford? He said you were not interested in any part of the business and it was too good a deal for him to pass up." Nick could see that she was surprised, but already knew what her response would be.

She was briefly stunned, though she tried not to show it. It took a moment for her to recover. "No, I was not aware of that. But it's not a crime to use a different name, unless you are committing a fraud. I am sure he changed his name only to protect me. I just wanted that part of my life to be over and was very firm with him about it. He saw the business opportunity and took advantage of it."

"That's what I thought you'd say," Nick replied as he stood up. "I'm going to take a quick shower and then we'll continue." He stopped and looked down at Dena. She appeared pale, but that was no surprise given the circumstances. He wanted to know about her childhood, which was obviously unhappy, and about the murder charge. He wasn't sure if it had anything to do with what was going on now, but every avenue must be checked. He put his hand under her chin and tilted her face up to look at him. "Are you doing OK?" She gave a slight smile and nodded. "Let me go shower and I'll come back and make you breakfast, then you can take another pain pill. Which you really will need after tasting my cooking."

"Thanks, Nick," Dena said, putting her hand on his arm. "For everything." What more could she say? He really was a decent and compassionate man. Though he was just doing his job, his concern was still comforting. Doug was the only one who was ever this caring and gentle with her, but that was just brotherly love. This felt more...intimate. It must be my inexperience showing through, she thought.

Later that afternoon, after what seemed like hours of rehashing information on every person she had known since kindergarten, Nick declared it was time to take a break. "Let's go for a walk, get some fresh air. Go put a sweater on, it's chilly today," he said as he grabbed his well worn leather bomber jacket off the back of the chair.

Once outside, Dena took in a deep breath of the crisp autumn air. It was one of those extraordinary fall days that looked like a picture on a calendar. The wind was tossing leaves at their feet and the sun heated their backs as they walked in silence. Dena's hair danced lightly around her face in the breeze and she tried hard not think of the multiple stitches and cuts that were now throbbing.

It was Nick who finally spoke. "So, do you want to tell me what happened to you when you were a child?"

Dena stopped, unable to go any further. She should have known this question was coming, but somehow, she didn't. Her stomach knotted and for a minute, she thought she might be sick. "What exactly do you want to know, Nick?" she asked, willing herself to be calm. "I mean, there's not much to tell. Girl has unhappy childhood, grows up and moves away. Starts a new life." She shrugged to show it was no big deal.

"Well, there is a lot I would like to know, but more precisely, whom did you murder?" Might as well go for the big fish first, Nick thought.

The gasp was loud. Her shock apparent, she was unable to even try to pretend otherwise. She was speechless.

Of all the things she thought he might ask, this was not one of them. How could he have found out? Doug would never breathe a word of that and it was kept out of the papers. Her family saw to that. "I was under the impression that a sealed record was just that. How did you find out?" The impact wearing off, she was now getting angry.

Nick shrugged his shoulders. "I'm an investigator," he replied. "We can't rule out that all this doesn't have something to do with your past."

"That was all a long time ago. And what happened has no relation to what is going on now. The only thing that would happen if my past got out is that it would ruin my reputation. I could even lose my license."

"How can you be so sure it has nothing to do with what is

going on now?" Nick's voice was getting louder now. "It never occurred to you that maybe a family member or a friend of the victim might want revenge for their death?" He resisted the urge to shake some sense into her. "No matter what the circumstances were, some people get a real chip on their shoulder when their loved one has been murdered." His usual cool facade was gone, his temper making its way through.

"I am sure. There are no family and friends left, dammit!" Dena yelled back. She was shaking. She had just talked more about her past than she ever had, and she was not prepared for this. He was making her so angry.

"How do you know there isn't a brother or ex-lover out there that just found you and wants justice?" He said this through clenched teeth. Nick knew many ways to get information out of people without losing his cool, but for the life of him he couldn't remember any of them. "These things happen all the time, Dena! So I'll ask again, how can you be so sure?"

"Because he was my father, God damn you!" Dena blurted out. "I killed my father."

Chapter Ten

Dena stayed locked away in her office for the remainder of the afternoon with the intention of doing some paperwork and to perhaps call Brad to check on a few patients. But what she was really doing was hiding. She knew Nick would have more questions for her and she could guess what he must think of her. She saw that look in his eyes and wondered if he would treat her differently now that he knew she was a murderer who had killed her own father.

And what in the world possessed her to blurt out the truth anyway? She paced around her office and swore at herself. So what if he had gotten the information that she had killed someone. The entire nightmare was sealed and there was an excellent chance he would never have known the rest.

She wanted to talk to Brad. It was *Dr. Braxten* when she needed to speak with him professionally, but the true issues that were tormenting her were those she could not share. Not even with her doctor. She could talk about her miserable adolescence, dissect some of her most wicked dreams and blame all her idiosyncrasies on her mother as most people in therapy do.

But never about what happened to that little girl she had known so long ago. She had disassociated from that child, so much so that over time Dena began to think of her as someone else. She even had a different name.

It was much easier to keep those memories tucked neatly away. That way she did not have to remember her life back in the small town of Elmurst where she had once lived, in one of the town's largest and nicest homes, and then one day, murdered her father.

No, she could not share that with Brad. The secrets you share in session were always to remain confidential, that would be guaranteed. But Dena did not want to put him in the position of knowing a colleague was also a murderer with an offensive past.

Dena made a few calls to her patients to be sure they did not feel abandoned. She listened to each one a few minutes and encouraged them to keep up their sessions with Dr. Braxten. She held back from offering any opinions or advice so she would not interfere with Brad's treatment.

Finally, she gave up trying to concentrate on her paperwork and had to acknowledge that this time she was unable to block out her past. She was angry with herself for not only losing control, but for giving away a part of herself she had kept successfully buried for over twenty years. She felt naked and exposed. She had lived with the fear of someone finding out for so long, but had always reassured herself that sealed records were just that, and she could finally find peace in her new life.

What she needed now was a good friend's shoulder to cry on and she had an overwhelming urge to talk to Marcy. She was a true friend who understood her better than anyone. Marcy had firsthand knowledge of what had happened to her when they were growing up, but Dena rarely talked about it. She immediately picked up the phone to call her and was disappointed when her machine picked up. She left a message for Marcy to call her when she got in.

She left her office in search of Nick and found him sitting

on the couch in front of the TV. ESPN was giving the day's scores for almost every kind of sport imaginable. Only Nick's gaze was not on the television but slightly above it, staring at a picture of her taken with Marcy at a party last year. He jumped up when he saw her but didn't move forward to meet her. She walked over slowly and stood in front of him, unsure of what she wanted to say or even how to begin.

It was Nick who spoke first. He kept his voice soft and calm. He had sisters and knew how to talk to them and always felt like a shit when he made them cry. "I'm sorry I lost my temper. I know your past is painful for you, and God knows I don't even know all of it, but this is very frustrating for me." He ran his hand through his hair. "It's like trying to put together a puzzle that's missing several pieces. Without your cooperation, I'm afraid I won't be able to figure this out, and you will get hurt. I want you to trust me enough to talk to me. I realize that's asking a lot, we barely know each other, but I want to help you."

Dena could see he was sincere, and much to her surprise, she felt like unburdening herself and releasing her past. This single thought startled her, that after all this time she would consider confiding her darkest secrets with someone. Someone she barely knew.

There was something else she realized. She wanted him to believe her. She wanted this tall, incredibly handsome man to stand by her and take her side. And for once, she didn't want to be alone.

"For some reason I do trust you, Nick, and I've surprised myself by wanting to tell you...everything. But I don't know if I am capable of that. It's been such a long time. There are things I've never told anyone, including my late husband. Some things I do not even remember myself, horrible things I believe I chose to block out." She sat on the couch, suddenly feeling drained.

"But you're a psychologist, Dena, how can you hope to help others when you can't even deal with your own past?" He asked this gently, but his mind was still on the fact she had shared none of this with her spouse.

"I know. You are not telling me anything I haven't told myself a hundred times. However, I do help others. All I've ever wanted to do is save others from their suffering, and by doing that, I feel it has helped me heal. It's just easier to focus on someone else's grief than my own." She paused for a second. "I can't undo the past, Nick."

"No, but you can let go of it," he said as he pulled her into his arms and held her. He couldn't have stopped himself even if he wanted to. It occurred to him that he had spent the last few days trying to keep from wanting her, and directing his thoughts so they stayed focused on work.

He was awake most of last night staring up at the ceiling while reminding himself that he did not want to get involved with someone like her. Someone that carried so much baggage. An ex-husband and children would be one thing, but a dead husband, a murder charge and a troublesome past that he wasn't even sure he wanted to know about, was a little more than he cared to take on.

But now, all those pesky little details escaped him as he felt her heart beating against his chest. His eyes locked with hers and for a moment, he just enjoyed the feeling.

Ever so slowly he put his hand under her chin and tilted her head up to look into her eyes. He took his time and studied her face, taking in every exquisite detail. His eyes settled on her mouth as he brushed his thumb over her bottom lip. He felt her tremble, but not resist. He felt his own heart beating like a drum and his pants growing increasingly tighter.

Slowly he brought his mouth to hers and lightly kissed her lips, just enough to get a taste of her. The soft, scarcely audible moan that came from her did not escape his notice and set off a wild impulse in him. He pulled her even closer to deepen the kiss.

And, as his luck would have it, his cell rang, breaking the spell.

He mumbled a curse word while yanking his phone out of his pocket.

"What?" Nick barked into the phone. He watched Dena move away and disappear into the kitchen.

"Hey Nick," Hank said, ignoring Nick's rough greeting. "I have just about finished with Greenly and he checks out OK. I must say though, I thought he was up to something. I mean, he is your typical money hungry lawyer, but he ain't breaking any laws. He does handle some work for that Trask company, but nothing shady that I could find. Looks like Paul Davis got him the business, maybe as a courtesy to Dena. Who knows? And I don't think he would try to harm the doctor; from what I see, he's really got the hots for her. They go way back."

He didn't know what he hated hearing more, that Greenly was innocent or that the two of them might have a history.

"OK, Hank. Thanks a lot." He was sure that if there was any dirt on Greenly, Hank would have found it. "I gave Edward a list of names to check that are tied to this case, why don't you get a copy, along with anything he has come up with. See if you can find some connections that I am missing. I guess it wouldn't hurt to check in with the detectives that Dena first talked to, see what, if anything, they have come up with. Detective Begley and the other one is Thatcher, a woman I think."

"I know Begley. He's been around a while. I'll go pay him a visit after I talk with Edward. I'll keep in touch." Hank was secretly pleased he was still on the job, as he just hated loose ends. There would be no golf or crossword puzzles until all the ends were tied up neatly together.

Nick sat down on the couch to think. If Greenly was innocent, that meant he was way off and really didn't have a damn clue who was after Dena. If he was going to stay here and play watchdog, then he would have to pull another person from the office in to help. He could coordinate from the house here, but the legwork would have to be done by someone else. He wasn't about to drag Dena all over while he questioned suspects; that only worked in the movies. He needed to check in with Margaret anyway and so he dialed her direct line.

"Good afternoon, Margaret," Nick said into the phone. "How are you this fine day?"

"Nicky dear, how good of you to check in," Margaret replied, mocking his tone and giving him a friendly laugh.

"I trust all is well at the office?"

"Fine and dandy," Margaret said as she reached across her desk for a pile of messages for Nick. "Since I am sure you did not call just to inquire about my day, I'll read your messages to you." She quickly ran through the stack, only giving him the ones that she could not handle herself and needed his attention.

"Thanks Margaret. Is Pete in by chance?" Pete Capaldi was his former partner in the police force and lifelong best friend. They grew up together, joined the academy together and now both were co-owners of O'Neal Investigations. Nick had started the company when he first left the police force and Pete followed him the next year, saying the job was just not the same without him.

"As a matter of fact, he just got in. I'll put you through. Nice chatting with you, Nick. Do call again," and she transferred him over to Pete.

"Pete Capaldi," he answered the phone while still typing on his computer. He was the master of multi-tasking. He could easily juggle hunting down a report buried on his desk and conducting a background check on his computer all while deep into a conversation on the phone with another call holding. Sometimes he even amazed the incredibly efficient Margaret.

"Hey Pete, how's it going?" Nick said to his friend.

"It's going fine with me, buddy," Pete said, chuckling into the phone. "I hear life is treating you pretty good these days. You were last seen three days ago leaving with a beautiful lady and haven't been back since. Where have you been hiding?" He stopped typing and put his feet up on his desk, glad for this interruption.

"Don't listen to office gossip, Pete," Nick said sternly but with a grin. "It's beneath you. But yeah, I've been holed up with a client, who is, as a matter of fact, easy to look at. However, she is having some trouble and I need to hang around here and keep an eye on her. That's where you come in, friend." Nick's voice turned serious as he brought him up to date on the case. "How is your work load right now?"

"Nothing major that can't be moved around." His hands were back on the keyboard, his fingers flying. "I can have Ben finish up some reports and tie up a few loose ends for me," Pete said, thinking out loud. Ben Waters was the only part-time employee they had. Still a full time police officer, he was moonlighting at O'Neal Investigations a few nights a week. He got paid under the table and put the money directly into a college fund for his four children. It was a nice arrangement that was working out fine for both parties.

"I need you to take a trip to Georgia," Nick said.

"Great. I love the South. I'll leave tonight." One thing about Pete, he never wasted time. He also had the ability to make quick decisions.

After his call to Pete, Nick was feeling better. Maybe now he could figure out what the hell was going on.

He picked up his laptop and fired off an e-mail to Clarissa to let her know that Pete would be in town and was taking over the case. Something was disturbing about that whole Trask business. The wife of the owner of the company was missing. Paul Davis had Trask Industries for a customer and Greenly had them both for clients. It could just be one big coincidence, but since he really had no faith in the word, he doubted it.

Delicious smells were drifting in from the direction of the kitchen, suddenly making him ravenous. A glimpse at his watch told him it was almost 6:00 pm, a good excuse to take a break and see what Dena was up to. He found her in front of the stove working her magic, a glass of white wine next to her. Her back was to him and he took a moment to enjoy the view. She had an incredible bottom. Firm. Round. True eye-candy.

This kind of thinking was not wise. Reminiscing about the kiss they shared earlier was not a good idea either. He hadn't gotten that turned on from a kiss since he was in high school.

"What's cooking?" Nick asked as he poured some wine in the glass she had left out for him. "It smells heavenly." With a boyish grin on his face, he walked over to her Viking stove and lifted a lid off a pan.

He had resisted the overwhelming urge to walk up behind her and wrap his arms around her waist and settled for peeking inside the pan instead. This whole playing house routine was going to get to him. Maybe it would have been better if he went to Georgia and let Pete keep watch here. But when a picture of his friend standing here helping himself to wine and anything else he wanted formed in his head, he promptly kicked out the idea. On second thought, he liked the idea of his bachelor friend, and known womanizer, on a plane headed south and far away from Dena.

"Chicken Cordon Bleu, asparagus with Hollandaise sauce and a salad. That sound all right to you?" Dena asked as she went to the sink to rinse the leaf lettuce. "Oh, and hot rolls with butter and apple pie for dessert. The pie I pulled out of the freezer, no time to bake today."

That left him stunned. He thought only his mother knew how to cook. Well, his sisters too. But that was only because they were forced to learn at birth. An Italian thing. But a single, childless, professional woman with culinary skills?

"That sounds wonderful." He tried to hide his surprise. "Can I help you with anything? I'm no chef, but I am not without skills."

"No, just have a seat and enjoy your wine. Did you find out anything when you were on the phone?" Dena asked casually. "I'm wondering if they have a suspect in mind." But instead she only wanted to know if he discovered anything else about her. She feared that one day he would tell her something vile about her past that she would not remember. Or worse, maybe then she would.

"Nothing helpful. Greenly checked out okay, which I know does not surprise you, him being your good buddy and all." Nick blurted this out with a little more sarcasm than he had intended. He saw her raise an eyebrow, but she said nothing. "I am sending Pete from the office to Georgia to check out a few things regarding Trask Industries. Ever hear of it?" Nick threw out the long shot.

"It doesn't ring a bell. Should it?" She was chopping up

vegetables on a board now while still managing to talk. Her eyes were alternating from the knife to him. He wanted to yell at her to pay attention, but she seemed to know what she was doing.

"Not necessarily. Just trying to connect the dots here," he said draining his wine glass. Dena automatically reached for the bottle and gave him a refill. It was dark out now and she went around the house lighting a few candles, more out of habit than anything else. After she lit the third candle it occurred to her he might think she was trying to set a mood. *Oh well, I like candlelight, it relaxes me,* she thought.

When she returned to the kitchen, Nick was staring at her thoughtfully, lightly tapping his fingers on the table. "Here's what I think we should do," Nick said softly.

She felt her face get hot. He does think I am trying to be romantic. She had just spent the last hour telling herself she would pretend nothing happened between them. And really, nothing had. But the thought of that kiss made the blood rush to her cheeks. She cursed her face for always giving her away.

"Dena, are you OK?" He noticed her face flushed; maybe it was one of those hot flashes women get. She nodded, so after a pause he continued. "Well, first of all, we have eliminated your patients and friends from any possible wrongdoing. Family is usually at the top of the list for suspects in most cases. But you say you have no family left." He saw her face visibly relax and wondered what was going on in that mind of hers.

"So," Nick continued carefully, "let's talk about the family you did have." Now the bright color of her face drained instantly, leaving in its place a frightening shade of pale that reminded him of death.

"My family...you want to talk about dead people, why?" *Why does he always have to come back to my past?* "How could that possibly help?" Her voice shook with anger.

Nick had guessed this would be her reaction, though he hadn't expected her to practically pass out. "Just work with me on this a minute, please." His tone was patient and gentle and he continued as if she had promised to cooperate. "There could be a connection. Now, let's start with your immediate family. Did you have any brothers or sisters?"

"No." Her voice came out in a whisper. She pulled a chair out and sat down and took in the view of the backyard. The patio light was on, casting an eerie shadow over her deck.

"When did your mother die?" He pulled out a chair and sat down across from her.

"My mother?" Dena asked, staring down at her hands as if searching for the answer. Perhaps it was better to just get this out once and for all. Then it would be over. "My mother is not dead. She still lives in Elmhurst, in the same house I grew up in, and we have not spoken in almost 24 years."

Thoughts of Nick's own loving mom came to mind and he couldn't imagine not being in contact with her. He should call her. He was sure to get an earful for not coming over for dinner this past week. "Why did you say you had no family alive?"

"My mother disowned me after...after what happened to my father." Dena looked up and met his eyes now, her eyes a little sad. She thought instead of her grandmother. A few fond memories of the sweet woman who took care of her and tried to protect her came to mind. She hadn't thought about her in a long time, because she was afraid if she allowed good memories through, the bad ones were sure to follow. "I am sure there must be a few distant cousins, but no one we were ever close with."

"Well then, I guess you should tell me about your mother. Tell me everything you can remember about her," he added before she could protest.

She struggled for a moment with what to say. She realized she did not know much about the woman who gave birth to her other than she was cold, unloving and just a bystander in her life.

"She, my mother, came from a wealthy family. When she married my father she insisted on the best of everything. The biggest house in town, becoming active members at the best clubs, but most of all, having the perfect family." She stopped and took a deep breath in before continuing. "I am not sure why I didn't have any siblings. Appearances were everything to Mother, and I always thought she would want to have at least two or three children to complete the blissful picture. I also learned that I could never discuss our private business with anyone. I learned that lesson early on." Then she spoke in a whisper he could just make out. "The hard way." She stared out the window as memories flooded in that she did not want.

"What kind of private business are you referring to?" Nick was almost afraid to ask, but he had to know. Even if this had nothing to do with what was going on now.

Dena kept gazing out the window with a distant, glassy-eyed look. "All kinds of business." She spoke slowly and softly. "Finances, family secrets and that my father... used to abuse me." Then she looked at Nick, her eyes meeting his. "That must be why I killed him."

Chapter Eleven

Early the next morning, Hank made his way through the Chicago police department in search of Detective Begley. His former home away from home. Not many would miss this eyesore, but he did. The beat up desks, the walls that were in dire need of a paint job and the permanent smell of stale coffee that penetrated the air made him nostalgic. He would recreate this décor in a second in his office at home if he thought his wife would let him.

He located Begley's vacant desk and had a seat in a sorry looking chair that was meant for visitors. Moments later, the missing detective turned the corner with a steaming Styrofoam cup of coffee. He stopped in his tracks when he saw he had company.

"Morelli. Couldn't stay away, huh?" The beaming detective stretched out his hand to greet his friend. "Still passing up retirement and working for O'Neal?"

"Yeah, you know me, not one to sit still for very long," he said as he shook his hand.

Begley blew on his coffee before taking a sip. "Hey, do you

want a cup? They're still trying to pass it off as coffee, though I'm not really sure what the hell it is."

"No, thanks. I left my Maalox at home. I wanted to talk to you about a report you took a few weeks back from a Dr. Davis. Someone broke into her house..."

Begley held up his hand to stop him. "Yeah, I remember. Classy lady. I felt sorry for her, but there was little we could do. I gave her O'Neal's business card, so I'm guessing she got in touch."

"Just curious if you came across anything."

"There wasn't much to go on, but I believed her story. My guess was she walked in on a robbery in progress; my partner didn't agree, however."

"What didn't I agree on?" Detective Thatcher said as she walked in on the tail end of their conversation. "Talking about me again, Begley?" she asked as she sat on the edge of her desk with a confrontational look on her face.

"Oh relax, Thatcher. You're wound too tight," her partner said as he turned back to Hank. "This is my partner, Detective Thatcher. Thatcher, this is former Police Detective Hank Morelli. He is asking about the report that doctor filed a few weeks ago. The lady with the break in." She nodded her head at Hank, but made no effort to shake his hand. She had heard of him. He was something of a legend around here among the older cops.

"Yeah, what about her?" Thatcher asked, glancing at her watch. Not that she really cared, the doctor and her break-in was a big waste of everyone's time. So was sitting around chatting with an old has been that still wanted to play detective.

"Did you come up with anything interesting?" Hank addressed them both.

"We didn't come up with squat, interesting or otherwise," Thatcher answered for them both. "That's because there wasn't anything to come up with. The *doctor* has an overactive imagination. Maybe she should have been a fiction writer instead of a shrink."

"We did check out her house, of course," Begley interrupted before his partner could say something they would both end up regretting. "There was some kind of scuffle, it appeared, by the front door." At that, Thatcher rolled her eyes and plopped down into a chair.

It must be a barrel of laughs having to work with her every day, Hank thought. Poor Begley, nice guy too.

"So, I take it that you two don't know that someone climbed a ladder and crashed through her bathroom window the other night? Surprised her while she was taking a bath." The cup of coffee halfway up to Begley's mouth was put back down; neither cop said anything. "She got off easy though with only twenty-something stitches on her backside. O'Neal broke up the party before it really had a chance to get going."

Thatcher stretched in her chair, doing her best to look bored, though the mention of Nick's name had her attention. "That break-in was probably legit then. Tough break about her back and all, but that has nothing to do with the episode that brought her in the first time. Now, if you will excuse me, I've got work to do."

Hank got up to leave and as he did, he stared at Thatcher for a long two seconds, causing her to squirm under his scrutiny. Then he turned back to Begley.

"Begley," he said. "You have my deepest sympathy."

* * *

That same morning Doug Greenly arrived at his office at the predictable time of 7:30 am. He had his habitual cup of coffee from Starbucks, which he had served in his own special travel mug. He particularly detested drinking coffee out of disposable cups of any kind. He fiddled at his desk and waited until a more reasonable hour to call Dena.

He decided 8:00 am was reasonable enough and picked up the phone to call her. He had been worried about her since the visit from that thug of a detective. But, she was a grown woman and a psychologist to boot, so she must know what she was doing. Still, he wanted to check in.

"Good morning, Dena," he said cheerfully, pleased that he

had not gotten her answering machine.

"Doug!" she exclaimed, immediately recognizing his voice. "I have been meaning to call you." She was sorry she did not phone him earlier, he must have been worried sick about her.

"I heard you have had some excitement in your life finally. Although, I must say this was not what I had in mind for you. Is everything okay now?" She could hear the concern in his voice.

"I am sorry if you were worried or inconvenienced in any way. I know an investigator came to see you. I told Nick we were lifelong friends, but he still felt the need to have you checked out."

"Oh, I don't care. If it helps you, then fine." For the next question, he tried his best to sound casual. "Who is Nick?"

"Nick O'Neal is the owner of the investigative firm I hired."

"I see," Doug said, though he felt she was leaving something out. "So, have they found out anything yet?"

"No, but I had another visitor the other night." She filled him in on the last break-in. "Well, one positive thing has come out of all of this; it's forcing me to finally go through Paul's things I had in storage. After he died, I had everything of his put away and I haven't taken a look since. So, today I start sorting and tossing." She said this while looking around at the boxes on her office floor and twirling the phone cord in her hand. "I am sure there's not much here of value or that would be of use to anyone." She let out a long sigh at the thought of the task ahead of her.

"What kinds of things did you save?" He was curious she should save anything at all. She wasn't exactly sentimental when it came to Paul, or anyone else, for that matter.

"Mostly work stuff, files, his planner, and endless amounts of paper. It was just too much to deal with at the time so I shoved it all in boxes and stuck it into storage. All his clothes and personal items from home I had the church thrift shop pick up a while ago." She stood back up to get to work.

"His planner?" Doug asked nonchalantly. "You mentioned

to me last month you came across it in a box of Paul's possessions you stuck in the back of your closet."

"Did I?" She reached out and pulled her late husband's
constant companion out of the box. It felt odd to see it again.
"Well, I guess I just thought it was in there. That box had his
wallet, address book and the entire contents of a drawer he
used in my desk. I just emptied the drawer into the box and put
it aside."

Then, eager to change the subject, "Let's do dinner next
week, Doug, we haven't spent any time together in ages."

Doug smiled into the phone. "That sounds marvelous.
There is a new little trendy restaurant that just opened; we can
be one of the firsts to check it out. Hey, do you want to come
and stay with me a few days? You really shouldn't be there
alone, Dena."

For some reason, she felt funny telling him she wasn't
alone. "Actually, the private detective I hired is staying here
with me. He insisted but now I am glad he did." She realized
then just how glad she was that Nick was keeping watch.

"Oh. Well, I do feel better knowing that you are protected."
His hand formed a death grip around the receiver. "I will call
you next week for dinner." He was eager now to get off the
phone. They said their good-byes and he sat unmoving at his
tidy desk for almost a full half hour while he thought about his
dear Dena.

Dena stood in the midst of the clutter, realizing the extent
of the chore ahead of her, but her thoughts were on Doug. Her
mind slipped back in time to when they were little. It seemed
she had always known him. They lived on the same block.
Doug, Marcy and Dena would all hang out together, and almost
always at Marcy's house. Her home had an open door policy
that made everyone feel welcome, whereas Dena's house was
more like a cold, forbidding museum.

Doug had no home. Not his own anyhow. His widowed
mother was the head housekeeper at the Whitfield mansion
near the end of their street. The Whitfield family's backyard
was reserved for their own children, not the hired help's and it

was preferred that their housekeeper's son stay out of sight.

She always felt sorry for Doug's mother. She was on the heavy side and Dena recalled her as always looking old and tired. She wore an odd, sad expression like that of someone who is remembering bittersweet memories of a life that had passed her by. She worked long, hard hours and was continuously exhausted. And even though she was given the title of head housekeeper, it was more for appearances, for there was less than a handful of staff to head. So, most of the work was given to Doug's mother, Lilly.

That left Marcy's as the natural place to hang out. They took care of each other, and Doug became Dena's protector. Once, when he called for her outside her bedroom window, as he often did, he heard her crying out in pain. He waited a few minutes, unsure what to do. He could hear her father yelling at her and Dena whimpering and he became filled with rage. He wanted to kill the man, do something, anything to help. But, as a skinny boy of eleven, he didn't know what he could do. So, he waited. And when she came out, he took her hand and walked her over to Marcy's. Together they would bandage, wrap and ice her wounds. Unfortunately, it soon became a routine. The trio kept it a secret and hid a first aid kit in the garage.

Dena had learned at an early age that other adults could not be trusted. They would not believe her and no one was going to rescue her. In fact, they would hold her responsible.

She had taken the chance once with a young teacher she was particularly fond of, whom she had come to have faith in.

Ms. Matherson was everyone's favorite teacher; she had a way of making you feel special. One day after school, while erasing the blackboards for Ms. Matherson, her sleeve fell back to reveal an ugly black and blue bruise. As she reached up high to get the last of the day's lessons off the board, she heard her teacher gasp.

"Dena!" she cried. "What in the world did you do to your arm?" Her father took care not to leave a mark when disciplining, and if he did, it generally was in a place that clothes concealed.

The seconds dragged by and turned into minutes before she could find her voice. Her shoulders were slouched downward, but her head remained facing the blackboard, as if the advice she sought might materialize in front of her. Finally, she decided she should trust her teacher whom she truly loved. She didn't want to get her father in trouble. She just wanted him to stop. "My father does this to me," she whispered softly. "When he gets mad at me."

Her teacher thought long and hard before replying.

"Well then, Dena, I suggest you try not to make him mad." Yes, she understood what Dena was trying to say to her. But getting one of Elmhurt's most prominent and honored citizens angry with her would not only get her fired, she would most likely have to leave town. She had a job she loved, her own little home and most important, a new boyfriend. Things were becoming serious between the two of them and she couldn't bear the thought of leaving him.

So, the best thing she could do for Dena was to just advise her to stay out of her father's way.

She nodded her head and left, never bringing it up again. So her teacher thought it was her fault too, just like her mom said. Maybe I am to blame, she thought as she walked home. But I try so hard to be good. She concentrated on holding back the tears. She did not want to be a cry baby.

So immersed in her flashback was Dena that she was unaware of Nick standing in the doorway. He stood as a silent observer watching tears stream down her face. But other than tears, her face held no other emotion or expression.

"Dena," he kept his voice low in hopes that he wouldn't startle her. "How's it going in here?" It had to be tough going through her dead husband's things.

When she finally acknowledged him, she knew she was going to tell him. Not for her sake. No, for her friend, Doug.

"I just got off the phone with Doug, and as I sat here a bittersweet memory came to mind. I usually don't spend time reflecting on the past, I try to stay focused on the present. I know you think that Doug might have had something to do with all this, but he couldn't have." Dena motioned for Nick to have a seat while she took a deep breath in and exhaled slowly.

"As you might have already guessed, my childhood was not filled with merriment." She made an attempt at a smile. "My father was a well known and highly respected member of the community, but behind closed doors, he was a monster. Sometimes, for a reason no greater than leaving a book on the floor, my father would roll up his sleeves and let me have it." She turned her chair slightly so she could look past him and out the window at her beautiful yard. Just like she had seen her patients do when they were reliving their horrors.

"My mother, though she never physically hurt me, did not help me either. If she was in the same room, hard at work on her needlepoint, she would quickly set her project down and excuse herself from the room. She would mutter something about needing to check with Cook about dinner. She pretended nothing was wrong. Her job was to keep up appearances and make sure the house ran smoothly. We always had hired help and she left all my care, as well as that of the house, to them."

Nick said nothing, but a cold rage was building inside him. He wanted to reach out and hold her or track down her heartless mother and choke her. But instead he used restraint and sat and listened.

She continued her story as if this meant nothing to her. Keeping her voice flat and even, she did not allow herself to get emotionally involved in the story she was telling. She did not want to fall apart in front of Nick.

"If I struggled or resisted in anyway, I knew it would be fifty times worse. Various types of torture were used on me, from cigar burns to electrical switches." Her voice sounded so casual and matter of fact, it was as if she was discussing something as mundane as the weather. "As you can imagine, wounds of that nature might become infected if not properly taken care of. So, I would go find Doug if he wasn't already waiting outside my door for me, and we would head to Marcy's house. The two of them would patch me up and do their best to comfort me. I always thought Doug would become a doctor, he was so good at bandaging me and calming me down." She smiled as if this was a happy memory. "Marcy, though, did not have the stomach for it. She would often run out and throw up behind the garage."

Nick was nauseous himself, and if she hadn't already killed that bastard of a father, he would have. He did not need to know the circumstances of his death, the man deserved to be shot. He could not even begin to imagine growing up in a house like that. His own childhood had been wonderful and he was surrounded by warm, loving people.

"Dena," he spoke like a police officer, taking down the facts. "Didn't you tell anyone, or try to get help?"

"You have to remember, this was twenty-five years ago. Times were different. Especially in a small, Southern town. I tried to tell a teacher of mine, but she didn't want to get involved. She was probably afraid for herself. My father was a powerful man." Dena pinched the bridge of her nose in an effort to ward off a headache.

"I think my grandmother knew. Not everything, but she knew my father was evil and she was afraid of him. She wanted me to live with her but my parents would not hear of it. To be honest, I didn't tell her everything, to protect her. She loved me dearly and that would have killed her. I was allowed to stay the night there occasionally, and it was heaven for me. I frequently had horrible nightmares and she would always come in to comfort me." Dena closed her eyes and allowed the memories to flood her mind.

"You take care, Dena," Grandmother whispered in the thick blackness of the night. Gently she tucked Dena's hair behind her ear. *"I know your daddy has a dark, evil side that frightens even me. You take care to stay out of his way."*

They both sat quietly in her grandmother's little guest bedroom. After a few minutes her grandma got up and turned on a little crystal lamp that sat on a chest of drawers.

"When you are home and you wake up afraid, you can turn on this little lamp to bring you comfort. I will let you take it with you," Grandma offered. It tormented her to see her pre-

cious granddaughter so fearful.

"No!" Dena said sharply. *"Daddy hates when I leave a light on at night. He says they are for sissies and he doesn't want me to be stupid and act like a scaredy cat."*

"Well then honey, you just whistle," Grandma stated firmly. *"When you wake up from a bad dream, you just give a little whistle and you will feel better."*

"Whistle," Dena finally spoke again, coming out of her memories. She wore a sad expression. "Grandmother used to tell me to do that when I was scared."

She was never sure if she felt better when she followed her advice, but nonetheless, she kept up the practice. For some reason she never thought to try it the other night when she had a nightmare about Paul; maybe there were just too many other things on her mind. Years later, when she was in college, she came across a thought on the subject by Sigmund Freud. "When the wayfarer whistles in the dark," he wrote, "he may be disavowing his timidity, but he does not see any the more clearly for doing so." I might not see any clearer, Dena thought, but I still try to whistle my nightmares away.

"So, anyway, that was my childhood for you in the Cliff notes version." She took a slow, deep cleansing breath in and waited for Nick's response. She tried to give him a little grin; she didn't want him to pity her. But unfortunately, she felt a tear start to roll down her face.

"I am so sorry, Dena." And he was. "Sorry that you had to suffer at the hands of your own father. Sorry that you never knew a happy childhood and that to this day, you are still tormented by your experiences." And because he did not know what else to do for her, he did what he could. Slowly, he walked around the desk, his eyes never leaving hers. He bent down and scooped her up in his strong arms and carried her to the living room where the fire he started earlier was now roaring in the hearth. He sat back into a big rocker, keeping his grip tight. There, he rocked her for what seemed like an hour, whispering comforting words and stroking her hair.

It was Dena who first spoke. "I've never told anyone, except my own therapist, about my childhood. Not even Paul. Of course Marcy and Doug know, but we agreed to bury it a long time ago."

"Why did you decide to tell me?" Nick felt strangely honored that she did. That she would share a part of herself she was unwilling to let anyone else see. But still he wondered why.

"I didn't want to keep pretending it never happened. It did happen and I guess I wanted you to know who I really am. But mostly, I wanted you to see Doug for the kind and gentle man he is. I owe him that."

She felt good in his arms. In his lap. Too good, and his thoughts were starting to go in another direction. He was staring at those lips again. Something about her mouth was mesmerizing. Ever so slowly, as if afraid to break the spell, he slid his hand behind her head. He kept his eyes open as he pulled her forward towards him. He was doing a fine job of ignoring his conscience that a little earlier had told him all the reasons why this was a bad idea.

His lips touched hers, softly at first, to test the waters. He felt a response that surprised him, but one that he did not take time to question. When her mouth opened slightly, he let out a groan and his hand quickly found her breasts. He could easily visualize them bare from his earlier glimpse of her, and it did strange things to his blood pressure.

A little noise escaped from her mouth that nearly sent him over the edge. He had been walking around semi-hard these last few days and he now felt ready to explode. He was getting up to carry her over to the couch when he heard the rap on the front door. Dena scrambled to her feet with a look of terror on her face and nearly fell on the floor.

"Relax," Nick said, swearing in three languages as he crossed the room to the door. "If someone is about to break in again, I doubt they would knock first," he muttered. But he discreetly felt for his gun while looking out the peephole. He hated surprises, especially the kind that might result in him having to shoot someone.

Nick opened the door frowning and mumbled a "come in." A handsome man strolled in wearing an outfit right off the cover of GQ and a big grin. He kept smiling as he looked at Nick and then Dena.

"Uh oh," the intruder said. "Looks like I have interrupted something. My bad. But I did phone first."

Nick scowled then patted his pockets for his cell phone but came up empty. He must have left it in the kitchen.

"Dena, this is my partner, Pete Capaldi, co-owner of O'Neal Investigations. Pete, Dr. Dena Davis," Nick said as he closed the door. He watched Pete fairly leap over to shake her hand.

"So, I see the office rumors about you are true. You are beautiful." he murmured as he took her hand. Nick was half expecting him to kiss it and bow.

"Sorry to break up your cozy evening." Pete said, though he looked anything but. "I was on my way back from the airport and wanted to fill you in on what I learned in Georgia." He sat down on the couch and stretched his feet out.

"Make yourself comfortable, Pete," Nick said sarcastically. "So, tell me what you learned." He motioned for Dena to take a seat in the rocker, the chair farthest away from his good friend.

"Go ahead," Nick reassured him when he noticed his hesitation to speak in front of Dena.

"OK. But I warn you, some of this gets ugly."

"It's OK, Pete. Please, speak frankly," Dena interjected. It couldn't be any worse than the countless sessions she had sat through with her patients, listening to their worst nightmares replayed week after week.

"Well, as you may now know, Nick was already working on a missing person's case when you hired him. Michaelene Trask has been missing for a little over two years. Her sister, Clarissa Beacher, hired us to find her. Coincidently, we discovered that your husband conducted a good amount of business for Trask Industries, and more importantly, had a unique relationship with the owner of the company, Haidyn Trask."

"Unique?" Dena asked when he paused. She saw Nick nod

his head for him to continue.

"It looks like your husband may have been running drugs for Trask. This guy has a heavy drug operation going on. The feds are investigating him now, which, by the way, no one else knows about yet. They have been trying to get enough evidence to bust Trask and had begun their investigation on Paul before he died."

"I can't believe that Paul was involved with something like that." Dena was shocked. "Money was never that important to him. He flew planes because he loved it. He knew he would never get rich from it and he didn't care. Business was good and steady. He made a nice living from doing what he wanted to do."

"Well, money makes people do foolish things. And this kinda money would tempt a saint. Anyway, we already knew quite a bit about Trask and his company because of the missing person case. He is not someone you want as an enemy."

"You think Paul's disappearance might have something to do with him?" It felt strange to have all this brought up again. She wasn't sure how to react. She had buried him and put this behind her.

"It could, yes. If Paul had tried to double-cross him in some way, Trask would be the type of man to take action. He might have had something done to his plane or had someone waiting at one of his stops."

"Did you speak to Clarissa while you were there?" Nick asked. Though she was genuinely eager to find her sister, she was not all that talkative with Nick.

Pete nodded. "She told me she knew her sister had been planning to go away for a while, like take a long vacation and not tell her husband. She didn't want Trask to send someone to fetch her and bring her back or him calling and harassing her. Clarissa said she knew her sister was deathly afraid of her husband. When she didn't hear from her sister after a month, she got worried. So, she started her own investigation."

"Well, you sure got a lot more out of Clarissa than I did," Nick said, amazed. That was Pete for you. He could charm the socks off just about anyone, and when it came to females, they turned to mush. He glanced over at Dena to see if she was mesmerized by his charisma. She was smiling at the bastard.

"Well, shucks, Nick," Pete said with a boyish grin. "Was that a compliment?"

Ignoring his friend's comment, he continued. "She could have been planning on leaving him for good, and might still be in hiding." A more chilling thought occurred to him. "Or Trask found out about her plans and stopped her permanently." Nick rubbed his chin as he processed the information.

"I didn't talk to Trask while I was there. I think it will be bad for our health when he finds out what we know." He paused for a minute while tapping his fingers on his leg.

"I assume you talked to Mr. Trask yourself?" Dena asked Nick. "What did he say about his wife's absence?"

"He said she left him and is probably out spending his money somewhere. And since he hasn't received divorce papers yet, he believes she is just taking a break. He went on about how they have been married awhile and couples need a vacation from each other now and then. He said he knew she would come to her senses and return home when she was ready."

"Did you believe him?" She wanted to know what his instincts told him.

"At the time I had no reason to suspect foul play and we only talked over the phone. But a report about a wife that has been missing for over two years obviously raises red flags." He paused and she could almost see the wheels turning. "I didn't get the chance to meet him in person."

She knew what he meant by that. He would want to see his body language. Look him in the eye. He would be very good at that.

"Oh, I talked to Margaret on the way over here," Pete said as he was reading the cover of a Newsweek he found on the coffee table while tapping his fingers on his leg. It was almost as if he had a song playing in his head while simultaneously reading a magazine and carrying on a conversation. All his energy was giving her motion sickness. "She said Detective Begley left you a message that a Bridgett Bonner's body was discovered last night."

Dena and Nick exchanged glances.

"You mean they found where their plane went down?" Dena asked. "They found their bodies?"

"No," Pete answered. "Her body was discovered right here in town. She's been alive and well until the other night. Then she was murdered."

Chapter Twelve

Early the next morning, Nick and Dena met at the kitchen table to try and figure out what to do with the news they had learned last night. And what, if anything, did it have to do with the trouble she was having now? It had been an endless night with no hope for sleep for Dena and the evidence showed on her face. Her brain had been on overload and it was just too difficult to shut down.

Her husband was really a money-hungry drug dealer.

His girlfriend, Bridgett Bonner, was just found brutally murdered.

"So, where has Bridgett been hiding all this time?" Dena asked suddenly. "And why?"

"Why what?" Nick asked, finally looking up from his notes.

"Why was she hiding? When she heard that Paul was missing and everyone believed she was with him, why didn't she come forward?" Dena got up to make another pot of coffee in hopes that it would lift the fog in her brain. "What could she possibly gain by pretending to be dead?"

"That's what we need to find out. Go get dressed, we're going to pay someone a visit. We'll stop for coffee on the way," he added when she gazed desperately at the coffee maker.

"So, do you want to tell me where we are going?" Dena finally asked while staring out the window of Nick's Tahoe. The sun was making its way through the trees in an effort to warm up a rather chilly November morning. How could it look like such an ordinary day when her world, as she knew it, was coming apart?

"We are going to see Bridgett's former roommate. You told me she once shared an apartment with a girl named Suzie, so I did some checking and found she moved not too far from here." When he saw her shudder, he kicked the heat up a notch.

They pulled up in front of a compact but well kept bungalow, just outside of Oak Park. It was a quiet, nice little family neighborhood where kids played on the front lawn and the people next door were your friends. The charming little house they walked up to did not seem capable of harboring someone who pretended to be dead.

Suzie Simms answered the door on the second ring. She looked as if she thought she ought to know the names of the two strangers standing on her porch.

It was obvious she had just crawled out of bed. She wore baggy, well worn flannel pajamas and her feet were stuffed in fuzzy slippers. Her hair had some major bed head going on that resembled a cartoon character Nick couldn't quite place. It was also just as apparent she had been crying.

"Suzanne Simms?" Nick asked, though he was sure he had the right person.

"Yeah, that's me," she said. She sniffled loudly and used her flannel sleeve as a tissue.

Nick winced and wished he had listened to his mother's advice of always carrying a handkerchief.

"My name is Nick O'Neal and this is Dr. Davis. I am a private investigator. Can we talk with you for a few minutes please?" He locked eyes with her and offered her a heart-stopping, lopsided grin.

"It's really not a good time for me right now," she apologized. "I'm not much in the talking mood." Suzie spoke directly to Nick, wishing she had never answered the door looking like this. Even in her grief she could not help but notice what a hunk this guy was. And his eyes. They were the most incredible shade of blue she had ever seen.

She was sizing up his physical attributes when she realized he was saying something to her. She ran her nose over the other sleeve this time and Nick frantically checked his pockets just in case a hanky should materialize. He looked expectantly over at Dena. Didn't women usually carry that kind of thing in their purses? Dena gave him a puzzled look, so he had no choice but to continue.

"So, Ms. Simms, may we come in and talk, please? I promise not to take up too much of your time," Nick asked, treating her to another one of his killer smiles.

"Sure, come on in," she said, moving out of the way to allow them to enter. "And call me Suzie." She walked over to a couch and love seat that sat opposite from each other and waved her hand for them to have a seat.

The décor had a rustic country appeal. It was cozy and inviting. Not quite what you would expect from two single modern women, but Nick liked it. The couches were plaid with a wood and iron table in the center and a smaller one at the end of the love seat.

On the coffee table, thank God, sat a box of Kleenex.

"I'm sorry I'm such a wreck," Suzie said as she threw herself back into the couch. "But my roommate just died." As she blurted this out, a fresh batch of tears started.

"Yes, we know, Suzie. I'm sorry." He was relieved that he did not have to be the one who had to break the bad news to her. He picked up the box of Kleenex and held it out in front of her.

"You do?" Suzie said with an alarmed look as she took a tissue.

"Yes. We know that your roommate, Bridgett Bonner, was killed the other night," Dena answered for them both. She felt she should say something; after all, she had known Bridgett.

Suzie quickly covered a look of panic that had washed over her, but not before Nick could recognize it. After years on the police force, he could detect and decipher a multitude of facial expressions. It's an essential trick of the trade when the majority of the people you deal with do not readily speak the truth.

"I think you are confused. My friend's name is...was Maddie Stevens," Suzie stated, forcing herself to remain calm. "She was killed the other night as she was leaving work. She was...someone cut her. Her throat." She put her head in her hands and her body began to shake.

"I'll get you a glass of water," Dena said and made her way to the kitchen. Her first reaction was to sit and comfort her, but she knew they were not there for a counseling session and Suzie was not her patient.

"I know who your friend was, Suzie, that she had changed her name and was hiding out. I want to know why. I am not interested in anything you may have done to help her and I will see that you don't get into any trouble." Nick leaned forward and looked into her eyes. "But I think she changed her name because she was frightened of someone, and that someone found her and killed her. And if they even think you know something, there is a good chance they may come for you next."

"Oh my God!" she cried, rocking back and forth. Dena came in and handed her the water and put her arm around her, telling her to breathe deeply.

"I warned her not to go ahead with their plans. It was crazy. Like something out of a movie. But no, she wouldn't listen to me." The thought that she could be in some kind of danger had indeed occurred to her. But to hear someone else say it, made it much more real.

"Why don't you start at the beginning, back when Bridgett first met Paul?" Nick suggested.

Suzie was still for a few seconds while she thought this out. She had no one left to protect but herself. And she had to admit, she was in way over her head. Training for a career as a hairdresser does little to prepare you for a life of crime and murder.

"It started a few years back," Suzie said softly. "Bridgett was having an affair with her boss, Paul Davis. I don't really know how the two met. I think it was through the hospital where she once worked. She was a nurse. Anyway, he owned some kind of charter service and one of his planes was an air ambulance. He hired Bridgett to care for the patients while they were in flight. It was a good job. The pay was good, she got to travel, and she was really crazy about this guy. He was married but his divorce was already in the works." Nick couldn't help but glance over at Dena to see her reaction, but she appeared lost in thought.

Suzie ran her hands over her wild mane and continued. "Then Paul got into some kinda trouble. I don't know all the details, but it had something to do with one of his big shot clients. You see, Bridgett had discovered that Paul had been stealing a little merchandise from each delivery he did and was selling the stuff himself. She was worried because this was someone you didn't want to cross. I don't know his name. But he owned a big company and was worth a lot of money. I think he came from the South. Bridgett jokingly referred to him as J.R., like the guy from that old show Dallas. Anyway, Paul suspected that his client was on to him as well as the feds. And, after a couple of guys from the FBI came to his office and started poking around, Paul decided to stage his death. Bridgett said if the J.R. character and the authorities were on to him, he had no way out. If the feds didn't lock him away for life, the other guy would kill him."

He could guess what their crazy plans were. "So they decided to start fresh, huh?" Nick sounded intrigued with their brilliant idea, when in reality he was anything but. Only in Hollywood can you pull off living with a different identity and living happily ever after while sipping Pina Coladas under the palm trees. In the real world, especially without underworld connections, you'd get caught sooner than later.

"Yes." Suzie gave him a look of admiration for his quick

reasoning. "For the next few months Paul and Bridgett worked out the details on how they would fly away and just disappear. You see, Bridgett was really the smart one. She spent hours planning where they would go, where money would be wired, that kind of thing. And supposedly, Paul had a bundle of money socked away. Bridgett took everything she had and away they went."

"So, she did go away with him then," Dena interrupted.

"Well, no. About a week before they were to leave, she learned that Paul had been cheating on her. She found something in his office that made her suspicious and she began to realize that he had never intended to take her with him. She believed that Paul was taking this other woman with him instead of her, and that he had been just using her to help set things up. At first she was so mad, she was spitting fire. She was going to confront him, but then had second thoughts. I convinced her to go to the police and tell them everything. She knew all about his plans and his secrets. She knew everything. Then she realized, there was no way he was going to leave her behind."

"You mean she thought Paul would kill her?" Dena asked, stunned. She was certainly seeing a whole new side of Paul, but she had a tough time believing he was capable of murder.

"Yes. Especially when she learned who the other woman was. She was, and get this, the wife of the businessman he was in trouble with. Bridgett figured his new girlfriend would be able to bring a hefty amount of money with her when they ran away as opposed to the measly $5,000 she had tucked away. This was about money and a big time scam, and she knew he was not going to let her walk away. She knew she had to go to the police, even if that meant she got into trouble for originally helping him."

"How come I never heard anything about this then? If there was a police report on this, I'm sure someone would have mentioned it?" Dena asked. She may have felt like pulling her hair out, but she had years of practice sitting still and listening to other's nightmares. This one just happened to be her own.

"She never went to the police," Nick stated calmly, keeping his eyes locked with Suzie's. "Who changed her mind?"

Surprise flickered on Suzie's face. "No, she never did. And you are right, someone did change her mind. Some man contacted her and asked her not to go to the police. He said he was collecting evidence himself and when he had what he needed, he would turn Paul in. He convinced her that going to the authorities now would only incriminate her. It was all very creepy."

"How so?" He gave her an encouraging smile to continue.

"Well, he seemed to know all about their plans, but Bridgett could never figure out how. She never told a soul, other than me, and she was sure Paul wouldn't have said anything. He said they would let Paul and his mistress go off together and think they were safe. He wanted Bridgett to hide out until they left on their scheduled trip, then he suggested she change her name. He said he was representing the man Paul cheated. He would handle everything and make sure Paul was brought to justice and the woman returned to her husband. He also said his client knew all about Bridgett and her role in helping Paul disappear. He hinted it would be better for her health if she disappeared for a while."

"Who was this guy?" Nick asked.

"At first we thought he was a cop. But when he said he was representing his client, we assumed he was a lawyer," Suzie said.

"I don't suppose you remember his name or where he worked?" Nick gently coaxed her. When she shook her head no he tried again.

"What did he look like?" He had a pretty good idea who the lawyer was. But without proof, he couldn't even whisper the guy's name in front of Dena.

"I never really saw him." She was shaking her head no, her wild hair flying about her face. "And I am just awful with names. I'm sorry," Suzie said, wishing she could offer something of value to this incredible male specimen.

"Anyway," she got back to her story. "He gave her some

money so she could lay low for awhile and helped her change her name. In return, she gave him all the information she had on Paul, his business, how he planned on disappearing and where he had money hidden. She even gave him the names of the people who bought the stolen merchandise. Bridgett then became Maddie Stevens, and we both moved here together and started new jobs. I am a hairdresser, so I can find work anywhere, and this guy helped Maddie get a new job as a private nurse for some old lady. In fact, the old lady just died a few days before Bri..I mean Maddie died." A fresh batch of tears started and Suzie shook her head as if to stop them. "She really liked that old lady, ya know? She felt real bad when she died."

"Do you know the name of the woman Maddie worked for?" Nick asked hopefully. "Or her address?" He knew it was a long shot. And most likely she was paid under the table, so they weren't going to find tax records.

"Not her real name. Maddie used to call her Flur or something like that. Anyway, it was some French name that this lady liked to be called. I think Maddie made it up or used it to make the lady feel special."

Nick pulled out his business card and handed it to her as he gave her a grin. "You can call me anytime if you think of anything. Anything at all, even if it is just an impression you have, please give me a call." Nick stood. "Thank you for your time, Suzie, we appreciate your help."

"Sure, I am just sorry I couldn't be of more help. Do you think I will be safe here now?" Suzie asked.

"I honestly don't know, but it might be a good time for you to take a vacation," Nick said truthfully.

"Gee, thanks," Suzie said with a little chuckle as they made their way to the door.

On impulse, Dena turned back and handed Suzie her card as well.

"I specialize in grief counseling, Suzie. Please call me day or night if you need to talk," Dena said softly as she touched her arm. "Sometimes just talking it out will make you feel much better."

* * *

The drive back to Dena's was a quiet one. The picture perfect blue sky that escorted them out of town was now replaced by cold, gray clouds. A light mist and a cold breeze turned it into an entirely different day. She could see Nick's brows knit tight in concentration.

"So, I don't suppose you speak French?" Nick asked doubtfully.

"Je ne parle pas tres bien le francais," Dena replied.

"Excusez-moi?" He asked with a raised eyebrow.

Dena laughed. "I said I don't speak French very well. However, I think the name Maddie had for the old woman was fleur." She spelled it out for him. "It means flower in French."

"Hmm. You never stop surprising me," he said with another smile. "Hey, how about surprising me again tonight?" Then, "With dinner. You're a good cook," he added quickly when he saw the shocked looked on her face. "Gee, what did you think I meant?"

"I don't know what I thought exactly, but all kinds of possibilities ran through my mind," Dena said, laughing. It felt good to laugh, even to flirt, Dena thought. Although she didn't have much experience in the flirting department, she was old enough to recognize it. "What are you in the mood for?" she asked.

He raised his eyebrows at that and chuckled.

"For dinner, Nick. What would you like me to make? Something French or Chinese? I know a few German dishes as well," Dena asked, mentally examining her pantry at home.

"What, no Italian? You don't like Italian food?" Nick sounded surprised.

"I love Italian food. But I'm sure I cannot compete with your Italian mother, so I won't even try."

"Well, she is a great cook. And speaking of her, I had better call her right now," Nick said as he began dialing his cell phone. "I haven't so much as checked in with her in days, so

I'm bound to get an earful. She will want me to come for dinner."

"Hey Dylan. How's the new business?" Nick clicked on the speaker phone as he mouthed to Dena, "my brother."

"Good. Great, actually, Nick. Got some new software you will be interested in for your office." Dylan was the owner and brains behind his new successful software company. He provided Nick's office with the newest devices and equipment, keeping O'Neal Investigations on the cutting edge of technology and one step above any other private detective agency. It was one of the reasons his firm was such a success.

"Talk to Edward. Tell him I said to order whatever he likes. He practically lives at the office, so you can call now if you want. After I speak to Mom, that is. Is she around?"

"Is she around?" Dylan teased. "She has been hovering around me since she heard your name. Talk to you later, Nick," he said.

"Nicholas O'Neal!" his mother shouted into the receiver, causing Nick to pull the phone away from his ear or risk serious damage to his eardrum. "You're too busy to call your own mother? When are you coming for dinner?"

"I know Mother, and I'm sorry." Nick winced. Yes, he should have put in a quick call. Only there was no such thing as a quick call when he phoned home. One of his siblings was sure to answer and he would have to talk to one or more of them before he could even get to his mother. "I am working on a case where I need to act like a bodyguard, so I have been with my client night and day." He felt Dena giving him a look.

"What is this client's name?" his mother asked with suspicion.

"Dr. Davis," Nick answered quickly. He was ready for her.

"I see. Well, bring her with you tomorrow night for dinner. I will make all your favorites. Next time, don't wait so long to call me."

"What makes you think Dr. Davis is a woman?" He grinned into the phone.

"I didn't think you would spend night and day watching

over a man. You would send Pete for that assignment. You signed up for this job, so this one I want to meet. See you both tomorrow."

"You win. See you tomorrow." Nick smiled as he hung up the phone.

Chapter Thirteen

He looked over at Dena who had been studying his profile while he was on the phone. He wanted to ask if she saw anything she liked, but that sounded a little fresh. And probably not a good idea.

"You are going to see your mother tomorrow?" Dena asked, hoping to get out of it.

"*We* are going to see my mother for dinner tomorrow. My mother, father and, I am sure, all my brothers and sisters will be in attendance."

Her face took on a look of horror. "I am not used to big family gatherings. Actually, I am not used to families at all. How many brothers and sisters do you have?" Dena asked in one lungful of air.

"I am one of six. Three boys and three girls. There is Anthony, Meghan, myself, Maria, Dylan and the baby of the family, Shannon. And you will get to meet them all. I am not leaving you alone." His tone was final and firm.

"Sounds like your parents took turns naming their children. Half are Italian names, half Irish," Dena said with a nervous laugh. "But this is a family gathering. I think I would be in the way." She did not want to admit to him the whole idea terrified her.

"You're right, they did take turns naming us. Anthony, the oldest, was named after my mother's father, whom they both loved, so it was a mutual decision. After that, they took turns." Nick reached over and patted her hand. "Don't worry, they will love you. They will make you feel right at home."

The remainder of the afternoon they were each busy with their own agenda: Dena nestled in her office doing patient follow-up calls and billing; Nick checking in with Margaret, who brought him up to speed on the entire day at the office in less than ten minutes.

Nick returned a phone call from his agent who was inquiring when he might expect at least the outline of his next book. He committed to Marcus that he should have it next week. That sounded very promising, but in reality it was one big fat lie. He hadn't even started it yet. Sure, an outline could be done by next week, if he was actually working on it now. He had a few ideas spinning around his head before Dena walked into his office. But after spending a day with her, a new story began to unfold. So he pitched his old ideas and began writing notes in a folder he carried with him. Jotting down ideas for a book was the only time he ever really took notes. He never had a problem remembering names and numbers for the business. But if he didn't catch the thought for a character down on paper, it would be lost. Tonight, he reasoned, he would transfer some of his scribble into the start of an outline. Marcus would be happy.

* * *

Later that evening, after a simple German meal that consisted of sausage, sauerkraut, potatoes and of course German beer, they settled in front of the fireplace. Nick had his laptop, cell phone and several files spread out in front of him.

Dena was sorting through a box of Paul's papers she had

brought out from her office. A black garbage bag lay partially full next to her chair. She was half tempted to haul the box over to the roaring fire Nick had built and toss it in.

She peeked up from the papers in her hand and her eyes rested on Nick, who was typing on his laptop. God, he was gorgeous. You could never get tired of merely watching him, and she wondered why he wasn't married. Maybe he was. He never said one way or the other.

"Are you married?" Dena blurted out before she could stop herself. Shocked at what had just come out of her mouth, she wondered why she suddenly felt like an adolescent.

He stared blankly at her for a moment and she was hoping he hadn't heard her.

"Married?" he asked with a devilish grin.

"I was just curious." She wished now that he would forget she had said anything. Or the phone would ring or someone would come to the door. Maybe a small earthquake.

"Not at the moment. Why, are you interested?"

"No..." Dena started to say.

"No? You've been staring at me for the last fifteen minutes," Nick interrupted.

"Well, if you would let me finish, please," an exasperated Dena cried. "It's only that we are spending day and night together and I hardly know anything about you."

"What do you want to know, Dena?" He enjoyed seeing her flustered and the pink already on her cheeks. "You already know what I do for a living. You're going to meet my family tomorrow and you've even been to my condo, what else is there?" Nick paused for a minute. "Or is it my love life you are interested in?"

"I am not interested in prying into your love life, Nick," she said, trying to hold back the irritation. Well, she started this. "I thought you might share how you started your business, why you chose this profession, things like that. You know, we could have a conversation."

"Oh. Conversation. Sure." He shrugged. "I would be delighted to share my history with you. But I warn you, it's not that exciting." Not to him anyway.

She was about to tell him to forget it and run upstairs and take a bath, but before she could get the words out, he started talking.

"I left the police force because I felt I was limited in what I could do and got tired of following rules when the bad guys got away with murder, literally. I opened O'Neal Investigations to have a source of income while I pursued my true passion, which is writing." He hesitated only slightly when he saw her raise her eyebrows at that. "The business grew fast and my good buddy and former partner joined me and we branched out into other areas. We handle security for businesses, missing persons, collections, and a few child custody cases. We are also on retainer with a large law firm in the Chicago area--we handle just about everything for them. But even after I got a little more established in my writing career, I decided I would keep the business. I still enjoy that kind of work and it often sparks an idea for a book. Plus it provides a nice income for some good people I know. Most are former police officers who enjoy working without all that messy red tape and politics."

"How is your writing going?" asked Dena. "Have you published anything? I am not much of a fiction reader, but I do enjoy a mystery or a good thriller now and then." She was sure if his face was on the jacket of any book she had read, she would never forget it. It was his eyes, she decided. They were not only captivating, but made his face unique.

"I've published a few things," he replied and left it at that.

"When I asked if you were married, you said not at the moment. Does that mean you were once married?" Dena hated herself for asking, but for some unknown reason it was gnawing at her.

"Once, yes, and that was enough. What can I say? I was blinded by her. And once I could see straight again, I saw her for what she was; a shallow, spoiled little rich girl. We parted ways, the divorce was amicable and we still talk from time to time. Meet for drinks, that kind of thing." That was all he felt like dredging up. Talking about Leslie produced a pain in the back of his neck that reached around to the tip of his forehead.

"Well?" Nick asked.

"Well what?" She shot back.

"Are we done with the Spanish Inquisition?" Nick asked, but was laughing. "Because if we are, I'd like to call it a night. I'm beat."

"Yes, you're right. It's late," she said as she got up quickly from her chair, feeling mortified by her intrusion into Nick's private life. In her haste to make a speedy exit from the room to the safe haven of her bedroom, she sent the contents of her lap flying to the floor. She dropped to the floor in attempt to clean up her mess and hide her face that was burning with embarrassment. She stopped when she saw Nick's feet in front of her. Maybe she could just crawl out of the room and he wouldn't notice.

Slowly, he bent down and seized her by the arms, pulling her up so he could see her face. Since she appeared to be fascinated with his feet, he cupped his hand under her chin, bringing her eyes up to meet his. Her face was red as raspberries and he thought she looked adorable. Still holding her chin, he leaned forward and kissed her. Slowly at first, but with confidence. And practice, she thought. To get that good, he must have had a lot of practice.

His kiss deepened and she felt an unfamiliar but pleasant fluttering in her stomach. He tasted incredible and she felt her body betray her, responding in a way she thought was not possible. His solid muscular arms supported her and she knew she would let him do just about anything to her. Her pelvis had a mind of its own as it rubbed up against his leg, causing a moan to escape from her lips.

Nick let out a loud groan and then a curse as he picked Dena up in his arms and headed up the stairs with her, his lips never leaving hers. He tumbled on the bed with her and fought back the overwhelming urge to rip her clothes to shreds. He had to see her naked, feel her soft skin.

A sudden ringing rudely interrupted them. Actually, the loud ringing did not seem to come from the same source. It sounded like an invasion. The house phone, his cell phone and the front door were all buzzing away at the same precise moment.

Something had gone down. He cursed fate and jumped off the bed.

Nick ran down the stairs to the front door while answering his cell phone, leaving Dena to answer hers.

"Yeah?" Nick barked into the phone, while zipping up his fly. How had that happened?

"I gather it's not a good time to chat, but in case you haven't checked your voice mail on your cell phone, I wanted to be sure you got the message I left you earlier. I wasn't sure if it was important or not," Margaret said into the phone.

"No, that's fine, Margaret. What's up?" Nick said, trying to make up for taking his frustration out on his secretary. He looked through the peephole to find Pete standing on the porch, waving at the tiny opening.

"You got a phone call from a Ms. Simms. She said she remembered the name of that lawyer her friend met with. It was Hartman or Hartford or something like that, she said. She didn't remember the first name, but said you would want to know immediately. It appears that something on a letter in today's mail triggered her memory. I am assuming this makes sense to you?" Margaret asked.

"It does. Thanks, Margaret. You're a gem," Nick said as he impatiently waved Pete in. "Yes, I am. Goodnight," she said cheerfully and hung up.

"What brings you here unannounced and uninvited for the second time this week?" Nick scowled at Pete.

"Well, if I didn't know you better, good buddy, I would think you weren't happy to see me," Pete said with a mischievous grin on his face, which broke out into a bigger smile when he looked down at Nick's shirt. The buttons on his shirt were not matched up correctly.

"I see you two have been doing more than talking," Pete said as he plopped himself down on the couch and made himself comfortable. Knowing he was irritating his good friend seemed to make him very happy.

"Well?" Nick all but yelled. This better be good or he was going to pick up his good buddy and throw him out on his ass.

"I was nosing around the station this evening and just happened to be checking out Suzanne Simms..." Pete started to say.

"Yeah, yeah. I already met with her today," Nick interrupted him with annoyance.

"What I was going to say before I was so rudely interrupted," Pete continued, "is that there was a 911 call from her house tonight. When the boys got there, she was already dead. Throat slashed."

All humor was wiped from his friend's face now, revealing a seldom seen solemn side. Pete, the playboy and fun loving and ever-smiling charmer, took his job very seriously. The casual observer would never guess that he worked day and night with a vengeance on every case he had ever handled.

No words could form in Nick's brain. He felt like he had been punched in the gut. Had he put her in danger by going there today? He should have insisted she leave town that minute. *I've been thinking with my dick lately and got an innocent woman killed.*

"My answering service called," Dena said as she walked into the room. "Suzie Simms had wanted me to call her but I couldn't get an answer at her home. I'll try her back later." She saw a look pass between Nick and Pete. "What's wrong?" Dena was almost too afraid to ask.

"It's Suzie, Dena. She was killed tonight." There was only one way to give bad news, Nick believed, straight on with no beating around the bush. Giving it slow and easy does not spare the receiver any pain, it only drags it out. He saw her turn pale and paused for a second before continuing.

"But before she died, she called my office to tell me she remembered the lawyer's name. She said it was Hartman or Hartford."

"Mark Hartford was Doug Greenly's alias that he used when he bought half of D & D Aviation," Nick said to Pete, but was locked in a stare with Dena.

"And there is something else that has been bothering me. It was the old woman that Bridgett worked for who recently died. Suzie said her nickname was Fleur. What did you tell me Doug's mother's name was, Dena?" Nick asked, though he thought he remembered.

"Lilly," Dena said calmly. He would have made that connection sooner or later. She had remembered immediately of course, that Lilly always had a fondness for all things that were French.

She just didn't believe that the old woman Bridgett was taking care of could possibly be Doug's mother.

Chapter Fourteen

Darkness was the only thing Dena saw when she opened her eyes the next morning. A peek at the clock radio on her nightstand confirmed it was still rather early. Barely 5:00 am. She snuggled deeper in the covers as she heard the wind howling outside and a steady song of rain tapping against her window.

She had gone to bed last night and left Nick and Pete out in the living room still working. She did not have the stamina to stay up and defend Doug or the stomach to think about poor Suzie Simms.

Things certainly did not look good for Doug. She did not believe for a second he was involved with any of this mess. He may have dabbled in some unsavory business schemes, but she would never be convinced he was capable of murder.

And for some reason, Nick had it out for him from the beginning. It was almost like he was hoping her friend was guilty and going out of his way to prove it. Maybe he simply didn't like lawyers. She felt she owed it to Doug to at least warn him.

Doug grew up so poor, so wanting of the things that others

had and took for granted. She could see that perhaps he might feel he deserved more, but she could never believe he would hurt someone to get it.

Knowing Doug as long as she had, she could not believe that he would have become a thief and a cold-blooded killer. Suddenly, a thought did occur to her that she didn't like. It was a notion that flashed in her head. What if she had been so wrapped up in her own misery and pain as a child that she missed what was happening to her friend? She certainly had been blind when it came to Paul.

What was his home life really like? She could not say for sure. The memories that kept replaying in her mind were of Doug rescuing her, taking care of her. Was it possible that she was so self-absorbed in her own miserable childhood that she did not see her friend was suffering somehow as well?

"It's time to have a talk with Doug," Dena said out loud as she got out of bed, turning on the crystal lamp on her dresser. She was walking out to the kitchen to put the coffee on before jumping in the shower when she noticed the guest room door was open. The bedroom was empty and the house, she noticed, was very quiet. She was alone. When Nick was here, his presence filled every room. She wondered where he was and what time he left.

One hour later, Dena left the house wrapped in a fashionable trench coat and leather dress boots. She made her way to Doug's office, knowing he would start his day early. She had always thought Doug's actions were so predictable. Today she was not so sure.

As she swung left into the parking lot of Doug's office, she saw that he was already there. His silver BMW was the only car in the lot and was parked where it always was. A sign at the foot of the space had his name flamboyantly printed on it and announced that violators would be towed.

She got out of her new black Audi and entered the building. She made her way through the quiet narrow halls back to his office and stopped just before she got to his door. A man's voice was echoing through the empty office, and something in his tone made her stop. It took her a second to realize it had to be Doug on the phone, though his voice sounded odd.

His speech had a controlled anger to it. She could tell he was trying to sound composed and calm, but to her it sounded like he wanted to choke whoever was on the other end.

I told you I have been looking, but it's not that easy. I just can't walk in there and take it. Besides, it may not even have anything incriminating in it. And, there is a chance it may have been thrown out. There was a pause and then, *OK, I will find something out in the next day or so and get back with you.* No good-byes, Doug just pounded the phone back down into the receiver. Dena waited before going in, giving him a minute to cool off.

It had been a while since Dena was at Doug's office and she noticed he had made some changes. From the receptionist's area right to his door, everything had been updated and remodeled. Expensively too, she noted. New plush carpet, beautiful brass lamps and solid oak filing cabinets. Although she was not familiar with the artist's name on the bottom of the framed artwork, she could tell it showed real talent. She was happy for him. He deserved nice things.

But she couldn't help feeling a little hurt. Her good friend just had his entire work space lavishly transformed and he never mentioned a word about it to her.

Doug's door was ajar already as she walked up and tapped lightly on it. He took a second to look up and the irritation on his face quickly turned to delight.

"Dena! What a surprise. Come in, come in," he said all in one breath. He stood and came around the desk to greet her. He gave her a big hug then, while grasping her hands in his, stepped back to look at her. "To what do I owe this unexpected visit?" Doug asked, then added, "Not that I am not pleased to see you."

"I needed to talk to you about a few things, Doug. Do you have a minute?" Dena asked.

"For you? Always. Let's sit down." Doug pointed to the leather couch and Dena sank down into it. "How about some coffee? I have a special blend I put together myself," Doug said proudly.

"No thanks, Doug." Dena felt nervous now that she was here and didn't think her stomach could handle anything, not even coffee.

Doug brought his own mug over from his desk and sat down next to her, his brows knit tightly together as he looked at her.

"Is something wrong, Dena?" Doug asked, concerned.

"I know you are aware that I have been having some problems lately. Strange things have been going on that I believe have to do with Paul." Dena filled him in on the events of last night. She was carefully watching his face. Observing his body language. "And what is strange, Doug, is that your name keeps coming up." She deliberately paused to watch him, waiting to see what his response would be.

"My name?" Doug asked with a confused look. He started to pull at his collar as if it was suddenly much too tight.

"Doug, I am your good friend. You know that I love you like a brother." Did she see a look of pain sweep across his face or was she trying too hard to read him? "I don't care that you made money by buying the other half of Paul's business. I made it clear I wanted nothing from the business. But can you please tell me what you know about his disappearance?"

For a lawyer, Doug did not possess a great poker face. Not even a mediocre one. But at least he was smart enough to know it. He quickly got up and took long strides to the window, keeping his back to her long enough to recover.

"Dena, I am sincerely hurt that you would think..." his voice trailed off when he turned to look at her and saw her holding up her hand.

"Stop, Doug. Before you say anything else, I want to tell you what I already know." She didn't think she could bear to hear him lie to her. She stood up, eye level with her friend. *How well do we ever really know someone?* Dena thought. "I know that Paul was planning to run off and fake his death and bring his employee, Bridgett, with him. Then Paul either had a change of heart or perhaps never actually intended to bring her and just used her. Instead, his plan was to bring Michaelene and her money with him. I don't need to give you the last names, you know who these people are. Don't you, Doug?" Dena asked. She had to hear him admit this to her.

"Yes. I do," he answered softly, meeting her eyes.

"You were, and probably still are, working for Mr. Trask, Michaelene's husband. You paid off Bridgett, helped her change her identity and find a new job." Dena hesitated and wondered just how far she should go, then figured she might as well get to the bottom of this. "I am sorry to hear that your mother passed away, Doug. Did Bridgett take good care of her?"

He was looking at her like she had lost her mind, but said nothing. She was beginning to feel she had made a big mistake and ruined their friendship, when he spoke.

"Well done, Dena. It looks like you're certainly getting your money's worth on that private eye." A feeble smile came across his face as he walked towards her, stopping inches from her face. She could smell the coffee on his breath. "Now does he give you a discount for fucking him, or does he charge extra for that service?"

* * *

Nick had a bad feeling in his gut. It was a sensation he had learned to trust and it usually proved accurate. He was on his way back to Dena's when he called her to check in and got no answer. He wanted to check the reports Edward had run for him, as well as speak to the homicide detectives handling Suzie's murder. He was sure that Dena would be fine alone for an hour or two. But now he was not so confident. He had been calling her for the last thirty minutes with no answer. She could not be in the shower this long.

Nick picked up speed while keeping an eye out for the police. Not that he still didn't have enough connections to get out of a ticket, he just did not want to waste valuable time getting pulled over. He flew up her driveway and leaped out of the car in one fluid motion. He pounded on the door just in case, though when he left this morning, her car had been in the driveway. Mentally kicking himself for not having a key or even her cell phone number, he yanked his own phone out of his pocket to call Pete.

"I lost her. She left while I was out," Nick stated angrily into the phone.

"Where would she go this early?"

"Maybe she just ran to the store, went to breakfast. Hell, I don't know!" Nick yelled. "I guess I'll just have to wait here until she returns." With that he sat down on the hood of the car, unsure what else he could do. That's exactly what he would do, sit here and wait and pray she was okay.

* * *

Dena was shocked. Never in her life had she heard Doug speak to anyone that way, let alone her. She was rendered speechless for a minute while she collected her thoughts. From the minute she had walked through the front doors of Greenly Stone Law Firm, she felt like she had stepped into the Twilight Zone.

She wished now that she had waited for Nick to come with her, or at least left word for him where she was. But this was Doug. Her good friend whom she had known and loved most of her life. Perhaps he was just in way over his head and the pressure was getting to him. Maybe she had said enough for one day.

"Well, I think it's time I got going, Doug." She made a motion to look at her watch. "I know how busy you are and I don't want to take up any more of your time." She gathered up her handbag and re-tied her coat. "I'll call you later." She tried to give him a reassuring smile as she made her way towards the door.

"What's the hurry, Dena?" His voice sounded resentful as he pulled her back by the arm, twisting it behind her back. Pain shot up sharply through her arm and traveled to her shoulder blade. Her knees began to give slightly. "Anxious to get back to your bodyguard? Where is he anyway? I thought you two traveled in pairs. But then you thought you would be safe and sound with good old Doug, didn't you?" He let out a bitter laugh as he increased the pressure on her arm.

"It's so nice to know you love me like a brother, Dena. I've taken care of you and protected you all your life. You make the mistakes and I do the cleanup. God knows you were always too stupid to take care of that yourself." Dena could feel his rage.

"Doug, let me..." Dena tried to speak. She was starting to lose feeling in her arm, and attempted to loosen his grip.

"Shut the fuck up!" Doug screamed in her ear. "That's all you want to do is talk, talk, talk," he said. "Well, save your psycho mumbo jumbo for some other idiot. I had great plans for us, Dena, but instead you had to marry that loser. And once again I had to clean up your mess."

"Doug, you are hurting me. Let go of my arm and we can talk about this, please," Dena practically begged, but she wanted to appear calm. "I want to hear the plans you had for us. You never told me," she went on, desperately trying to think of something to divert his attention and calm him down. She strained to turn her head around and look him in the eye.

"Don't patronize me, you little bitch!" he shouted. "You don't have any interest in what we could have had together. You're already wet for that ex-cop. Your own little private dick, huh, Dena? I want to know how far this new fling has gone. Are you going to marry this loser as well?"

"No, it's not like that, Doug, honest..." She couldn't believe this was Doug she was talking to. And for the first time in her entire life, she was terrified of her friend. She hadn't thought for a moment that he had anything to do with Bridgett's death, but now she was not so sure.

"You lying little slut!" he shouted as he moved with her, picking up speed and ramming her head into the wall. The side of her face made contact with his new expensive art, and shattered glass once again found its way into her skin. Blinding pain shot through her head and she swore she heard her father yelling at her. Darkness was closing in on her as she screamed for her father to stop. As she fell to the floor, she prayed that Nick would find her.

Nick heard Dena say his name as he stormed through the door. He had made it just in time to see Doug smash her head against a fancy piece of art. Like a slow motion dream, he saw what was going to happen before it actually did, but still he was unable to reach her in time. He saw her collapse like a rag doll as he entered the office. She had been counting on his help, and once again, she was hurt on his shift. Some body-guard.

A rage that he had never known raced through him. He ran over to Doug and yanked him up by the collar to throw him across the room when he changed his mind. Instead, he threw a punch so hard he heard bones crack and was unsure if the source was Doug's jaw or his hand. Not that it mattered either way.

Then he threw him across the room towards the window, deeply regretting it was not open. He bent down and scooped up Dena and sat with her on Doug's imported leather couch. He got some satisfaction that if Dena had to bleed, it would be on one of Doug's prized possessions. He almost wished Doug would wake up to see it, but it was better not to have to deal with him yet.

Nick pulled out his cell phone with one hand and punched in 911. He requested an ambulance and the police, all the while rocking Dena and gently calling her name. The gash didn't look too deep but he still wanted her checked out. She was just coming to when the police arrived with the EMT in tow. The med-tech saw the two downed bodies and Nick's nod indicating he should start on her first.

When he looked back down, he saw Dena was staring up at him, confusion on her face.

"What am I going to do with you?" Nick asked softly. "How are you?" He gently moved her hair away from her fore-head so the tech could take a look at her.

"Fine," Dena croaked, then cleared her throat. "But I have a killer of a headache." She closed her eyes to shut out the pain. Then she opened one eye. "What are you doing here?"

"I took a shot that you might have come here to warn your friend. I wish I would have thought of it a little sooner." He tried to smile at her, but she could see he was genuinely concerned. "I am going to let them check you out while I go over and chat with the police officer." He carefully lifted her off his lap and placed her on the couch.

She nodded slightly and from the corner of the room they heard Doug moan. The medical technician's partner was now working on him and Nick heard him say something about a broken jaw. *Gee, that's too bad*, Nick thought. A little chuckle escaped his lips even as he flexed his stiff and sore hand. He hardly noticed the pain.

Officer Hines was standing in the center of the room with his notepad and pen in hand. He had seen it all in his ten years as a police officer, and not much surprised him anymore. Another domestic disturbance, the lady was probably here to file for a divorce, and the husband took out his anger on the lawyer. And since Officer Hines never met a lawyer that he liked, he didn't feel too bad for the guy. But boy, his jaw sure was messed up.

Nick walked over and introduced himself to the officer.

"I think you will want to call Detectives Begley and Thatcher and bring them up to speed on this," Nick suggested.

"Oh yeah?" Officer Hine's right eyebrow went up slightly. He just loved advice from civilians. "Why's that?"

Nick gave him some of the basics on the case. He did not want to piss off the officer, but he did not want to have to go into the whole story when it was the detectives he needed to talk to. After a few minutes of listening, the officer nodded and requested into the radio attached to his shoulder that dispatch locate the detectives and send them over.

Hines was just finishing up his report when Begley and Thatcher entered the room. Nick swore he thought he saw the female detective roll her eyes when she saw Dena lying on the couch.

"How's it going, Nick?" Bob Begley asked.

"It's been better, Bob." Nick gave him the details of what happened today, as well as the other activities he thought Doug was involved with. "I should have gone after him myself; I disliked him from the beginning without ever meeting him. But Dena has known him all her life and somehow managed to convince me that although he might be a little greedy, he was actually a swell guy."

"I have to say, Nick, I did check him out. After Hank Morelli paid me a visit, he got me thinking about this guy. I couldn't come up with a thing. He's clean. Maybe he is smarter than I thought and I'm dumber than I look. I obviously didn't dig deep enough."

Just then Thatcher, who had been checking out the place and speaking with the other officers, approached them. Begley introduced his partner to Nick, though he knew exactly who she was. The descriptions from Hank and Dena fit perfectly and although his first reaction was to lay into her for not helping Dena, he knew better. You definitely get more flies with honey, so he laid it on thick. And since he was not with the department anymore, he needed her help.

"Nice to finally meet you, I have heard a good deal about you," Nick said offering his hand. He held it for a second longer than necessary and locked eyes with her. "I know you have been working hard on this case, Detective Thatcher, and I want to tell you I will cooperate with you in anyway that I can." Begley looked like he might throw up.

A flustered Thatcher was for once at a loss for words, and much to her mortification, she realized she was blushing. Blushing, for God's sake!

"Thank you, Mr. O'Neal. We appreciate your cooperation and your willingness to share information. This has been a very puzzling case." She knew she sounded like a sappy teenager. Even her partner was giving her a funny look.

"Please, call me Nick. I'm sure you have been putting in some long hours on this one, detective," Nick said with a grin that said he felt sorry for her. He thought for a minute he might choke on the words. He was sure she had not put in five minutes, let alone an hour. "Let's set up a time for us to get together and go over what we have so far." He noticed her usual stone face took on a dreamy look.

Then Nick added, "Call me later today and I can give you the rest of the information I found on the money laundering and drug transferring, as well as the name of the man at the top. I am sure the FBI has already contacted you on the other things he is involved in, so we won't have to waste time going over that." Maybe this was more fun than chewing her out.

Thatcher's pleasant look was replaced with one of sheer panic. She mumbled her good-byes and went out into the hall with her notebook. What the hell, the FBI? Could that dumb shit shrink really be in trouble? She would look like an idiot herself as well as kiss off that promotion if this turned out to be something big and she did nothing. Time to make some phone calls and do some research before meeting with Nick. She realized she had a sudden desire to impress him, plus she did not want to look like one of those jerk-offs in her department she was forced to work with daily.

Begley, Thatcher thought, *I bet he has been taking notes on everything and doing follow through.* And since she bit his head off last time he brought the doctor's name up, he probably did not bother to keep her informed. Maybe he was planning on breaking this case himself and getting all the credit, and she was sure he could prove he did it alone. Although she had to admit, that was not her partner's style. She would simply have to ask him what he had so far.

One thing about Begley, he was anal about keeping notes about every phone call and nut case he talked with. She would have to eat crow to get him to share. Maybe she could snoop around his desk while he was at lunch. "Well, son of a bitch!" Thatcher said out loud and headed for their car.

The ride home was long and silent, but Dena knew he was furious with her. She never should have gone without him, but she never thought Doug would hurt her. She saw Nick's hands clenched tight on the steering wheel, his jaw rigid with anger.

He had been right all along. Not only did she feel like a fool, but how could a psychologist be so out of touch with someone's character?

After the medic did the butterfly bandage on her head instead of stitches this time, he told her to watch for signs of a concussion. Other than instructions on how and when to change the bandage, he advised her to go to the hospital for an examination since she was unconscious for a time. Oh, and you will most likely have a bad headache. Gee, you think? Dena wanted to say, but only smiled and declined the hospital visit. *Visiting the ER once a week is enough for me,* she thought.

Dena's head was pounding and she unconsciously lifted her hand up to touch the bandage. She grimaced as she recalled her face hitting the glass.

That was more than Nick could take.

"I'm sorry, I never should have left you alone. I should have known you might want to go and talk to Doug yourself." He was still beating himself up over what had happened. When he awoke at four and was unable to get back to sleep, he thought he could run out and get something accomplished before Dena got up. He would be gone two hours tops, and honestly thought she would be safe. He didn't count on her leaving.

"This isn't your fault, Nick." She was surprised he would think it was. She had been waiting for the lecture and the I-told-you-sos. If she would have at least thought about the incriminating evidence with the possibility that some of it could be true, none of this would have happened. "I can't believe, given my history with Doug, and my profession as well, that I never saw that side of him. And now I realize the man I was married to was a stranger." Maybe it was time for her to find a new career.

That was a depressing thought. Dena fondly remembered all the people she had helped over the years and she couldn't seriously think of doing anything else. All her patients that were wounded physically and emotionally and had withdrawn from life all together were now living happy, productive lives because of her. She believed her success rate was due to the fact that she surely could relate. She wasn't just handing out advice and shaking her head, pretending she knew how they felt. She did know their pain, only too well. Maybe what she needed was a long break, time to do a bit of serious soul searching.

Nick looked like he wanted to ask her a question, but said nothing.

"What?" Dena asked. "You look like something's on your mind."

He shrugged his shoulders. "It's nothing. I was wondering about your late husband. In these last few days, you not only found out he was a crook, but cheating on you. And planning on running away with someone else. And yet, after learning all this, what bothers you most is that because of your professional training you're worried that you missed it."

"Well, that does bother me. I was sitting here thinking maybe I ought to consider a new career." She wondered how he could tap into precisely what she was thinking.

"My point is, you don't seem broken up about learning the love of your life was not who you thought he was. Or that he was taking his affection elsewhere." There, he said it. He knew it was none of his business, but it had been bugging him. He thought she was the grieving widow when he first met her, now he was not so sure.

"I never said he was the love of my life," Dena replied quietly, and at that moment, she realized how true that statement was.

Nick appeared confused, but said nothing.

"When we began dating, Paul was very romantic. Then, when he asked me to marry him, I said yes."

"So, you married him even though you didn't love him?" Nick asked. At least he thought he loved Leslie until he learned she was a spoiled, self-centered she-devil. Never again would he confuse great sex for love. He believed in the institution of marriage; he just wasn't sure it was for him.

"Yes, I guess I did marry him even though I did not love

him. But at the time I thought it was love. I had never known love before, so when we started dating and he said he loved me, I thought that was what love must be like. When he kissed me, I felt nothing. I remember thinking, what's all the fuss about? Then after he died, I was left with guilt that I didn't love him enough." She felt her cheeks get warm as she recalled Nick's kiss. That was what a real kiss should feel like. At least she had the opportunity to experience it once in her lifetime.

"Why do you think Paul married you? I mean, couldn't he sense you were not head over heels in love with him? Do you believe he loved you?"

"I think he did love me in the beginning or maybe it was what he thought love was. Perhaps he thought we would grow to love each other. We were happy enough in the beginning, and we each had our own careers. I loved my job and Paul was happy building his business. I knew they had financial difficulties when he first opened D & D, but then all small companies do. He didn't live to see the business truly take off; at least I don't think he did. Maybe he is still alive out there somewhere." Then an appalling thought came to her: she would still be married if he was alive.

"When did the business start doing well?" Nick asked.

"Sadly enough, it was after the terrorists' attacks on the World Trade Center. Business travelers, celebrities and even your average citizens felt more secure flying in private planes. I heard Bob, Paul's former partner, added a luxurious jet complete with air-to-ground telephone and modem capability and a state of the art entertainment system. They stocked the plane with all the clients' favorites and special requests."

"I wonder why Greenly wanted half of the business anyway. You said it was doing well before, but you just said it didn't pick up until after the terrorists' attacks. It seems unlikely that someone who knew nothing about the aviation business would want take on such an adventure," Nick speculated out loud.

Unless it was the unthinkable. It would have been a great time to get into the private aviation business. That is if you somehow knew what was going to happen to change the industry.

"You can rest when we get home before we go to dinner; I have some calls I need to make," Nick said, glancing at his watch.

"Dinner?" Dena asked, her eyebrows arched high.

"You didn't think a little bump on the head would get you out of my mom's dinner, did you?" Nick asked with a grin. "Besides, her cooking can cure anything."

"Yeah, I think I will need a long rest when we get home," Dena replied, sinking down in her seat, letting her eyes close.

Chapter Fifteen

Dena could have sworn she saw several pairs of eyes peeking out the front window as they pulled up in Nick's parents' driveway in his SUV. All five of his siblings just happened to be hanging out in the living room when they walked through the door.

If anyone had a problem with her crashing in on what was clearly a family night, they didn't show it. They all seemed genuinely happy to meet her and watched her with open curiosity.

Nick made the round of introductions, though she doubted she would remember anyone's name. They were all talking at once, jumping up and down around them and they were loud. Extremely loud. She couldn't imagine growing up in such a noisy household. Dena touched her head unconsciously as her head began to pound.

"Oh my God!" screeched his sister Meghan. "What happened to your head?" she asked, tugging gently on Dena's arm and pulling her into the light so she could get a better look. The room suddenly became silent as everyone turned to Nick for an explanation.

"She had an encounter with a bad man," was all Nick said. "All right, everyone, let's back off the guest here and at least let her take her coat off." Nick helped Dena with her coat and then handed it along with his own to his sister Shannon. "Here," Nick said to her with a grin, "go make yourself useful."

With gentle pressure to her lower back, he let his hand guide Dena into the living room to have a seat. He noticed his sisters all exchanging knowing glances and nodding. He gave them the evil eye to warn them to not be pests. You'd have to be a blind idiot not to see they were already planning his wedding. He rarely brought a female home to meet his family for this reason, because they were so annoying. Maybe bringing Dena here was not such a good idea after all. However, if he didn't get around to showing his face here for dinner soon, his mother would send one of his siblings out to get him. And, since he didn't want to leave Dena alone, here she was.

"Nicholas, you're here!" his mother said as she made her way into the living room, drying her hands on a dish towel. Nick stood up and hugged his mother. She then turned to Dena, beaming.

"Mother, this is Dena Davis. Dena, my mother," Nick said as Dena stood up next to him, his mother reaching for her hand.

"Thank you for inviting me for dinner, Mrs. O'Neal," Dena said softly. Nick's mother held her hand in both of hers and gave it a light squeeze. His mother had the most beautiful olive skin she had ever seen, along with dark brown eyes and a loving smile.

"It's so good of you to join us, Dena dear. Oh, and look at the size of that bandage on your head, you must have a dreadful headache. Nick, take her to sit by the fire with her feet up while I go and make her some tea. Do you need an aspirin, dear?"

"I have some pain medication with me I could take, but thank you anyway," Dena replied, never having experienced this kind of mothering except the few brief times she spent with her grandmother. She found it soothing and almost allowed herself to feel comfortable.

"Then you just sit and take it easy by the fire, dinner will be ready in a few minutes. I hope you're hungry, dear. We've got lots of food." And with that his mother retreated back to the kitchen waving at her daughter Maria to come join her.

Dena relaxed back into her chair and took a deep breath, then choked on the exhale when she glanced around the room. The O'Neal family had all taken seats around her, each face happily watching her.

"So Ms. Davis, Nick mentioned you are a doctor. What do you specialize in?" Nick's brother Toni asked. Being the oldest, he had been down this road several times himself and was willing to give Nick a hand. His sisters were a nuisance. Until he met and married his wife Cindy, he had put up with their meddling for years. After he finally tied the knot, the refrain became, when are you going to have kids? Plus, Nick as the third oldest had already endured more than his share of his wretched sisters' interference. Now if it was their younger bookworm brother Dylan, he would be on his own. The only thing he ever brought home was his laptop.

"Please, call me Dena. And I am a psychologist," Dena replied to Toni's question. She silently hoped, but doubted, that this would be the last of their questions.

"Here you go, Dena," one of his sisters said as she stood before Dena, a steaming mug in one hand and a glass of water in the other. "The water is for your medication," she said as she handed the glass to her and set the hot tea on the table next to her.

"Thank you..." Dena said as she struggled to remember Nick's sister's name. It would have been so much easier if they wore name tags.

"Maria," she supplied happily. "And you're welcome." She took the seat across from Dena.

Just then a man walked into the room and smiled over at Dena. He was tall and handsome with gray hair and Nick's blue eyes. Nick was the only child of the family that was the perfect blend of both parents, Dena noticed. The others either looked all Irish or all Italian.

"Hi Dad," Nick said, standing to shake his dad's hand. "Are you done tinkering in the basement or did you just come up for dinner?" Nick asked, obviously pleased to see his dad.

"I put everything away when I heard the prodigal son had finally returned," Mr. O'Neal said jovially. Then he turned to Dena. "And I have already heard all about our guest while I was in the kitchen. Dr. Davis, it's a pleasure to meet you. Don't let Nick's sisters scare you off, they are in fact harmless."

Dena laughed. She liked this man already. Actually, she liked everyone.

"Please call me Dena," she replied as she shook his hand.

* * *

On the ride home Dena found herself feeling happy. The dinner had been wonderful and she had enjoyed being part of a family, if only for one night. And for at least a little while, she was able to forget her nightmares. Past and present.

That was until Nick's cell phone rang, reminding her that she was not a date he brought home to meet his family. He was someone she paid to watch over her.

Nick had caller ID on his cell phone though he rarely used it. But at this moment he didn't feel like allowing work, family or friends to intrude. That just about covered everyone who had his cell phone number. However, when he saw it was Pete's number on the display he hesitated, swore under his breath and answered it. He had forgotten to call him back after he found Dena and wanted to fill him in.

"Hey Pete, what's up?"

"Nothing much. How's the hand?" Pete grinned into the phone. He has been a witness to Nick's temper on more than one occasion and it wasn't a pleasant thing. Especially if you were the one on the receiving end.

"Gee, good news really does travel fast."

"I happened to be poking around the hospital when they

were wiring Greenly's jaw shut. I stuck my head in to say hi
and that seemed to cheer him up a bit. I think he was sending
his regards, but I couldn't be sure with all that metal in the
way."

"I'll bet," Nick chuckled. "What were you doing at the
hospital?"

"Well, actually I was at the morgue next door when a little
birdie told me about Greenly."

"Just out of sheer curiosity, who's your spy at the
morgue?" Nick asked. A woman, no doubt. Pete had informants everywhere, most of them female. But he couldn't even
begin to guess who he knew over there.

"I could tell you, but then I'd have to kill you," Pete joked.
"Now, do you want to know what I found out or not?"

"I'm all ears."

"They just finished the autopsy on Bridgett Bonner. She
was three months pregnant," Pete said. "They are going to run
Greenly's DNA to see if he was going to be a daddy. It won't
look too good for him if he was. He can't deny knowing her
then."

"But if he comes up clean, that leaves us with the possibility someone else could have gotten rid of her." Nick frowned
into the phone. Just when he thought things were starting to
come together, they began to unravel before his eyes. This had
more twists and turns than any book he had ever written. He
thought briefly of the manila folder he had been dragging
around, shoving into it each new turn of events. Now if he
could only turn the contents of his dossier into an outline, it
would make his agent a very happy man.

"Did Bridgett's roommate mention she was seeing anyone
before she died?" Pete asked.

"No. The only man Suzie mentioned Bridgett having contact with was the man who hired her to watch the old lady,
which by the way did turn out to be Greenly's mother." Nick
hesitated for a minute. "I wonder if she ever met Haidyn Trask,
or if Greenly was always the go between."

"That's a long shot. But if Bridgett was going to have his

baby, that would be a definite connection between the two. One that could be proved, if she wanted to do that. She would have become a liability. In fact, if that was the case, I am surprised she lasted as long as she did."

"Well, we better keep our thinking caps on because there is no way Trask is going to hand over his DNA on a silver platter. A man like Trask will have a fortress of lawyers around him, and without solid evidence, we won't get anywhere near him."

"If we wanted to get his DNA, I could do it. It wouldn't be legal, but at least we would know."

"That could be tricky, Pete."

"I'm a tricky guy."

"Let me think on it. Trask's a dangerous man to mess with. I can't see how you could get close enough to him to collect hair samples and not get scalped yourself. We need something more on him, but we gotta be careful. If his people ever get wind of us fishing around, we're done like dinner. He knows we were hired to find his missing wife, but remember, it was his sister-in-law that requested our services, not Trask."

Pete was silent for a moment. "You're probably right. Okay, we go through the back door then. I'll get Edward on this and have him check out Trask, his companions, his friends and his enemies. Also, every connection Trask has with Greenly." He had a thought. "You know, Greenly's only a modest player in the game. Trask probably considers him a loose cannon now and is making plans to get rid of him as we speak and Greenly is smart enough to know it. He might cut himself a deal, being the savvy lawyer that he is, and start talking. That is, when he can use his mouth again."

"Well, that would sure be the easier way." *And safer,* Nick thought. "Let's see what Edward can dig up and then we will pay Greenly a visit. You should probably let Bagley know what we are up to and let him in on anything that turns up. He will need to be there for any deals we might make anyhow.

"Oh, and talk to his partner Thatcher for me as well. I put a match under her today and got her going. She just left me a message. See if she found out anything. And check with your

FBI buddy and see if you can get a lead on this drug smuggling connection. The more we know for sure, the better."

Dena was listening to Nick on the phone. When he mentioned Doug's name, regrettably, the events of the day started to play out in her head. His angry face, twisted with rage, leering at her. The cruel accusations that he shouted at her still stunned and hurt her. Her mind almost refused to believe that this was her childhood friend. However, she was too experienced and educated to allow herself to fall into denial. Not this time. In fact, replaying her encounter with Doug helped her remember something else that had bothered her about her visit.

She waited until he was off the phone to tell him.

"When I arrived at Doug's office today, he was on the phone. He sounded agitated, so I waited in the hall until he was finished speaking," Dena said.

"Do you know whom he was talking to?"

"No, but he said that he had been looking and it wasn't easy. That he could not walk in there and take it. I got the impression the person on the other end of the conversation was angry with Doug for not finding whatever he was searching for," Dena said. "Doug also said it might have been thrown out."

Nick glanced over at her. "I gotta believe that he must have been the visitor at your storage unit." He frowned for a moment. "Think about it. Has anything that used to belong to Paul been brought up inadvertently in conversation lately, even if you were the one that brought it up?" Greenly would know how to weave a question into the conversation without causing suspicion.

"No. We haven't talked about Paul in ages. We talked about you and meeting for dinner..." Dena stopped mid sentence when instantly she knew. "When he called me, I was going through a box of Paul's things. I was in my office with the things we took from the storage unit while I was on the phone. I told him what I was doing."

"Anything specific of Paul's come up in conversation?" Nick asked, though this was enough to make him comb through each and every box.

"Well, I did mention I found Paul's planner. I remember because I was surprised he didn't have it with him. He carried that thing around like a woman with a purse."

"Let's go check it out. Unless someone already beat us to it," Nick mumbled under his breath, but loud enough for Dena to hear.

"Doug's been at the hospital all day and with the police. There is no way he could have gotten to it, or even called someone to have them go get it," Dena said, thinking about Doug's jaw. It would also be unlikely he would send that kind of message through someone else.

Nick mentally debated telling her. For her own safety, she should know. These were evil men they were dealing with.

"I think your friend is mixed up in something pretty wicked. These people he has been dealing with, Dena, they have ways of knowing things. They use things like wire taps, bugs and spies and have many informants. They have extremely deep pockets and endless resources. And, if I am correct, they will be watching Greenly and us, very closely." He didn't add that Greenly was a lucky man. If he wasn't in police custody, he would most likely turn up dead.

"What?" Dena gasped, not able to accept any more of this whole cloak and dagger thing.

"We need to be careful," he said with a solemn voice and a hard look in his eyes. He prayed he was wrong. Maybe Greenly was just another greedy lawyer bending the law for his own financial gain and trying to cover his tracks. Perhaps he only worked for Trask and they knew nothing about Dena. Hank had said the man had the hots for Dena. This could have nothing to do with Trask, and only be Greenly taking out his frustrations because he felt rejected. Didn't it always come down to love or money?

"Well, shouldn't we tell the police?" Dena asked, her voice cracking slightly.

"They know," Nick replied calmly.

"Oh. Good."

"There is another fact to consider," Nick continued. "If Trask or his people knew about the planner, he would already have it in his hands. They wouldn't waste time or wait patiently for Greenly to get it. If they came looking for it, you would know. He might be working with someone else. Could be he didn't want to get his hands too dirty and there is a middle man."

A minute later, Nick cut the Tahoe's lights and navigated it slowly up her driveway, parking directly next to the side door. He hadn't wanted to risk the sound of the garage door opening, though that would have been so much easier. Nor did he want to stand out there and open it manually like a big bulls-eye target.

"Wait here and lock the doors," he said, as he slid out of the car and followed the drill similar to last time. Only this time he wasn't on the lookout for a stalker or crazed family member of one of Dena's patients. They would be restricted by their limited skills, experience and even income. That type of criminal could only run so far without getting caught.

This time he would have to dig deep and rely on everything he had ever been taught. He thought of the hours of research he put in for his books and thanked God, not for the first time, that he decided to become a writer. It was time to relocate and lay low in for a while, Nick thought, as he checked the door for any explosive devices. Sometimes, a little paranoia went a long way in saving one's backside.

He entered so quietly that it would make a cat burglar proud. A professional thief, as Georgie called himself, would be pleased to see his lessons carried out so perfectly. Nick once gave him a break on a few lesser charges in return for some tricks of the trade. At the time he considered it research for a future book. If he got out of this unscathed, he'd have to call up to say thanks.

Nick held a small pocket flashlight near the lock to check for wires then watched for a red flashing light to start once the door was open. That would be a pretty sophisticated device to find around here, but then again, he reminded himself, he wasn't dealing with kids.

He wondered for the hundredth time if he was overreacting. This was more like an episode of a bad police drama and he felt like an idiot. He believed in always expecting the worst and in following your gut instincts. He reminded himself that was all he was doing. Better to feel a little foolish than a lot dead.

The door was clear and the house felt empty, but he disliked surprises of the dangerous kind so he continued his search. Top to bottom, he checked out every nook and cranny. He moved silently through the dark spaces with his gun handy, safety off. When he gave Dena the all clear, she came in with her brows knit together in question as she glanced over at the door.

"What were you looking for on the door?" Dena asked.

"A calling card," Nick said as he pulled the kitchen shade down and turned on a small light over the stove. "All right, let's go grab everything in your office that was Paul's and then pack our things. We can't stay here," he said as they headed to her office.

"Where are we going?" Dena asked. "I am getting tired and my head hurts. I just want to go to bed. And don't you think you should have asked before you order me to pack up and leave my house?"

"To a friend's cottage and you can sleep in the car," Nick said as he threw her late husband's things into a box. "Oh, and can I please try and save your life like you hired me to?" Nick said with a little sarcasm thrown in. He was tired himself and wanted to stay sharp. Needed to stay alert. He wasn't up to having to pacify her as well. "Go throw some stuff together and I'll meet you in the kitchen in ten minutes," he said as he left the room.

Fifteen minutes later they were ready to go. She hadn't said anything to him after his last comment and he could tell she was brooding. *Well, it's a long drive. She'll get over it.* He finished packing the car as Dena came out of the house with a bag of garbage in her hand and frowned when she realized she forgot to open the garage door. She turned and went back in the house to hit the switch while Nick watched her from where he stood loading up the trunk.

He felt himself getting annoyed with her, but maybe it wasn't her fault totally. He had held back telling her what he really thought so it wouldn't terrify her, but what the hell. She had hired him and he should report it all. Maybe then she would take this more seriously and not worry about trivial things like taking out the trash.

Dena hit the garage opener just as Nick closed the trunk, giving him a clear view of the inside of her tidy garage.

A warning bell sounded in his brain.

"Shit!" Nick yelled. He hadn't counted on that. But he should have. He knew that Dena usually used the garage entrance, so it should have been the first place he looked.

Running towards Dena, he grabbed her and threw her in the front seat, and before he could even close the driver's side door, he was high tailing it down the driveway in reverse.

"Get your head down," Nick ordered.

A thunderous noise rocked the car and blinding light filled their field of vision. In front of them, where Dena's house used to stand, stood a blistering inferno.

Chapter Sixteen

The astonishing beauty that filled their vision was in such sharp contrast to the disaster sight they left behind, that it seemed surreal. Nick had immediately phoned Pete as he fled the scene and they both agreed it would be best for him and Dena to quickly disappear.

The cottage looked so exquisite, resting at the end of a spiraling dirt lane, that it resembled a page from a fairy tale. The wintry scene looked like something you might find on a postcard or perhaps on an advertisement for a ski resort. And because they were further north, a light dusting of snow covered the grounds and the sky held a promise of more to come. Enormous trees that were now barren of their leaves framed the enchanting path that led to the summer home's front door.

The little cabin, as his friend had referred to it, was anything but small. The tremendous log cabin was two stories high with five bedrooms, three bathrooms and had all the comforts of home and then some. And behind the cabin, sat a small, but perfect-for-fishing, manmade lake.

Nick's mind however, was not on the breathtaking scenery.

Instead he was rehashing what he did and didn't do. And now was faced with what he could and couldn't do. He might have gotten them both killed. For a while there he had started to feel a little ridiculous, surmising that his writer's imagination was just working overtime. Now he didn't know if he felt better or worse for being right. The only thing he knew for damn sure was that he needed help.

His own power and resources were extremely limited compared to what he was dealing with. He had an office and staff fully trained and extremely knowledgeable to fight the bad guys and keep them away. But that was usually about protecting a client from one lunatic, not one wealthy business man with ties to drug lords and the underworld and God knows what else. Now that Trask knew for sure he was being investigated under a microscope, he would be sure to eliminate every loose end. That meant any documentation that belonged to Paul as well as any person that knew him. He was sure somewhere on that list would be his own name. It was time to accept that this was out of his realm of expertise and that he needed to call in the cavalry. He would have to sit back for a while and work from the sidelines. But how long would that take?

"This is lovely," Dena said. "Is it yours?"

"No, it belongs to a friend of a friend. There's no way it could be traced back to me." He glanced around the property as if seeing it for the first time.

Dena got out of the car and stretched after the long drive. "What do we do now?" she asked.

"Drop out of sight," Nick said as he started to unload the trunk.

"For how long?"

Good question. "For as long as it takes."

Or until they were no longer safe. In the meantime, they were stuck here together.

He had his laptop. It would be the perfect setting to start and possibly complete a book. He'd done it before. After an episode with writer's block, he had used this place to get a jump start and the words flowed so easily, he stayed until the entire book was completed. But he was alone then. Anyway, his job now was to protect Dena. He could not very well get caught up in a fictional drama when he had one of his own playing out in real life.

Dena started to head towards the front door when she turned back to Nick. "Whom exactly are we hiding from? It can't be Doug, he's still in the hospital."

She deserved some kind of answer. After all, she had lost her friend, her house and probably a bit of her sanity all in about a day.

"I'm sorry, I am not able to tell you just who the main players are at this point. But I believe it is in our best interest to stay out of sight for a while until I can figure this out." Well, that was the truth.

Dena looked at him like he was deranged.

The inside of the cabin was just as charming. If her life was not in such shambles at the present moment, she might even be able to enjoy herself, Dena thought. But she could not shake the memory of her house, and more importantly, her office, being blown to bits. She would have to call Brad. He would have to take her patients for a while longer. Some, she thought sadly, should probably stay with him for good. She knew that her patients were getting comfortable with Brad and making some progress; it wouldn't be fair to interrupt them again. And Marcy. I need to let her know I'm okay. Plus I could really use a friend right about know. And some caffeine.

"I would love a cup of coffee. Do you think I might find any in the kitchen? I suppose we should have stopped for groceries." They had passed a quaint little country store in town, but neither one had felt like stopping.

"I had the kitchen fully stocked while we were on our way up," Nick answered while putting a fire together in the massive hearth. When he noticed the questioning look on her face he added, "I called a friend on the way up. He owes me one. Help yourself to anything you like."

Dena walked into the huge country kitchen, equipped to please any chef. If she could have designed the kitchen she wanted, this would be it. Gleaming copper bottom pans hung from a rack in the center of the room, just above an efficient work station. Perfect for someone helping you without getting in your way. The island had a sink, a chopping block and a drawer stocked with every utensil you would ever need plus a few she wouldn't have a clue how to use. And the counter space was every cook's dream. But the best feature, she thought, was the window above the sink that looked out upon the lake. The sun was just starting to set and spectacular rays of color were spiraling out onto the still water. She walked over to the window and took in the scene.

"Did you find what you were looking for?" Nick asked from the kitchen door. He had been watching her standing at the window, staring out into the darkness.

"I was looking at this incredible view and watching the sun set," Dena said, still facing the window.

"The sun went down over 15 minutes ago, Dena," he all but whispered.

She turned to him and forced a smile as her hand searched her wrist for her watch. She was losing track of time again. "So it has."

"Why don't you go and unpack, maybe rest. I'll make us something for dinner." It was more of an order than a request. She looked like she was coming unglued and he had no idea how to help her. Maybe she should call her doctor friend.

"Go find a room you like," he added.

She nodded her head and left the kitchen in search of a bedroom to call her own, if only for a few days.

The room she chose should belong to Nick, she thought. But she was drawn to the blackness beyond the sliding glass door that she knew come morning, would have an incredible view. The large bedroom also had a fireplace and colossal four poster bed. Next to the hearth, with an afghan thrown across it, was a wonderful chair and ottoman, inviting one to come sit by the fire. Yes, one felt comfort just being in this room, Dena thought, as she stripped naked and crawled beneath the cool, crisp sheets.

When it was quiet for too long, Nick peeked in on Dena to find her sound asleep. He put aside the dinner plans he had and settled for a gigantic roast beef sandwich to tide him over until she awoke. With his snack in one hand, he grabbed a beer from the fridge with the other and sat at the table along with the boxes from Dena's house.

He hadn't wanted to take the chance his cell phone could be monitored, so he e-mailed the office and Pete. There was always the possibility someone could be watching that as well, but Edward had assured him the computers at the office were well guarded. He gave out numerous and endless assignments to just about the entire staff asking that they receive the highest priority. In other words, folks, drop everything, help save my ass. And he knew they would. Though he wanted to turn everything over to someone else to handle, he didn't feel secure putting his life entirely in another's hands. Particularly Thatcher's.

He had risked a quick call to Pete on the drive here. They both agreed it would be better if everyone thought they hadn't made it out of the house. It would buy them a little time. But, for God's sake, he had told Pete, stop over at his parents' house ASAP and tell them the truth. It was also decided Pete would tell Detective Begley, knowing they needed the backup. He could be trusted. They requested Begley hold off telling his partner anything until Pete had a chance to talk directly to her first. And though they knew the FBI and the ATF were already deeply involved, they were having a hell of a time getting someone from either agency to talk to them. Even to Begley. No big surprise there. The Feds are not known for playing nice with other law enforcement agencies and hate to share information.

After he finished sending out assignments, he read his own mail that had been waiting for him. The first was from Pete.

Hey, can't get the lovely detective Thatcher to return my calls (I'm hurt), so she must prefer that I visit her in person. Greenly was not going to be a daddy...and have no leads as to who the other candidates could be. Still don't know what charges he will face yet. Need to find out before we can strike a deal. So far, only charge is for assault. Also, he sent word that he wants to talk to Dena. He doesn't seem to know about the accident yet...or maybe he's just trying to be clever. Pete

I'll bet he does. The thought that Greenly would wheel and deal himself out of no jail time made Nick's stomach knot up and his hand ache to smash the man's jaw again. He scrolled down to the next e-mail, which was from Edward.

Sir, this is what I have so far on Trask. It's not a lot, but what I do have is infallible. As you know, he is the owner and CEO of Trask Industries, Inc., which manufactures various types of electronics such as computers, TV's, stereos and surveillance equipment.

He is also involved in real estate in Georgia; condos and a shopping mall. He has as many friends as he does enemies. He went to school with the Chief of Police in his town who, by the way, just officially called off the investigation on the missing Mrs. Trask. The closing report stated she ran off with another man, taking a large amount of cash and all her jewelry with her. I'll keep digging. I have forwarded copies of this e-mail to all O'Neal employees, as the reference to surveillance equipment is noteworthy. Edward.

Well done, Edward, Nick thought, as his mind then drifted to Trask. Haidyn Trask did not appear to be the type of man who would want others thinking his wife left him, especially for another man. Unless he would rather have everyone believe he had been robbed and then dumped for another man than to focus on what really happened to her. The question was: did Trask know whom his wife was having an affair with? Sure he did, and Nick would bet his last dollar that was why they both were missing.

Two out of the remaining e-mails were from Margaret and contained a variety of reminders and phone messages from his family and agent. The last message on his screen was from Hank. That was a surprise. Hank hated computers.

"Nick...as we originally thought, Greenly was a busy boy. Only under the Hartford name. I have some things to show you. Give me your fax number and I'll send them. I'm writing from

a print shop, just in case we got a shadow.

P.S. I abhor computers. I would rather send out smoke signals than peck away at this contraption. HM"

Nick replied back with the cottage's fax machine and silently prayed Hank would watch his back when going to find a fax machine.

* * *

Detective Thatcher was not having a good day. Earlier she had spilled hot coffee on her new white designer blouse while simultaneously trying to scarf down a fast lunch and read reports at the same time. Since her conversation with Nick, she had been hauling ass trying to just get up to speed on that shrink's case.

And now as she rushed through the precinct, the front desk sergeant notified her that the captain wanted to see her when he got back from lunch. And since her perpetually bad-tempered boss did not call you in to give you a pat on the back, only a kick in the ass, she knew this day was really going to suck.

The heartburn caused from her greasy lunch was making its way to the back of her throat and she prayed she had Tums somewhere on her. She stashed them everywhere. Her desk, pockets, and her police vehicle. So, you would think the most logical place would be her handbag. She kept up her sprint through the office while rummaging through her purse in search of relief when suddenly she came to an abrupt halt.

Speechless, she stood looking at her desk.

"Your desk is a mess," the man stated simply. He had his feet propped up on her desk and was leaning back in her chair, his arms linked behind his head.

"Who the hell are you?" Thatcher snapped at the man with a tone that usually made grown men jump.

"Pete Capaldi," he answered with a boyish grin, making no effort to get up.

"Do you mind?" she said, pointing to her desk. The audacity of this imbecile was amazing. Why do good looking men think they can get away with anything?

"No, I don't mind. However, I do feel that perhaps if you were more organized, you might be more proficient at your job."

"Get out of my chair and away from my desk, you ass-hole!" She walked around the desk to come face to face with him.

Pete slowly got up and shook his finger at her. He leaned in towards her, invading her personal space, and spoke softly. "My, what foul language you use, Yvonne. And you've got quite a temper too. Not a good combination for someone look-ing to be promoted to Detective Sergeant."

Shock registered on her face as she stared at the handsome man in front of her. "Who the fuck are you?" she asked again, this time her voice more guarded and mixed with disbelief.

Pete straightened up and the grin was back and mischief danced in his eyes. "I told you, Pete Capaldi."

"Did you go through my desk?" she asked through clenched teeth. Who the hell did this pretty boy think he was? She wanted to get out her gun and shoot him between the eyes.

He shrugged his shoulders nonchalantly. "Just passing the time. I was bored. After all, you kept me waiting for over an hour."

"You're in a lot of trouble, dickhead. You do realize that you are in a police station? Now, I hate to cut this little party short but I am going to call one of the officers and have you booked for breaking into my desk." She picked up the phone and started to press a button. Normally she would thrive on knocking this grinning idiot down a peg or two, but today she just could not spare the time.

"The captain wanted to see you as soon as you got in. Should I escort you in? But I have a little tip for the ambitious, career-minded detective: you may want to talk to me privately first." He winked at her and smiled, like they were old friends. "And that advice, Yvonne, is on the house."

She was so enraged, it actually felt like steam was coming out of her ears. She wanted to Karate-chop his face to pieces.

But the voice of reason inside was beckoning her to shut up and listen. He knew too much about her and she needed to know how. She also wondered how in the hell he was able to just walk through a police station and sit at her desk for an hour with not one of her fellow officers noticing.

Her heartburn kicked up five notches at the mention of her captain. A sinking feeling was slowly washing over her as some of the pieces started to fit together.

"What do you want?"

"I work with Nick O'Neal, which by the way, you would have known already if you bothered to return my calls." He did not miss the spark in her eye, and then pain, when she heard Nick's name. He tucked that little tidbit away for later when it might come in handy. Information of any kind was a wonderful and useful tool. So was blackmail.

He paused and gave her another award-winning smile before continuing. "I want to know what you found out on the Davis case. And before you say something silly like there is no case, let me remind you that this is big. Being involved in this matter, on any level, could indubitably help your career. Working with me would clearly be to your advantage." He saw the wheels turning. She may be a bitch, but he knew she was a smart cookie. He had made sure of it first.

She pursed her lips together in concentration. She knew the jackass was right, though it would kill her to admit it. She liked to do things on her own and hated to accept assistance of any kind. Women who took help from men appeared weak. However, this time she could bend her own rules slightly since it would be advantageous to her career.

"Okay. We will work together. I will give you what I've got so far." She almost choked on the words, but she got them out. "You are taking over now that Nick is...dead?"

"He's not dead. But we would like to keep up that assumption, if you will," Pete said, making his meaning clear. He saw the stunned look on her face but continued on. "And, since you just started actually working on this case only yesterday, I doubt you could give me anything I don't already know. But when you do come across something useful, I expect you to get on the horn pronto."

She started to deny the accusation but Pete simply held his hand up and shook his head. "Don't bother denying that, you'll just waste my time. And I hate to piss away time, Yvonne," he said in a grim tone, his face losing its ever-present smile just long enough for effect. With his charm back he continued. "So, why don't I just give you the lowdown? Come and sit behind your desk and get your notepad out, you're going to need it."

Amazingly, she did as she was told. As if in a trance, she pulled out her notepad and gazed up at him. She said a silent prayer that Taylor, who sat on the other side of her cubicle, was at lunch. She realized then that Begley must have made himself scarce. What a chicken shit; she would deal with him later.

"First of all, the incidents that happened to Dr. Davis *are* of importance. Whoever broke into her storage unit and her home on three different occasions was looking for something. The third time they decided to just blow up the place. That would get rid of any evidence as well as the two people who might know something. We think they were after a planner or some other type of documentation that belonged to Paul Davis, which could tie Greenly to some very bad people. You already know that Paul had an affair with his nurse, Bridgett Bonner, who was supposed to have died in the plane crash with him. Her turning up dead the other day, just as Greenly was going under the spotlight, makes him look guilty enough. But what we need to do first is find some concrete evidence of Greenly's guilt to use as a bargaining tool to get him to talk. Without him, there are things we may never know, until it's too late."

"What about the nurse being pregnant? Greenly could be the father," she asked, more to show she *did* know what was going on.

"That report came back yesterday." He glanced down at her cluttered desk and shook his head. "No dice."

Shit. "Okay. So I'm a little behind here. I'm a quick study. Now who are the big bad guys you are talking about?" So far, she couldn't see how nailing the squirrelly lawyer to a cross would do anything for her but make her smile.

"Terrorists," Pete stated simply. Now that he had her attention he knew she would listen. And get to work. "We want the link between Greenly and the big cheese he works for, Hydian Trask."

* * *

Dena's eyes flew open when she heard the floorboards creak in her room. Someone was in here with her, she was positive of it. And whoever it was, they were walking softly towards the bed. She knew she was defenseless just lying, there but for the life of her she could not think of what to do. The room was pitch black, not even the moon was around to cast a shadow. Think of a plan, dammit. Her heart hit like a hammer against her ribcage and she was sure whoever was in the room with her could hear it.

She could roll to the far side of the bed and get to the floor and try, in this maze of darkness, to find the door. Then she could scream for Nick. Fast as she could, she started to move across the bed only to find herself entangled in the sheets. Hands grabbed her shoulders as she violently tried to free herself from the nest of sheets.

"Good. You're awake," the voice said. "Dinner is ready, let's go downstairs."

"Nick?" She gasped. "Is that you?"

"Were you expecting someone else?" His voice held a trace of mischief. But the chuckle died in his throat when he saw her face.

"What's wrong, Dena?" he asked firmly, his eyes scanning the room for signs of trouble.

OK, breathe. "I heard you come in. I thought it was..." her voice trailed off. She felt relieved and foolish at the same time.

"I am sorry I scared you, but you're safe. No one here but us."

"How can you see anything?" she wondered out loud. She felt herself being pulled towards him, through the thick raven ink air. He rested her head on his abdomen and cautiously stroked her hair. The moment, for some reason, had a sense of déjà vu to it.

"I see just fine." He smiled. It was an ability that had saved his butt on more than one occasion. Chasing some loser through an unlit, abandoned house. Watching him try to blend into the night.

"What are you, a bat?" Willing her eyes to adjust, she still could not see her own hand in front of her face. Or him, for that matter. Yet here he was, unbinding the twisted covers that were wrapped around her torso. The bed sheet loosened and dropped to her waist. Abruptly his hands stopped moving. She heard his sharp intake of air.

"Something like that," his voice sounded thick.

"What's..." she started to ask what was wrong when instantly she knew. She was stark naked. She mentally cringed as she recalled discarding *all* her clothes before she fell into the bed. Why she should choose to sleep in the buff, especially here, was beyond her. She always slept with something on. In fact, she preferred it that way.

She froze like a deer caught in the headlights. He might know she was nude, but at least there was no way he could see much of interest.

He couldn't seem to remove his hands. Or his eyes. When the sheet fell from her, her entire glorious body glowed like she was under a spotlight. His mind grew hazy as he fought with his inner demons. He wanted to touch her. Never in his life could he remember wanting something to this extent.

But it wouldn't be fair play. She was vulnerable right now, having lost pretty much her entire life. She would probably hate herself afterwards. And she damn well would hate him.

That would be assuming she wanted anything from him other than friendship and comfort, which he knew was all she needed right now.

His fingers had been unconsciously stroking her back, in light, little circles, traveling up and around her neck to find the soft and delicate skin behind her ears. The sweet moan that escaped her lips made him groan in frustration. He could smell her hair. It reminded him of sunshine and flowers.

Okay, now would be a good time to stop. Tell her dinner is ready. It's getting cold...

She guided his hand to her mouth, and began kissing it. Taking his index finger in her mouth, she began sucking on it. *Oh, hell.* Tentatively at first, as if to test the waters. Then faster, making her own rhythm. Like he could protest even if he wanted to, which he did not. He seemed to have been struck mute. He could no more stop her than he could stop breathing. So much for his noble intentions.

"Dena?" he said, breathing too fast. There, he finally found his voice. End this. Tell her now before you throw her on her back and pound into her.

"Hmm?" She laid back and took his hand, pulling him down on top of her. He was hard as a rock and centered directly between her legs.

"Dinner's ready," he choked out, barely recognizing his own voice.

"Good. I'm starved."

God, so I am.

They awoke hours later. A phone was ringing downstairs. Nick jumped out of bed in search of his jeans, which had somehow found their way to the other side of the room. He looked at his watch.

Who would call at 4:00 am? Dena started to get up with him.

He gave her a pat on her bottom. "Go back to sleep," he ordered. She let her head drop back down and hit her pillow like a brick.

Halfway down the stairs, Nick realized it was the fax machine that had been ringing. He could hear the machine humming as it spit out its message.

Good. He went over to the machine in the cottage's office and pulled out Hank's report, not bothering to sit as he scanned it over.

Greenly has another office that is registered to Mark Hart-

ford. Edward found records of calls from the Hartford office to Trask (the company and to his home's unpublished, private line.) In his office I found some documentation referring to D & D (the following pages), but suspect the really good stuff is on one of the computers here (Ed's turf). Of course none of this is legal, so we will have to go through more proper channels. Also, he has one employee here whom I would like to talk to. Dr. Davis may know her or at least have met her once. There is a picture on the desk of Dena, another woman, Greenly and one other man. (I'm guessing the other man was the late Mr. Davis.) Hank

Nick sat down at the desk and read Hank's report again. His brows knit tightly in concentration.

He wondered how seriously Greenly took his alter ego and what else they would find when they dug deeper under the Hartford name. He shook off a sudden chill as the realization dawned on him that they could be dealing with a dangerous psycho on top of everything else.

Trask Incorporated probably ran a legit business, keeping their noses clean and running things by the book to stay out of the spotlight. The Hartford office was most likely the only domestic outlet he used to sell the specialized merchandise from his electronics company. High tech, super sensitive listening devices, phone taps, microscopic video cameras, night vision goggles...the list went on. All very handy toys to have for guys like him, but in the wrong hands, they were deadly. Not to mention illegal.

Nick would also lay odds that Trask had an international distribution ring set up. Proving it would be another thing. Some connections were starting to come together. He could see Trask providing his equipment and knowledge to the worst criminals imaginable. Not caring that they would, in turn, use their purchases to kill Americans. He was sure this was the activity Pete's friend in the FBI was watching when he said they were closely monitoring the situation.

He set down the report and stared into space, his mind already slipping back to last night, before his visit to her bed.

He knew he shouldn't have done it. But he couldn't quite bring himself to regret it.

It started innocently enough. While waiting for Dena to wake up he got caught up with work, went through the boxes and planner and after realizing he really needed her to look at this stuff, got bored. With idle hands and all that, he did what came natural to him and took out his yellow legal pad and began to write.

At first he didn't even realize he had been writing about her. The words just kept coming.

Then he could not stop. He started with the day she walked into his office and left off where they were having wild, incredible sex.

Jesus. He put his head in his hands while the realization dawned on him. Talk about a self-fulfilling prophecy.

He wrote a juicy sex scene with her and literally put down the pen, walked into her room and jumped her in bed. He may have been trying to talk himself out of it, but the seed had already been deeply planted.

He would, of course, have to change a few things before anyone, including his agent, could read this. He left way too much personal information in the outline, just trying to get the feel of everything on paper first.

He also left his handiwork on the kitchen table. Not a good idea. He got up to go retrieve his work when he heard a gasp from the other room.

Shit. Too late.

Slowly he rose and walked towards the kitchen, sending up a silent prayer he was wrong.

She stood at the table wearing nothing but a man's white T-shirt and socks, and from where he stood, it appeared she left her panties upstairs. She looked young and incredibly sexy. And very angry.

Laying the last page back down on the table she lifted her head and locked eyes with him. Hurt and accusation were in those eyes and something more. Almost, defeat.

"Once again someone I trusted totally blind-sided me. I

never saw it coming." Her words came out in a whisper laced with self loathing.

"It's not what you think..." his voice trailed off when he realized how dumb his words were. It was exactly what she thought it was.

"I was going to change the names, even the location." Gee, that was much better. He shook his head as if it would make him stop saying these unbelievably stupid things.

"Well, that was thoughtful of you. I suppose I should thank you for considering my professional reputation. But in light of everything that has happened, I have been considering changing my occupation anyway." She tilted her head to the side slightly as if listening to an inner voice. "That's why you took me as a client, isn't it?"

"Yes." That and she intrigued him. But that was most likely because of the writer in him.

"It must have really paid off for the starving artist. Murder, mystery and mayhem all rolled up into one foolish woman in distress." Her voice finally started to match her anger.

She was dead right, except for the starving artist comment. But he thought it best to let that slide. How could he convince her he didn't write for the money? Hell yeah, the money was nice. He sure wasn't going to give it back. But how could he explain to someone else that when he sat down to spin a tale, he could allow himself to get lost in the lives of his characters? Not to mention that all the crimes were solved by the end of the book. It was a most satisfying profession.

"And detective Begley?" Her brows tilted up. "I suppose he is on your payroll for scouting out hysterical, damsel-in-distress types and sending them your way?" She had put it in the form of a question, though she already knew the answer.

"Something like that, yes," he answered honestly, still keeping his voice calm.

"And how do you see your little story ending?"

"Happily, I hope. But it is still too early to tell." He paused for a second. "Listen, Dena, I know this looks bad. But I really just went into your room to wake you for dinner. I know the idea was planted in my subconscious, but my intentions were honorable. I may have taken you on as a client for writing material, but I am in this as deep as you are."

"Well then, let's get to work so you can finish your book. Who knows, maybe you'll have a bestseller on your hands?" Not trusting herself to meet his eyes, she turned to the boxes on the table and started pulling papers out.

She was determined not to show him how much he hurt her. She felt used and foolish. When she had made love with Nick, she thought it was earth shattering, the best sexual experience she had ever had and she had wondered if he felt it too. Now she knew it was just research for his book. She suddenly felt sick to her stomach.

Just then the fax phone rang again, breaking the thick tension.

Nick walked back to the office to see what was coming through. It was from Hank.

I went back to the Hartford office and borrowed that photo I mentioned. See if it rings any bells for the Doc. HM

"We found an office that Greenly kept under the name of Hartford." He looked up at Dena who had followed him to see the fax. "This photo was on one of the desks that Hank thought belonged to a woman. Recognize her?"

Dena took the sheet and stared down at the grainy photo in her hand. She blinked away the tears that were starting to pool in her eyes and saw Doug, Paul, herself and her best friend all looking ten years younger.

"Marcy," Dena said softly. "My friend Marcy." Her eyes were fixed on the photo as she remembered the day it was taken. In front of Paul's new twin engine plane he was so proud of. Happier days, or so she had thought.

"Dena," Nick hated to ask. "What does Marcy do for a living?"

Chapter Seventeen

Dena reached out for the chair next to her, grabbing its back for support. Her world was spinning, yet she refused to sit down or let go of the fax sheet she still clutched in her hand. She wanted to tell Nick how far off base he was, that she had known Marcy forever and that she was closer than a sister to her. That if she was working in an office Doug kept under another name, she would know about it.

But she said nothing. Because somewhere, in the back of her brain, ugly thoughts were starting to surface. Looking over the events of Marcy's life this past year, she wondered how she could not have suspected something.

Marcy had left her job last year as a Special Ed teacher to become the office manager at...where? She couldn't remember the name although she talked to her often while she was at work. Now that she thought of it, Marcy always called her. This phenomenal new job allowed her to move to a newer home in a nice neighborhood. A new sports car, vacations and a complete new lifestyle. Not to mention she looked better than ever; in fact, last time she saw her she practically glowed. She never thought to question this before, but how much would an office manager, without any experience, make?

What a fool she had been. So accepting and trusting of everyone. Always so focused on helping others with their pain she could not see what was going on around her. She briefly wondered if Marcy and Doug laughed about her naiveté.

She gradually allowed her gaze to move from the now wrinkled photo to Nick who had been uncharacteristically quiet. He stood watching her, waiting. Most likely trying to study her reaction to this latest horror to later put down on paper.

What she really needed was some time alone. Some space to sort out all the emotions running through her without someone observing her every move. A chance to lick her wounds and to heal because right now her heart was beyond broken. She felt a physical pain deep inside her chest.

She wanted to put as much distance between this man and this place as possible and she promised herself she would. As soon as this was over.

She took in a deep, calming breath as new determination surged through her. She had enough of being a victim and an idiot. Filled with grit and tenacity, she vowed she would find out why all the people she cared about chose to ruin her life, and most important, why she let them.

And then she would create a new life. Move to the other end of the earth. Discover a new profession. Reinvent herself totally. A place where she knew absolutely no one and she could start fresh.

But she knew that first, they would need to figure out what the hell was going on here. Suddenly, she was eager for her new life to begin. It was like the promise of spring after a long, cold winter.

"Let's go through these boxes now," she said abruptly, turning to the box in front of her and pulling out paper. She found it physically painful to look at him, those damn blue eyes of his. She remembered staring up into them as he thrust into her, their eyes locked through the entire, glorious ride. That was all it was, she reminded herself, a ride.

If she was going to get through this, she would have to push all personal thoughts out of her mind, and stick to business.

"Get a garbage can so we can dispose of the obvious junk now," she ordered Nick without so much as sparing him a glance. "Then we will sort into three piles. One for anything pertaining to D & D, one with any name I recognize and the other to research. The rest we throw away." She was careful not to meet those eyes and just remain focused on the box in front of her.

He wondered what was with the sudden change. She probably came to the conclusion she was stuck with him until this was over, and the sooner she had all the answers, the sooner she could get rid of him. Maybe that wasn't such a bad idea, but he should clear the air so they could work together. And try to explain, without putting his foot in his mouth, that this wasn't just a roll in the hay for him. He wasn't exactly sure what it was, but what happened between the two of them was definitely not research.

"Dena, I am sorry..." he tried to get out before she cut him off.

She held up her hand to stop him without even glancing up. "I'm sorry it happened as well. But it did, and we were both consenting adults so let's just move on."

That wasn't what he was going to apologize for, but he let that go. Suddenly, he longed to have his old life back. He had built an existence that gave him everything he wanted. He put in a few hours at the office doing a job he loved, would meet a few friends or family for dinner or lock himself away at his place for days if he wanted to write. He dated when he wanted and had an uncomplicated but satisfying sex life. Or so he thought until last night.

Now he was holed up in a cabin with a woman who hated him and was stuck rifling through dirty boxes of what looked like scrap paper. Not to mention someone had tried to kill them, and would, most certainly, try again.

An hour later all he had to show for his efforts was a headache and a stiff neck. He got up and went to the kitchen and grimaced when he saw the now spoiled dinner he had left on the table. Left there while he went up to wake Dena, and instead did the one thing he promised himself he wouldn't do. He dumped the food in the garbage and made scrambled eggs and toast. He brought out two plates and set one in front of Dena, who was still hard at work.

"I'm not hungry," she said with her head buried in a box.

"Listen, if you don't eat, you won't be able to keep up your strength. And that will slow us down." The words came out a little sterner than he intended, but she got the message and started eating. Too bad, he was half hoping he would have to force-feed her.

When he finished eating he built another fire. He'd had enough of the hard wooden kitchen chairs and would rather sit by the fire and be comfortable.

Dena watched him make four trips out back for wood. He had put on a red and black flannel jacket and looked very much at home in the country. When she found she was actually admiring how great he looked, she got annoyed with herself.

"Hey, Paul Bunyan, what's with all the wood?" Her curiosity got the better of her.

"We're expecting a snowstorm. I'm just taking some precautions, that's all," he replied casually as he piled up the wood next to the hearth.

"And how do you know that, do your corns ache?"

"Just my bad luck to be stranded with an angry smart ass," he murmured under his breath. "I had the radio on in the kitchen while I was making breakfast. It started snowing during the night and they are predicting about a foot of snow before it's done. We couldn't leave here even if we wanted to. The roads back here are not on a list to get plowed. Only the town's main roads have that service."

She wasn't laughing anymore. "What about food?"

This time he laughed. He had to force her to eat her eggs and she's worried about starving to death.

"Stop staring at me like you think I will turn into a cannibal. There is a freezer in the furnace room stocked with food, not to mention the dry goods in the kitchen pantry. We could stay here two months without ever leaving and do fine." He mumbled a curse under his breath declaring it had better not come to that.

"Oh. Well, then the storm would also make it harder for someone to find us, right?"

"Yes. But not impossible. I moved the car into the shed and soon the tracks will be covered up. I guess if someone was determined enough they could hike up here on foot. But I am hoping they still are under the impression we are dead," he said as he moved their work in front of the fire. "I am going to take a shower, make coffee and then I'll get back to work. Why don't you take a break as well?" With that he left the room, not waiting for an answer.

As he stepped into the shower, he briefly wondered what she was doing down there alone. Relaxing, he hoped. Left to his own devices, he knew he would be snooping through the drawers and rummaging through the cupboards. But that was him. It was an occupational hazard, he guessed. He stood in the shower with his head bent forward and let the hot spray close his mind down for a minute.

Dena needed some time alone. She wasn't used to having another person under foot after living alone for so long. Even when she was married, Paul was away on business most of the time.

What she really needed was a hot bath, she thought as she looked out the patio door at the water. The sun was just starting to rise and it was an awe-inspiring view. It would be wonderful to live by the water, to have this superb view everyday, she thought as she made her way to the bathroom attached to her room. She shuddered as she recalled the last time a bath seemed like a great idea, only to end up with twenty stitches in her backside. Well, she wouldn't waste time being afraid. Nick was here and she felt reasonably safe. Besides, she needed this time to think, and to put together her new future.

She frowned as she thought about the healing stitches on her back. A long soak probably would not be a good idea, so she would stay in only for a few minutes.

She must have fallen asleep. Nick's voice startled her as she sat up, noticing the water had turned cool.

"Hey, did you fall asleep in there?" Nick asked.

"I'm just getting out now." She stood and grabbed a towel, shivering.

"Good. Come downstairs and get back to work."

While Nick waited for Dena to finish upstairs, he e-mailed Hank and Pete about Marcy. He gave them her last name, address and the connection to Dena. What he couldn't give them was why? Money would have to be his guess. Friends have killed friends over money before. Greed and the want for more can turn even your soul mate into a murderer.

Identifying Marcy gave them a foundation to build on. He asked Pete and his new friend Thatcher to start the negotiations.

He then went back to the blasted planner they had thought held so many secrets. So far it had given him nothing but eye strain and an urge to throw it in the fire.

"Find anything yet?" Dena stood before him drying her hair. She had pulled on a pair of gray leggings, and a pale pink oversized sweatshirt with apparently no bra. She looked about sixteen.

"No. Nothing earth shattering. He has phone numbers to Greenly's law firm, home and to Trask's office. And of course appointments, but nothing I can connect to anything illegal."

"Maybe it's written in code. You know, in case someone should find it."

"Well, shoot, I left my secret mystery decoder ring at the office."

She rolled her eyes at him and put her hand out. "Let me take a look."

Chapter Eighteen

Marcy McQuade enjoyed living alone. Especially in a new home that was all hers, that she had picked out and decorated herself and did not have to share with an overweight couch potato. Simply thinking about her new life brought tears of joy to her pretty face.

She moved quickly across her living room floor, her high heels clicking loudly on the bare, newly refinished wood floors. She paused in front of the mirror in the foyer to double-check her appearance before she headed out the door. She smiled as she thought of the handsome businessman that came into the office last week for a bugging device and left with her phone number.

She had used the upcoming date as an excuse to splurge on a black pair of strappy Prada shoes which would have cost her a month's salary if she was still a teacher. Even with her new pay scale, they put a dent in her budget. So, when shopping for something to wear, she settled for an off the rack black cocktail dress. It was a well made classic and gave her what she hoped was an air of sophistication.

She thanked her lucky stars for this job. She never met anyone when she was a teacher except other teachers or the janitor. She felt a little stab of guilt, enjoying life and going on a date when her best friend had been killed. But, as they say, life is for the living.

She fluffed her new short, spunky haircut that she requested on impulse after deciding to part with the long, dark locks she had favored since childhood.

When a new career practically fell in her lap, she had come to the conclusion that life was giving her a second chance. Really, her only chance. And if she did not take it, she would be imprisoned in that life until the day she died.

Five minutes after accepting her new position as office manager, she rushed into the school office and resigned, phoned a lawyer to start divorce proceedings and then stopped in at a trendy day spa and signed up for a total makeover.

She had her hair cut and colored just slightly to give it a vibrant shade of shiny dark brown, her eyebrows waxed, a chemical peel and make-up lessons. The results were better than she expected and shaved ten years off her appearance. Her new job was salary plus commission and she worked like she owned the business herself. She hustled her tail off and before a year was up, had enough for a down payment on a new house.

Reluctantly, she tore her gaze from the mirror to grab her coat from the front closet when the doorbell rang. She frowned at her watch and wondered if she should just ignore it. Who would stop by at this hour anyway? She was meeting her date at the hotel where he was entertaining clients, and while she did not want to be too early, she did not want to be late either. It rang again and then was followed by a loud knock. Whoever was there was persistent.

The visitor saw the curtain move and he put on his trademark smile, which was at best, scary. Someone once said that when he smiled, he looked like an aging serial killer.

"Yes?" Her impatient voice snapped through the crack of the door. She had left the security chain on and was ready to slam the door shut if she needed to.

"Marcy McQuade?"

"Who's asking?"

"Hank Morelli. I work for a company that handles private investigations. Your friend Dr. Dena Davis had hired us. I am just following up on a few things." Marcy gasped loudly at the mention of her friend's name. She stared at him a few seconds then closed the door, undid the chain and opened it back up. Her eyes gave him the onceover.

"So, you are a private eye?" She pursed her lips together while scrutinizing him.

"Sure."

"You look like a cop."

"I was."

"You are not much of a conversationalist, Mr. Morelli," she said as she waved him in and indicated he should have a seat.

"Oh, I can be quite chatty when I want to be. How's the new job coming along?"

She raised her eyebrows slightly in surprise then quickly tried to cover it. She took a seat on the couch across from him. "Fine, thank you. Very different than what I was used to." She paused for a second, her eyes assessing the former officer in front of her. "But I am sure I do not need to tell you about my former occupation. I've got the feeling you know all about me." She said this with a flirtatious grin.

"Not all about you. But I will." He smiled again, but there was no humor in his eyes. "What exactly do you do?"

Her intuition told her he was playing her. That he had most of his answers already, but wanted to hear her version. He was a smart one, for sure. Dressed in an outdated, slightly wrinkled brown suit and with an overcoat that he threw down next to him, he reminded her of the TV detective, Columbo. And just like the fictional detective, Marcy was convinced several before her had underestimated this man's intelligence.

"I am the office manager at Hartford Specialties."

"And just what are Hartford's Specialties?"

Her eyes squinted slightly while she chose her answer carefully. "The company specializes in different types of surveillance equipment, security devices such as alarms and cameras. We also offer cameras that use biometrics. Some of our clients are Private Investigation firms like yours."

"Biometrics?" Anything with computers or advanced technology gave him a severe stomachache, but being a good detective, he knew he would have to suffer through it.

"Yes. It is an identification system that can be used at security checkpoints virtually anywhere. The system gathers information from scanners or recordings depending on what type of biometric information is needed." She wondered what the hell any of this had to do with Dena, but refrained from barking at the rumpled investigator. She did not want him to think she had something to hide. Then he would be here forever.

"Who is the owner of the company?" he asked casually. He often asked questions that he already knew the answer to. It was sort of a hobby.

"His name is Mark Hartford. He doesn't come in to the office much, and I've only met him once or twice. We handle most of the business by phone or e-mail." Fortunately, when it came to lying, she was one of the best.

"I'm interested in your clients, other than the PI firms you sell to." He watched her and waited for her reply.

"Well, apartment and professional buildings and some smaller stores. The larger department stores usually have their own people. We have a few wealthy citizens who want extra protection, maybe a few celebrities." She shrugged her shoulders. "I can't give you any names, of course, if that is what you're wanting."

"Why's that?"

"Well, because we value our clients' privacy."

"Do you run any background checks on people before you sell equipment to them, you know, to make sure they won't be doing anything illegal with it?"

"No. And we are not required to, either." She did not like where this was going, but she kept a smile on her face as she answered his questions calmly.

"What about your customers in other countries, say the Middle East, for instance?"

"I don't believe we have clients in the Middle East." She re-crossed her legs and began to fiddle with her necklace while she pondered his question.

"You didn't seem surprised that your friend hired a private investigator before she died." He phrased it as a fact instead of a question and leaned back slightly into the sofa to study her.

"You do jump around with your questioning, don't you? Is that your way of trying to catch the fly in the web?" She glanced down at the gold watch on her wrist and thought of her date waiting for her.

"Were you on your way out for the evening?" Hank inquired pleasantly, although he made no effort to speed things up.

"As a matter of fact I was. Is there somewhere you are going with this line of interrogation? Because if there is, I cannot follow it. Perhaps if you just come out and ask whatever it is you want to know, I could answer you and then we both could be on our way."

"I've already gotten most of the answers I need," he said, reaching for something in his pocket. "I hope you don't mind, but I borrowed this to show a friend."

Curious, she reached her hand out to take what looked like a picture, then yanked her hand back when she touched the frame, as if it where hot. She recognized it at once, of course. It belonged to her. Finally, she accepted the photo back and wondered exactly how much he knew.

The former detective said nothing, he only watched her, waiting to see what she would come up with.

"You took this from my desk?" Marcy asked, surprised.

"Yes."

"Did you break in?" She was still unclear on how he could get this and what it all meant.

"That would be illegal."

"Well, it's just an old photo. I can't see why you went through all the trouble of taking it." She pretended to look bored.

"I'm funny like that. I was just trying to put together a few pieces of this puzzle in my mind. Someone, including Doug Greenly, gave Dr. Davis a lot of trouble before she was killed. I already know that Greenly also operates as Mark Hartford and that he owns the company you work for. Yet you tell me you hardly know Hartford and have met him only once or twice."

She looked down at her new shoes as if trying to figure out how she could get the hell out of here.

When Marcy remained silent, he continued on. "So I'm guessing he came to you and offered you the job of a lifetime and you jumped at it, not asking too many questions." Hank paused to see if she would deny it. "And part of your job description is to make sure no one knows Hartford is really Greenly. But what about killing your best friend? Did you know you would be turned into a murderer when you took this job, or maybe it was just a hidden perk?"

She gasped loudly. "How dare you say I had anything to do with Dena's death! Or imply that Doug did. We loved her." Tears pooled in the corners of her eyes. "Doug started this business on the side and didn't want it to interfere with his law practice, so he used a different name. So what? That doesn't make him a killer." For the first time since she accepted Doug's offer, she was concerned for her future. This man was way too smart. She wondered if he was the one who discovered who Hartford was, because she knew for a fact great pains had been taken so no one would make that connection. If he found that out so easily, she had reason to think her new life was in jeopardy. She made a show of drying her tears on the back of her hand.

Hank leaned forward to peer at the woman who thought she could make him feel sorry for her. His eyes were cold as ice as they held hers. "Your *friend* smashed Dena's face into a plate of glass in a fit of rage. A young woman whom he hired to care for his mother and who was supposed to have died with Paul Davis, just got her throat slashed. Then her roommate, who just happened to remember the name Hartford, ends up murdered as well. Same gruesome method. Now Dr. Davis's house was blown to bits with her and my friend inside."

"I can't be convinced Doug would do anything to hurt Dena and everything else is just a coincidence." Even as she said the words, she knew they sounded lame.

"I don't believe in coincidences. Greenly is a liar and a thief and I think you know that, which makes you no better. But you are looking the other way and in some instances helping him. Selling yourself out for a little cash."

He saw her cool composure starting to slip. "Some might call you a whore." His face wore no expression, and he never raised his voice. It wasn't necessary. He knew how to get someone to talk, one way or another.

"Now just a minute!" She jumped to her feet and kept her fists clenched in anger at her sides. "Where do you get off calling me a whore?"

Hank remained seated and incredibly calm. "Actually, I wasn't done. I was also going to say that you are a murderer and traitor as well. You and you alone run that office. So what I want from you is information."

"I don't have to listen to this! You are not a cop and you have no right to come in here and make these accusations. I want you to leave, now." Her voice shook with anger.

He cast a smile at her that sent chills down her back. Then he stood to face her.

"I can leave now, but you won't be rid of me. I will give you more trouble than the headache that is now forming behind your eyes. Until you give me the proof I need to tie Greenly to Hydan Trask and to all the other mess he is involved in, I will be your shadow."

As if he planted the suggestion, a headache did indeed start to form deep in her skull. And she knew then that, without a doubt, this man would be the biggest thorn in her side that she had ever encountered. Well, even thorns can be disposed of without getting pricked yourself, if you are very careful. They also could ruin this wonderful new life she had worked so hard to create.

"Let's go to the office," she said with her teeth clenched. "I have some documents you will want to see." She caved because she knew this man was telling the truth, and if she didn't, she would never be rid of him. She would have liked to make Columbo here disappear permanently, but that was Doug's department and he was currently incarcerated.

She had indeed stashed away some incriminating evidence, in case the time should come that she would need to prove her innocence. She didn't have to give away all her secrets, just enough to get the heat off of her.

Chapter Nineteen

Dena's brows were knit tightly as she read the planner. Something was there of importance, only she couldn't seem to grasp it. It kept slipping away and memories of the night before with Nick came in its place. Then she thought of his book and her lustful thoughts died there, along with a piece of herself. There you go. If you find yourself daydreaming about him like a fool, just remind yourself of that. She forced her eyes back to the planner.

Then her eyes found it, the entry that had been nagging at her subconscious. May 20th, 2006, just three days before Paul disappeared, he had an appointment with Doug scheduled. The next day, he flew to Georgia although no one knew why. It was not unusual for Paul to take a day trip somewhere just for pleasure, after all, he was a pilot and loved to fly. Paul had "GA" marked on the page for May 21st and she had remembered Bob saying something about it after the plane disappeared. On the following day, May 22nd, Paul left to pick up an elderly client from Bermuda who needed to return home, and was never heard from again.

After several days of a search-and-rescue team coming up with nothing, the search was called off. The official statement released was that his plane went down somewhere in the ocean, near Bermuda. The newspapers however were a little more creative with their headlines, almost enjoying that another plane had disappeared into the "Bermuda Triangle."

Dena looked up just as Nick was walking into the room, his dark, thick hair still damp from his shower, and she noted that he had changed into what looked like a pair of favorite jeans. Faded and fitting just right. He wore a blue flannel shirt with the top two buttons undone, giving her a peek of his dark chest hair. Where in the world did this wardrobe keep coming from? He only arrived with the one duffel bag, and she doubted he had thought to stuff in all this country wear.

"Did you decipher any hidden clues, Sherlock?" Nick asked with a grin he could not help. He knew she was pissed at him and teasing her probably wasn't a good idea, but growing up in a house with three sisters made it a natural pastime.

She ignored what she thought was sarcasm. "Doug had an appointment with Paul just three days before he disappeared."

"Was that so unusual? I mean, Doug was your friend and a lawyer. Maybe it was over a legal matter." He sat down on the floor and leaned against the couch.

"Paul didn't care much for Doug, and vice versa. He used him for legal services when he first opened his business, but only because I made him. And Doug gave him a break on his fees, which at the time was necessary. But after that, they didn't see much of each other that I am aware of. But then, I hadn't been aware of a lot of things...." With that her eyes glazed over.

"Is there any indication of what the meeting was about?" he asked to get her back on track.

"No. But the next day he flew to Georgia by himself on a day trip. The day after that he disappeared."

"Did he frequently take day trips that didn't involve flying customers somewhere?" It looked like Paul had a lot of freedom to come and go, but what really interested him was the

Georgia trip only a day before he was planning to vanish.

"I don't know. He didn't tell me what he did each day. He flew planes. If I called the office and he wasn't in, it was safe to assume he was up in the air. I already knew he went to Georgia because Bob told me. There was an investigation after the assumed crash, but they were not asking the right kind of questions."

"Bob was his partner, right?" Nick saw where she was going with this now, and was impressed.

"Yes. I think we need to talk to Bob."

She watched him as he clicked the pen in his hand for a moment. "You know what, Sherlock? I agree. I would prefer to do it myself, but we will have to settle on sending someone else," he said regretfully.

* * *

Pete found D & D Aviation easily enough, but what proved to be more of a challenge was hunting down Bob. When he came through the front doors of the office, his eyes fell on a perky blonde in a tight pale yellow sweater who sat at the reception desk chatting on the phone. When she saw him walk in, she mumbled a 'gotta go,' hung up, and politely greeted him when he asked to see Bob Denton.

"I'm not sure where Bobby is at the moment, but he's here somewhere on the grounds. Have a seat and I will page him." She grinned at him as she chewed her gum.

"Why don't I just go take a look around for him?" Pete said, offering her one of his heart-stopping smiles. He knew with a little flirting and some charm, he could get last year's tax returns if he wanted to. She was truly every man's wet dream and it was a shame he did not have time to do more than flirt with her, but he needed to talk to her boss and get back to work.

Without Nick at the office, Margaret had taken Pete on as her pet project. She rearranged his office, changed his filing system and, it seemed, was steadily increasing his work load.

"I'm sorry, but that won't be possible. Because of the necessity for the increase in security, I cannot have you walking around unescorted," she said in a no-nonsense tone. She stood up to reveal a pair of incredibly long legs gift wrapped in the best fitting jeans he had ever seen.

He stood just looking for a moment, speechless. He didn't know why, but he thought for sure she would be wearing a mini skirt with six inch heels. Something he was sure *Bobby* would appreciate.

When his eyes finally connected with hers, he realized she knew what he was doing. And what he was thinking. And for the first time he could remember, he felt a little embarrassed.

He gave a low chuckle at his own arrogance. He had played her for a dumb blonde and had expected that she would fall for him because he had a nice physique and could pour on the charm. He knew what he had done, but what was worse, she knew it. He decided to play it straight and reached in his pocket for a business card. She raised her eyebrows in question when she read it.

"A private investigator, huh?" She stepped back and looked him over with an appraising eye. "I thought perhaps you were a model for GQ."

Pete let out a laugh. He had that coming he knew, but it surprised him. She maintained eye contact, watching him with a perceptive smile.

"Well, Mr. Capaldi, let me page Bobby for you." She bent over the desk, pressed a button on the phone and spoke, requesting that her boss call the office. "If this doesn't work, we'll go search for him. If he is working on an engine or with a noisy machine, he can't hear the page."

"Don't you have a mechanic that does that?"

"Sure, a couple of them, actually. But Bobby likes to do a little tinkering with the engines now and then. Kinda like a hobby. He says it relaxes him." She held up a finger to indicate he wait while she answered the ringing phone.

He didn't think he would like to be up in a plane that the owner enjoyed tinkering with as a hobby. He also wondered what else her boss enjoyed tinkering with. While the receptionist was scheduling someone for flying lessons, he took the opportunity to snoop around. A stack of textbooks piled on her desk caught his eye. Topics ranged from subjects such as Corporate Law to something about building important relationships at work. A couple of computer manuals and a highlighter were lying next to the textbooks. Maybe she takes a few classes at the local college, he thought. He looked up when she hung up the phone.

"I don't actually read those, I only look at the pictures," she said, pointing to the books.

He laughed out loud. This girl was not only beautiful and obviously intelligent, but she also had a sense of humor. This certainly hadn't come up before, he thought. She had raised her eyebrows and seemed to be waiting for him to say something.

"I guess I was a little surprised."

"What, that I know how to read?"

For someone who was known to have a way with women, he sure wasn't doing very well. *Time for a different approach before she clobbers me over the head with one of those textbooks*, he mused.

"You're a part-time student, then?" he asked, because suddenly he was intrigued. Not just making idle conversation, which would lead to her giving up her phone number.

"Full-time student, part-time employee." She stopped talking to answer the phone. "That was Bobby. He will be here in a minute to talk with you."

"Great. Thank you." He could smell her perfume, a light, floral scent.

"You're welcome." She stood for a few seconds then sat back down and began doing something on her computer.

Just then Bob Denton entered the room. He wore greasy denim work overalls and a friendly smile. Maybe he really did enjoy tinkering with those planes. He went directly over to Pete and stuck his hand out.

"Bob Denton. What can I do for you?"

Instead of getting a mental read of the guy he was supposed

to be questioning, Pete found himself wondering what the story was between Bobby and Blondie. When he realized Bob was looking at him with a strange expression on his face, he forced himself to snap out of it.

"Pete Capaldi. I'm a private investigator that works for the firm Dr. Dena Davis had hired." He paused for effect and to see what the owner and happy mechanic would say.

Bob Denton's smile vanished and he nodded his head. "I'll be out back, Jill." And to Pete, "Let's step outside. I need some air."

Bob lead the way through glass double doors that opened up to a small but pleasant courtyard. There were trees, flower pots, a couple of picnic tables and a small fountain in the center that was covered for the winter. He went over to a vending machine, paid for two Cokes and handed one to Pete. "A little oasis to escape to now and then, even in the cold," he said, as he took a sip of the soda. "I come here for a little peace and quiet, Jill likes to study here and the other employees eat lunch or take breaks here. Well, not in the winter." He laughed a little. "I'm the only one who comes out here in this weather. My wife designed it and planted the flowers," he said proudly and pointed to the ground where the flowers would bloom in the spring.

Pete raised his eyebrows but did not say anything and to his surprise, Bob started laughing into his Coke can.

"For an investigator, you are as transparent as an open door, Mr. Capaldi. I love my wife and am a happily married man with four children. Jill is a wonderful, competent receptionist whom I love as well. She is also my niece." Then his eyes narrowed slightly as he looked over his can at the man sitting next to him. "And I must say, I am a little protective of her."

An incredible sense of relief washed over him, which was immediately replaced with his feeling like an idiot.

"I am sorry, Mr. Denton. I didn't come here to find a date or to insult you." He really hoped this guy was innocent, because he just blew some major interviewing techniques.

A sincere look of sorrow washed over the man's face as he remembered why the investigator was there. He went over to the picnic table and had a seat as Pete did the same. "I know you didn't." He started to play with the tab on his Coke can. "And please call me Bob. I can't tell you how sick I am over what happened to Dena. She was a warm, loving woman and I always liked her. As a friend," he added quickly. "So, you said she hired you. Did that have anything to do with her death? I know the papers said a faulty furnace was responsible, but..." his words got a little choppy and he let his voice trail off.

Pete was an experienced and clever liar who could fib his pants off if he wanted to and usually, he enjoyed himself immensely while doing it. His job gave him the avenue to practice his skill and he considered it one of the many perks of his job. But he liked this guy and he felt rotten about being deceitful. When had he become such a softy? Maybe it was time for a vacation when all of this was over.

"An unknown person or persons were giving Dena a hard time, broke into her house on more than one occasion. First, she thought they were after her, but later began to think it was something else. Like they were after information or perhaps an item in her possession she didn't know was important."

"What in the world could Dena have that would put her life in jeopardy? She was as straight as an arrow." He shook his head in disbelief. "Unless it was something to do with one of her patients, you know, a crazy ex-husband. That sort of thing."

"We checked that out and came to a dead end. Were you aware that Bridgett Bonner just turned up dead a couple of weeks ago?"

Bob put his can down and his eyes widened in surprise and he began shaking his head. "You mean they found the plane finally? Where?"

"Bridgett was never on that plane. She has been alive and well and practically living within shouting distance from Dena." He could see Bob's shock was genuine and that he truly had no idea she had not been on that plane. "What do you know about Doug Greenly?"

"That lawyer?" He shrugged his shoulders slightly. "Nothing much. He did a little work for us when we first got started. If I recall correctly, he was a good friend of Dena's. Don't think Paul cared very much for him, though."

"Greenly helped give Bridgett a new identity and a job taking care of his aging mother." Pete could see his shock and a sudden wariness in his eyes, as if he knew the worst was yet to come. Either he was an excellent actor or he truly didn't know that right under his nose, his friend and business partner had planned to fake his own death.

"Bridgett helped mastermind a plan for her and Paul to fly away into the sunset with a lot of cash and make it look like they crashed. She put together a new life for them and then at the last minute, he gave her the slip. It turns out the entire time he was planning on taking someone else with him."

Pete watched the man process the information. His face went from shock to disbelief, then finally anger. He was a quick study.

"And leave behind Bridgett? Didn't he think she would give away his plans?" Bob finally replied when he found his voice.

"She was going to do exactly that when Greenly approached her and offered her a new life. He promised her there was another larger scam Paul was involved in, and when he had enough proof, he would go to the police. He also told her if she didn't change her identity, Paul would find her and kill her."

"Do you think her murder was somehow connected?"

"Yes." Pete didn't even blink an eye. He knew all these pieces of the puzzle were related. "A week after Bridgett was murdered, her roommate was killed as well. Someone was afraid of what they knew."

The winter sun was shining on Bob's face, causing him to squint slightly. A few lines appeared around his eyes and mouth when he smiled, which was often, even when talking about something unpleasant. "So now you want to see what I know and perhaps this is your way of telling me I could be next?" Pete nodded his head so he continued. "Everything you've told me today is news to me. I thought Paul and Bridgett had died in a plane crash. End of story."

"So you knew they were having an affair?"

Bob shifted uncomfortably in his chair. "I never said that."

"You referred to them as a couple instead of Paul and his nurse." He in reality had not made the two sound like a couple, but Pete was curious what he would say.

He started to protest and then stopped. "I guess it doesn't make any difference now, does it? Everyone it would matter to is dead. Yeah, they were having an affair. They would go off on trips together, just the two of them. I walked in on them once, and I wasn't real happy about it and felt bad for Dena, but it wasn't my place to tell her. He was my business partner and, I thought, friend."

Pete stuck his hands in his leather jacket to warm up; he didn't know about Bob, but he was getting pretty damn cold. This guy must be part Eskimo. "So, he didn't steal any money from the business when he left?"

Bob shook his head no. "I've been thinking about that. If he was planning on faking his death and living somewhere, he would have needed a lot of money. Unless he planned on taking up work as a pilot someplace else. He didn't take any from me, but he could have been pocketing something on the personal trips he took. He went every other week somewhere with Bridgett and said they were taking the day off. I guess he could have been flying another party." Bob's dark brown eyes narrowed as a thought occurred to him. "Or he could have been moving *something*. Something for which he would have been paid a good amount of money to ship. It has been known to happen."

Pete didn't say anything and just watched him.

"You already knew that, didn't you?" A look close to panic came over friendly Bob's face. "What in God's name was he doing?"

"We don't have the proof yet. But we think your partner was picking up things like high tech intelligence gadgets, guns and other goodies and flying them to a terrorist training camp in the Middle East. And I think Greenly set up the deal. But Paul couldn't have done all that in a day trip. Were there trips he would take when he was gone a little longer?"

"Yeah. About every other month, he would be gone for about three days. And around the time he disappeared, he was going every month."

"He would have needed to file a flight plan, wouldn't he?"

"Yes. But they wouldn't have a record of that after all this time."

"That's what I figured." Pete stood up.

"But I do." Bob said with a clever grin and stood up as well. "The only thing is, though, he couldn't have taken one of our planes that far. We'll go take a look at those records; at least maybe the dates and times might be helpful."

Pete shook off a chill and nodded.

"Come with me. You look like you're getting a little frosty sitting out here anyway."

As they walked back through the office doors Pete told himself he would not look at the blonde again. Jill. That was her name and he said it again to himself. But his eyes betrayed him and when he glanced over at her, he found she was watching him. Pete was unaware that he had stopped walking until he heard Bob clear his throat. He couldn't recall ever acting like a bigger fool over a girl, even as a teenager.

There was something about her. He didn't know what it was and he was damn sure he didn't want to find out. He would get the records that Bob kept and wave goodbye to Jill.

Chapter Twenty

Dena raised her head and massaged the back of her neck when she heard Nick talking in the other room. She stood up to stretch as he entered the living room, finishing up his call.

"I thought you said phone calls could be traced?" Dena eyed him suspiciously. She wondered if she would end up regretting the trust she had placed in him. Actually, on some level she already did. But that was on matters of the heart. Her brain continued to play the "what if" game a little longer as she imagined various scenarios that included Nick being the bad guy. Could he have been in on this from the beginning? Had their first meeting been part of the plan? It sounded far fetched and incredibly irrational, but then everything that had happened had been a real stretch for her imagination. But she had to admit, it would make great reading material.

"They can be. Cell phones are a little trickier and this one has a scrambler on it. But just in case, I kept it short." Now he knew that not only did she hate him, she no longer trusted him. That would make protecting her more difficult, because she would fight him and second guess his decisions. He had watched her stretching when he first came into the room. He stood silently while she lengthened her body, her hands lifting high over her head, causing her shirt to rise and give him a nice view of her flat stomach and navel. He quickly turned to face the window and forced himself to think about baseball. Not easy to do when all you saw outside was snow.

He held the cell phone out so she could see it. "The phone was research for a book I did," he offered as an explanation, but still she had a wary look in her eyes.

"Who were you talking to?"

"That was Pete. Bob Denton had copies of the flight planes that showed Paul flying to Georgia on several occasions and landing in a small airport ten minutes from Trask's headquarters. We are thinking when he landed there, he would switch to a larger plane and go on from there to the Middle East; or perhaps he only flew the merchandise halfway to a drop off point and someone else made the final delivery. That would ensure that the terrorist training camp location would not be made known."

"What good does this information do us now? Or is this merely research for your next book?"

Nick raked his hands through his hair. He was already working on little sleep, while his brain was taxed from sifting through endless papers and trying to figure out what importance, if any, the information had.

The last thing he needed was to have to continually justify his motives. He had learned long ago to control that Irish/Italian temper of his, but she was really getting under his skin.

"Any information we find is important, until we know exactly what happened. This is what investigative work is all about. It is a painstaking and meticulous process of gathering every scrap of information you can dig up. Then, the next step is to try and put it all together." He saw she was backing down a little, so he continued.

"And your friend Marcy provided us with a contact name at Trask who called and gave the orders. This guy would contact

Greenly with his request and arrange for Paul to deliver it. Eventually, Greenly set up his own office and branched out selling security systems and equipment to regular citizens. But what I need to know is, who is flying the equipment now that Paul is not around?"

"What do we do with this information?"

"We use it to get Greenly to talk. We need him to give us the names of those in charge on both ends. Once we have them, then we will be safe." Maybe. Nick looked down at the one remaining full box on the floor. "Is that the last box to go through?"

"Yes. Then we can go back and search through the piles to determine if anything is important. But really, it just looks like junk."

He squatted down next to the box and started pulling out papers. "Well, let's get this finished while I wait to hear back about Greenly. Pete's working out a deal to get him to spill his guts."

"Dena, what's this?"

"Hmm?" She pulled her eyes from the document she was reading.

"It's a deed to a piece of property in the city of Hert belonging to a Paul Davis. Looks like about twenty acres of land. Did you know about this?" He looked over at her to gauge her reaction.

She moved closer to him so she could read the document over his shoulder. He had that freshly showered smell with a hint of after shave, something spicy and slightly musky. She quickly sat back on her heels and took a deep breath to clear her head.

"No, I didn't know anything about that property. I never even heard of a city called Hurt. Where is it?"

"It's spelled H-e-r-t. It's about an hour away from here. It's a spec of a town, nothing much to it." He got up to absently gaze out the front window, his hand rubbing his chin while he mentally measured the snow.

"It looks like the snow's coming to an end." He glanced at

his watch. "It's already after 4:00 now and will be getting dark soon. First thing tomorrow we'll go have a look-see at that property and try to find out what's so special about it that someone would rather have you dead than come across it on your own."

"You think this is what they were after?" She looked intently at the piece of paper he held but what she was mainly observing were his hands. They were big, strong hands that made her feel safe. Funny that she never noticed them before and wondered why in the world she was thinking of them now. Maybe this was the first step to having a nervous breakdown.

"Yeah. Unless I find something else in this box or in one of your little piles there, I would have to say this is it."

"Aren't you afraid of leaving here? The tracks we leave behind might put us in danger and how will we even get out of here? Just look at all that snow." It was crazy to go out in this weather hunting down clues like Nancy Drew with one of the Hardy Boys. Even if he was a cop at one time and a Private Eye now, she wondered just how qualified this fiction writer was. It felt like they were in way over their heads.

"Not as dangerous as waiting here like sitting ducks. Eventually, they will find us." He stood up and pulled his cell phone out of his pocket, glad not to be sitting so close to her. He thought traipsing around out in a freezing blizzard might just be a welcome relief.

"Who are you calling?" No longer happy to sit back and let Nick take charge, she wanted to be an active participant in this investigation, which now involved her very life.

"Someone to come and plow a path outta here in the morning." And then, as if reading her mind, "He will make a path down the back roads, so anyone coming from the front won't see our tracks, not to mention they'd have a hellava time trying to get through all that snow." Even with it plowed, he thought, it's going to be a bitch getting through those trees. But he had to get to that property.

The next morning Dena heard the snow plow about two minutes before Nick banged on her door.

"Come on, Dena, get up," he growled at the door while knocking loudly. After the shitty night's sleep he had he felt like kicking it down. "And dress warm. There should be some women's stuff in the closet."

She rubbed the sleep out of her eyes and mumbled a response, wondering what put Nick in such a foul mood. She reminded herself that she did not care; her job now was to focus on finding all the answers, ending this mess, and moving on.

In her bathroom Dena washed her face and brushed her teeth so she could at least feel human. She wasn't going to bother with putting make-up on, but at the last minute decided a facial moisturizer and a lip balm might be a good idea before going out into the cold.

As she rummaged through the closet in her room, she did indeed find some women's clothes that were about her size and she briefly wondered whom they belonged to. She picked out a navy and white wool sweater and a white turtleneck to put underneath and wore her own jeans. There was a pair of winter boots on the floor of the closet that she pulled out. They were a size and a half too big but with a thick pair of socks, they should do the trick. They would have to do, because she hadn't packed any of her own.

She found Nick in the kitchen dressed in an outfit very similar to hers, leaning against the counter with a mug of coffee in one hand and a map in the other.

"There's coffee if you want a quick cup," he said without looking up. "Then we need to get going."

It would probably be a good idea to have a little breakfast with the coffee, but she settled on the caffeine she so desperately needed. It was clear he did not want her to waste time eating, which was just as well, her stomach felt as if it were tied in knots. It seemed to do that a lot lately whenever she was near him.

"All right, let's get going." He folded the map and walked out of the kitchen.

They paused at the sturdy wooden coat rack near the back door to put their coats on. His, she noticed, was a heavy duty navy parka. The kind you can stay out in for days in twenty-five degrees below zero weather and even build igloos if you want.

Nick scowled at her when she grabbed her wool coat and began to pull her arms through the sleeves. She was grateful she at least had gloves and a hat with her. They weren't made for the extreme cold, but they would be better than nothing.

"You better stay here. You're gonna freeze in that." His voice was clipped.

No way. She was not being left behind. "I'll be fine. I like the cold." Which was a big fat lie, she hated winter. But she could tell he really didn't want her to come and for some reason, that made her want to go all the more. Plus, she was tired of not knowing what was happening. This was her life and her problem, and she wanted an active role in finding the solution.

"Suit yourself." He yanked open the door and went out, leaving Dena to follow in his footsteps.

But as soon as she stepped out into the heavy snow, she knew she had a problem. Her boots were fine in the house, but out in the deep snow they were getting stuck and because they were way too loose, pulling off. She could feel the cold wind biting through her inadequate clothing but she did her best to pretend everything was fine. By the time she got to the Tahoe, Nick was already behind the wheel with the engine running.

She now had snow in her boots and was freezing. But she would rather die than give him the satisfaction of being right.

She could see he was still in a foul mood. It was more than just a mood, it was anger and it was directed at her. She could imagine that this was very inconvenient for him, and most likely putting a real damper on his social life.

She started to shiver a little and wished he would turn up the heat, but she wasn't about to ask. The cold had always been hard on her and she spent little time outdoors during the winter. She turned her attention instead to the winter wonderland surrounding her.

The view was truly breathtaking. Snow covered everything like a thick, white fluffy blanket. Only occasional branches of the tall evergreens could be seen peeking out here and there. A cardinal sat proudly on the wooden fence watching them drive by. The owners of this house were lucky to be able to escape here and enjoy this incredible view.

Nick couldn't seem to shake the mood he woke up with. A loathsome mood and a hard-on woke him up too early and knowing he was shackled to the source of his annoyance for a good part of the day wasn't helping any.

He never should have let her out of the house. She wasn't dressed for it and she didn't look like the type that would tolerate the cold well. Not enough meat on her bones to provide sufficient insulation. At the very least he should have allowed her to eat breakfast, knowing that her body would go through calories at a faster rate to maintain its temperature. Well, he had told her to stay put. But he knew even though he was mad at her, she didn't deserve to freeze to death.

When she came into the kitchen this morning, he had wanted to punish her. Penalize her for taking over his life, for invading his dreams at night and making him lust after her like a schoolboy. And having her once was worse than never having her at all. Now he didn't have to rely on his imagination to wonder how incredible her body was; he knew firsthand.

This line of thinking was bound to get him in trouble so he switched his concentration to the road. Jim had arrived at sunrise to plow a path behind the house as promised. It was no more than a clearing between the trees that would lead them out to a main road. It was not obvious to anyone, not marked in anyway, and not found on any map. Even if someone were looking for it, chances are they would drive right by it. It looked like nothing more than a small break in the trees. Jim was careful not to plow too close to the ground to draw attention, only to allow the SUV to clear.

The trail was narrow and bumpy and Dena put her seat belt on to keep from being tossed around like a rag doll. It was a relief when they turned onto the main road. After a long stretch of silence she asked Nick what he thought he would find at the property.

"Nothing. It is probably just a vacant lot, maybe a hunting shack there. But at least you will get to see the new land you just inherited. You ought to get a pretty penny for it when you sell it." And he hoped she did. He didn't want her living this close to one of his hideaways.

What made him so sure she wouldn't want to keep the land? It might make a nice retreat to come to once in a while, but she knew her immediate plans would be taking her far away from this area.

When they arrived in Hert, Nick pulled into the only service station to be found to ask for better directions.

A teenage boy walked out of the old time service station and looked eager to help them with whatever they needed.

"What will it be, sir?" The boy asked with a smile when Nick rolled down his window.

"Go ahead and fill it up," Nick said with a nod and a pleasant grin. While getting the car gassed, the young man cleaned their windows and checked the oil, all while casually sneaking peeks at Dena. Nick rolled back down the window and called him over to the car.

He held the deed that had the address of the land so the young man could see it. "Are you any good at giving directions?"

"Sure, I know every corner in Hert inside and out. That place you're looking for, though, is so far out, it's almost in the next town over." The young man pointed out the road from which they had just turned. "Just follow Main Street here about five miles or so to a road called Brick. Don't know why it's called Brick when it's not even paved. Anyway, turn left there and go down about two miles and it will be on your right. There's an old shell of a barn across the road from it and about the only thing you will notice is a no trespassing sign. There's no house or anything, at least not that you can see from the road, so just watch for the barn and you'll find it."

"Thank you. You've been a big help." Nick slipped him a twenty and watched his eyes grow wide.

"Anytime!"

Nick gave a nod and started to reach for the window button and stopped.

"Hey," he called the kid back to the car. "How did you know right where to find this property? It doesn't sound like much of a landmark."

"Some guy came around a while back. I helped him find it by pulling out some maps and calling the locals. He didn't tip like you, though, and I spent nearly an hour helping him. My dad said it was the right thing to do." He shrugged his shoulders.

They found the spot exactly as described by the gas station attendant. When they pulled up, all they saw were trees and snow. If there was a road or a driveway, it couldn't be seen under all the cover.

Nick pulled the Tahoe over to what he hoped was the side of the road. With the snow not plowed, it was hard to tell where exactly the road started and ended. He jumped out of the vehicle without saying a word to Dena, and started to scout around.

At first glance there was nothing to see, but if you looked more closely, you could make out a clearing through the trees. She saw Nick making his way towards that direction and scrambled to get out of the car. Clearly he intended to just ignore her and leave her behind. Fuming, her stubbornness took over her common sense and she raced after him, falling twice in the snow.

There was an eerie silence that surrounded them. The snow seemed to muffle out any sounds as they made their way through it. There were no planes overhead, no distant sounds of a highway, only what seemed like a noiselessness, an empty forest. Even though it was broad daylight, the utter stillness of the land was spooky.

He knew she was behind him, just as he was sure she would follow him. He should make her go back and wait, but he knew she would protest and he thought, if provoked, he would undoubtedly lose his composure. When he didn't bother to slow down or offer to help her, he realized he was acting like a moron. Now wasn't the time or place to analyze his feelings or motives, but if he was honest with himself, his actions were a knee-jerk response to being shut out and, more or less, dumped.

After another ten minutes of struggling through trees and snow, they came upon an old, once-painted white farm house with a large barn. Both were ancient and in need of either repair or demolishing. The house seemed to be about one hundred years old and at one time, might have been rather grand.

Nick went up what was left of the stairs and peered inside the front window. The house was totally empty and appeared to have been unlived in for a number of years, but Paul could have used it for a hunting lodge or even a meeting place.

"We didn't come across anything mentioning a house on this property. Still, if it's on your land, you must own it." He said this more to himself as he started walking around the house to the back, hunting for an easier way to get inside. The locks were old and not worth much, but he wanted to be able to lock up again when they left. He found it hard to believe their new friend at the gas station didn't know about this place. In a small town like this without much else to do, an abandoned house would be of prime interest to boys his age. Nick approached the back door and managed effortlessly to jimmy the lock with his pocket knife and in they went.

Dena followed him in. They went through each room searching for any personal effects left behind, but the house was totally cleaned out. Only worn, dirty wooden floors throughout the entire house. Aged, yellow wallpaper still hung on the walls with an occasional lighter spot indicating a picture once hung there.

The house was barren of all effects that make a house a home, but yet somehow, it seemed so familiar to her, like she had been here before. Which she knew was impossible considering she did not even know this house existed until about a couple of hours ago.

In her mind, she could see the house as it once had been and the many possibilities of what it could be if you were willing to sink in hours of time and pockets full of money. It was a large country house with a big porch in front and Dena had a vision of herself sitting on a swing there on a summer's day.

Convinced there was nothing to be found in the house, they left through the back door when Dena froze as something caught her eye to the right. In truth, she hadn't even looked in that direction, but she knew it was there. She felt it. She stood still, stunned, as the color rapidly drained from her face. Her stomach tightened and she was sure she would be sick.

Nick turned around and gave her an irritated look for not following him but stopped when he saw the odd expression on her face. Quickly, he reached for his Glock, a practiced move he knew would be faster than asking what was wrong.

"Dena?" He asked tentatively as he glanced around, seeing nothing out of the ordinary.

She shook her head no.

"For God's sake, what is it?" She heard a mix of mild anger and concern in his voice.

"The cellar." She still did not turn her head in its direction, but she was sure it was there.

For the first time he noticed there was a cellar and thinking she must have seen someone there, he went over to investigate.

"I'll go check it out. Stay put," he said, even though she was firmly rooted to the step she was still standing on. But when he approached the cellar doors, he could see the rusty padlock tightly closed, which probably could not be opened even with the key.

He turned back to her and she seemed to be coming out of her trance. "This is locked, Dena. No one could have gone in there."

Embarrassed, she wasn't sure what to say. She didn't understand her reaction anymore than he did.

"I'm sorry Nick. I don't know what came over me. It's just when I walked down the steps, I knew there would be a cellar there and for some reason it terrified me." She began moving towards him. "Maybe I was locked in a cellar in a past life."

She tried to make light of it, but Nick wasn't buying it. And knowing the kind of childhood she had, he was sure she wasn't that far off.

"Did you have a cellar at your house, Dena?" You don't have that kind of reaction for no reason, a fact he was sure she was aware of. Her face had regained some of its color, but for a while there she looked like she was going to faint.

"I don't think so."

"What, you don't remember the house you grew up in?" He stared at her like she was crazy, which he was beginning to suspect she just might be.

She looked him straight in the eyes, daring him to believe her. "Oh, I remember some things. Like the white lace curtains in my room or the apple tree in our yard. But, other images are vague." Then something flashed in her eyes. "My grandmother had one, though. But I can't think of anything bad that happened to me while I was there. I only have happy memories of my time there."

He let the topic drop for now. He was sure something pretty unpleasant happened to her in a cellar, but she wasn't going to remember it now and it most likely had nothing to do with what was going on today.

"We might as well check out the barn before we go," he said, already heading in that direction. He supposed he should wait for her, hold her arm and help her through the snow, but the fact was, he did not want to touch her. To make any unnecessary contact might stir his feelings or remind him of their night together. He wondered suddenly if he was always this immature or if this was a new development. He turned then to see if she was okay and she was just a few steps behind him, a look of determination on her face.

The barn door had a padlock holding the doors closed. Though it was slightly rusty, it was not that old.

"This lock is probably only a few years old. Maybe the visitor looking for directions left something for us," Nick said as he pulled out a set of lock picks and began to work on the lock. Dena raised her eyebrows, but said nothing. The unsophisticated lock popped open and he pulled the big barn doors apart slowly, allowing the light to fill the dark barn.

"Holy shit!" Nick muttered in disbelief. Beside him he heard Dena gasp in shock. Not thinking, or even looking at her, he reached out for her hand and held it.

Neither one spoke. They just stood staring into the barn, hand in hand, while the gravity of the situation settled upon them.

Waiting patiently to one day be discovered, was an airplane. And there was little doubt, the plane had belonged to Paul. Nick dropped her hand gently and opened the doors fully to allow as much light in as possible.

"Was it his?" he asked as he walked further into the barn.

"Yes." She was sure of it. The mental image of Paul in that plane had been burned forever in her subconscious when they were looking for him.

Nick did a full circle around the plane. "Doesn't seem to have crashed, does it?" He approached the door. "I'm going to take a look inside."

He pulled and tugged at the passenger door until it finally gave and released with a loud squeak from lack of use. As he opened the door all the way, it continued to groan as if in protest at being disturbed. Nick stuck his head in to see both the pilot and the copilot seats were empty. A stale and slightly unpleasant smell greeted him that is often found in a space closed up for a long time.

He climbed in to take a better look and then went through the cockpit to check out the rest of the plane. His eyes scanned the plane, taking it all in. Boxes and several suitcases lay on the floor of the craft. They were open and their contents thrown around as if someone was looking for something. He couldn't see much in the way of medical supplies, so they must have emptied the plane first to make room for their belongings. He made his way through the plane, stepping carefully over debris, to search behind the seats.

In the far right corner, behind the last row of seats, a white tarp that looked like it had been used as a dropcloth for someone painting, caught his eye. Carefully, he lifted up a corner to see what was underneath.

He stared for a moment and let the sheet of canvas drop back down. Not much surprised him anymore. In fact, he suddenly realized that this was exactly what he expected to find the minute he opened the barn doors and saw the plane.

He jumped down from the plane to tell Dena. It wouldn't be the shock of her life; still, it would give her heart a little jolt, he imagined. This pretty much confirmed it was the deed that someone had come looking for. Someone was eager to get that piece of paper before Dena discovered this land existed.

This had to be the work of Greenly. Being close to Dena, he would be aware that she had no idea this property was here. And when she started going through Paul's papers, he got nervous. Every day he found a new reason to hate that asshole. But why just try to get rid of the paper trail and not the real evidence? Unless you were a crazy bastard and this was all part of the plan.

He found her sitting on an old wooden crate, shivering. Well, she wasn't dressed for this weather, that's for sure. He was about to give her a lecture and remind her she should have stayed behind when he stopped. Something wasn't right. Maybe it was the combination of the cold and the shock of finding the airplane, but she didn't seem right.

"Dena?" he spoke softly, forgetting his anger. "Are you all right?" He squatted down in front of her so he could look directly into her eyes.

Her eyes flickered with what he thought was a response, but no words followed. Her shivering was becoming almost violent and he thought of hypothermia. What do you do for that when you're stuck out in an old barn?

"Okay, just relax, Dena. I'll be right back." Again he spoke softly, to reassure her or maybe himself. He ran to the plane to get blankets or something to cover her.

He tore through the plane, opening cupboards and lifting seats until he found what he wanted.

He wrapped one blanket around her shoulders and the other across her lap. He started to pull her boots off to rub her feet when a chunk of snow dropped out at his foot.

He let out a loud curse that echoed through the barn. Why the hell would she wear these boots if they didn't even fit? He tugged off the other boot to find the same thing. Both feet were covered in snow.

Gently but swiftly he removed her wet and cold socks. Standing with her in his arms, he carried her into the plane so at least she could be a little more comfortable. After he lay her down on the floor and arranged the blankets around her, he took his own jacket off and draped it across her. Then he began to work on her feet. He lifted up his shirt and placed her bare, frozen feet on his chest. He didn't flinch at the shock her icy feet gave to his system, he hardly noticed. He massaged her feet while keeping them pressed to his skin, his shirt covering them. The entire time he spoke comforting words with an occasional bit of advice on the importance of dressing for the cold.

"Cold," she said through chattering teeth, only not as violent as before.

"Really?" He gave a quick smile even though he still wanted to throttle her for the scare she gave him. "Let's get you out of here." He needed to get her someplace warm; they couldn't stay in this chilly plane. He bent down to scoop her up.

"I can walk on my own," she protested quickly.

"Shut up." He lifted her easily and got them out of the plane.

"My boots." She swiveled her head around and saw them on the ground as they went by. They were already at the barn door and he wasn't slowing down.

"Yeah, what about them?" was all he said and he kept going.

He managed to close and lock the barn doors with her in his arms, then made his way back to the car.

She was wrapped tightly in the blankets and his parka. He wouldn't take it back when she offered and instead barked at her to wear it and keep quiet. She must admit she felt much warmer than she had before, even though she felt foolish having to be carried all this way. And though she offered to walk, she knew deep down she would never have made it. Her feet were losing some of the numbness she felt earlier and now it was replaced with a painful stinging. Her legs felt like rubber and the rest of her was so tired, it was becoming an effort to keep her eyes open.

She should have listened to him and stayed back. She hadn't been dressed properly and was nothing but a nuisance. She remembered it was a long way back to the car.

"I'm sorry, Nick," she said into his neck.

She awoke a little while later as he was depositing her in the car. The long walk seemed to have helped work off his temper and he seemed more relaxed. Or maybe she was just hoping that was the case. Either way, she kept her mouth shut and stared out the front window.

They made it back to the cottage in record time. Again carrying her, he swept her in and placed her on the couch in front of the fireplace. He quickly removed her coat and re-wrapped her in the blankets then left the room without a word.

He returned a few minutes later with a basin of lukewarm water and put it in front of her.

"This will sting." His tone was rather matter of fact. He started to put her feet in the water when he noticed the bottom half of both pant legs were soaking wet. "These need to come off." He undid her snap and zipper then placed a hand on either side of her small waist and grabbed a hold of her jeans, removing them in one clean sweep, while she let out a little yelp of surprise, which he ignored.

A tiny, unhappy groan escaped her mouth when she placed her feet in the water. She was trying to be brave and not complain, especially after the trouble she had caused, but her feet hurt.

"Here, drink this," Nick said as he handed her a cup of something hot. "It's tea."

"Thank you, Nick." As she took a sip of the tea, her shivers were causing the hot contents of the mug to slosh around a little. She saw him frown at her and wanted to apologize again.

"I'm sorry. I should have listened to you and stayed back. I was just being obstinate and wanted to prove to you I'm no wilting flower. Instead, the only thing I proved was that I am a fool that has caused you a lot of trouble."

"You are a stubborn thing, I'll give you that. However, you can stop apologizing to me, you are forgiven."

"Did you notify anyone about finding the plane?"

"I called Pete, who will let his friend in the FBI know. I didn't want to call the local police and draw attention to us or this area. They will be as discreet as possible, but you know how small towns are."

"Well, there can't be that much gossip over finding an old plane. I mean, I don't think anyone even knew Paul or that he disappeared. So, there shouldn't be too much fuss over hauling an old plane away."

Nick reached forward and took her tea from her, setting it down carefully on the coffee table in front of them. She observed him with a puzzled, expectant look.

"It's not so much the news of finding the plane that bothers me, it's the body I found inside the plane that's bound to stir up some commotion." He watched the color drain from her face.

"The body?" she asked to be sure her ears were not deceiving her.

"Yes. I believe we found the remains of your husband."

Chapter Twenty-One

Dena slept restlessly in front of the fire, aware that on some level her head was pounding and her throat hurt. The chills had returned, and somewhere, deep in her mind, something was bothering her. A thought or feeling was lingering there in the dark recesses, only she could not seem to grasp hold of it. Whenever she got close enough to capture it, the thought would vanish.

Like Paul did.

Only he didn't really vanish, did he? He was murdered.

The cellar.

She admitted to herself that she had been scared to death of the cellar, but she had no idea why. Now, she desperately wanted to understand what had made her so afraid. She had spent her entire life living a lie; now she wanted answers and the truth, even if that meant what was revealed might hurt her.

In fact, she was sure that when her secrets did come to light, what was revealed would indeed be incredibly painful. After all, if they were pleasant memories, she would not have chosen to bury them. She shook her head and marveled at the fact she allowed herself, a psychologist, to get away with that for so long.

From his chair next to the couch, Nick sat quietly and observed her. He saw her fighting inner demons, and the obvious turmoil going on inside her. She had been tossing and turning for over an hour now.

And she was shivering again.

Shit. He leaned forward and touched her face and found it burning with fever. He felt inadequate to play the role of doctor or even caregiver. He had never been responsible for another human before, not even a pet. His ex-wife took care of herself, or hired someone to help her if she was sick.

He threw another blanket on her and forced her to sit up and take some aspirin to help bring down the fever. He did not even have a thermometer, not that he would have known how to use it anyway, so he used the back of his hand on her forehead like his mother used to do to him. He did not know what else he could do, so he sat beside her quietly, feeling desperately inadequate, and just kept watch.

* * *

Pete was leaning far back into his chair with his feet propped up on his desk, reminiscing about the social life he used to have. He wondered when he had even been on a date last and his memory automatically drifted to the beautiful receptionist he had met the other day. Beautiful and smart, he reminded himself with a grin. He would like to talk to her again and found himself wondering how old she was, where she went to school and what she was majoring in. He could find out easily enough on his own, but it would be fun doing it the old fashioned way.

This was undeniably new territory for him. Pete shook his head and laughed at himself, knowing that usually the only information he sought was a woman's phone number. Wow, he must truly be in lust and extremely overworked.

If he had been unconsciously looking for a reason to call

her, he just found it. He picked up the phone and punched in D & D's number. It was almost 5:30 pm and he hoped someone was still there.

"D & D," said a pleasant female voice. Jill's voice.

"Uh, hi. This is Pete Capaldi. The investigator."

"Hi Pete Capaldi, the investigator."

He chuckled a little. "So, where do you go to school, anyway?"

"Has your investigation switched to me now?"

"You could say that."

"Oh." She hesitated for a second before replying. "U of C, GSB."

"What, am I supposed to break some kind of code?"

She was smiling into the phone. She didn't know why, but she found him amusing.

"University of Chicago, Graduate School of Business," she said slowly.

"Got it. Very good. Is your boss still around?"

"He is. Do you wish to speak with him?"

"Please." Smooth. Very smooth. Nick would have a field day with this. Playboy and womanizer Pete Capaldi was having trouble talking to a woman. He didn't even realize his call had been transferred until Bob answered.

"Hi Pete. What can I do for you?" Bob asked, making him feel like they were life-long friends.

"I was just wondering, did Greenly ever take flying lessons?"

"Well...now that you mention it, he did. Yeah, about a year maybe before Paul disappeared, I think. It surprised me."

"What did?"

"Greenly wanting to learn to fly. He seemed...too uptight. Most people that take up flying do it because they have a passion for flying. They love to be up in the sky and can't get enough of it. It's like a drug." There was no mistaking Bob's feelings for the sport.

"So, he didn't seem to enjoy flying?"

"No. I would have to say he hated it. But for whatever reason, he learned to fly."

"Could he handle a plane on his own if he had to?"

"Well..." Bob thought for a minute. "Yeah, I guess he could. He was a quick learner. He wasn't what you would call a natural pilot, but he could handle it alone."

"Did you ever give him lessons?" Pete was curious why he knew so much about Greenly and his flying.

"No. I couldn't stand the guy. But I was watching. I make it my business to know who is getting on our planes and, especially now, who is taking flying lessons."

"Boy, it must have been a bitch to learn he was your new business partner. Makes you wonder if that was why he was taking lessons, because he knew one day soon he would be taking Davis's place. I mean, if you own an aviation business, you should at least know how to fly. Right?"

The phone line was silent so long, he thought Bob had hung up. "Bob, you still there?" Pete was puzzled until the light bulb went off in his head.

"What the hell are you talking about?" the normally pleasant Bob said through clenched teeth.

* * *

Nick answered his cell phone on the first ring. And even though he was half asleep, his voice sounded alert and ready.

"What's the latest?" he said quietly into the phone when he read the number on the small cell screen indicating it was Pete.

"Greenly knows how to fly. Paul gave him lessons."

"Huh." Nick stood up and went into the other room so he wouldn't disturb Dena. He could hear it in his friend's voice that this wasn't the worst of the news.

"My sentiments exactly. And, I just dropped a bomb on Bob Denton. He didn't know the new co-owner was Greenly himself. Shit, I feel like I just drove a knife into the guy's heart."

"You sure he didn't know?"

"He didn't know," Pete stated firmly, and wished he could

have found a better way to tell him. It just never occurred to him that Bob did not know who his new business partner was. Not that there would have been any way to sugarcoat it; no matter how you put it, it was not good news for Bob Denton. The business that you built from the ground up, that is your passion and life's ambition, is secretly co-owned by one of the world's biggest slime-balls. He truly felt bad for the guy.

"I'm thinking Greenly could have helped Davis stage his disappearance then double-crossed him. He could have been hiding on the plane, and once they were in the air, pulled a gun on him. Then he killed him and flew the plane to Paul's property, which only he knew about, and left him there. No one knew about that land, he was probably paying the taxes on it and thought it unlikely anyone would discover the plane in the barn. Even if they did, there was no way to tie it to him."

"Paul was leaving with a chunk of change on him and Greenly knew it."

"The cash was most likely a bonus. I think Davis wanted out of the business, and once you mess with these guys, you simply don't quit. Davis was the one person who knew what Greenly was up to and he couldn't have him out there unaccounted for." Nick pinched the bridge of his nose while he paced around the room. "Did they confirm it was Davis's body yet?" If it wasn't they were even further away from learning the truth, and that was a depressing thought.

"They are getting dental records now to confirm his identity, but they are fairly confident it is him. And I have some more news, we did get Greenly to talk, but of course he never mentioned knocking off his friend's husband and leaving him to rot in the country. Must've slipped his mind."

"What did he say?"

"He gave us a couple of names. The first was someone he dealt with at Trask, the other was the one he sold the merchandise to. He swears he was just the middle man and was shocked to learn the goods ended up in a terrorist training camp. We have nothing to tie him to killing the nurse that worked for Paul or her roommate. No physical evidence was left behind at all, but then we know how smart the son of a bitch is. He wasn't about to leave a calling card behind. And they are even dropping the assault charge from when he roughed up Dena, because she is not around to press charges. The lawyer's got himself a legal team working for him."

Nick made a fist and got a moment of satisfaction when he recalled breaking the bastard's jaw. But it wasn't nearly enough. He should have hit his nose hard, at just the right angle, to lodge a few bone fragments into his brain. And that would have been the end of Greenly.

"This guy is going to walk, Nick."

"But not far. Because when I find him I'm going to break his legs. Then I will kill him."

Pete was stunned. In the entire thirty-something years he had known Nick, he had never heard him talk like this. He was not a thug that ran around with a baseball bat breaking kneecaps. His guess was that his friend had more than just a professional relationship going on with the doctor.

"There is something else that's bothering me. Where the hell is Michaelene Trask? I mean, if that is Davis's remains you found out there, she should be there too, right?" Pete wondered out loud.

"That was the original assumption."

"I finally had to tell her sister that there was nothing more we could do. I hated not being able to give her anything."

Clarissa Beacher would not accept defeat for an answer; that much he knew. He wouldn't either if it were his brother or sister.

"I didn't expect to find her on the plane, and I'm still betting she never made it out of Georgia," Nick said.

"I think she is dead, and I don't think Greenly had anything to do with this one," Pete said, tapping his pencil on his desk while he thought. He had better call Detective Thatcher when he got off the phone and fill her in; she was too mean to mess with.

"I'd have to agree."

"Edward ran quite a stack of reports on Haidyn Trask and I

tell you, that's one mean S.O.B. He's a Southern good old boy with all kinds of connections. He's wealthy, well known and he wouldn't take too well to his wife trying to leave him for another man."

"When I first started investigating her disappearance, he was the prime suspect. Hell, he was the only suspect. The sister was convinced he did something to her. But when all this with Greenly came up and her affair with Davis was discovered, we got off track."

"I'm sure Trask knew his wife was running away with Davis, and that Davis would be killed. He might have even ordered Greenly to do it. So why wouldn't he let his wife go and the two could be knocked off together instead of him getting involved?"

"I think," Nick said as he clicked his pen a few times, "I think Trask wanted that honor."

* * *

He was a large man. He drove a big car, had huge hands and feet and always wore an enormous hat. A Stetson. He looked more like he was from Texas than Georgia and had a strong resemblance to J.R. Ewing.

Haidyn Trask loved the finer things in life that having unlimited wealth could give you. That was why he worked days, nights, weekends and often holidays. He did believe in taking vacations; that was, after all, part of the good life, but he usually worked during those as well. He labored endlessly to ensure that he always had, as he put it, money to burn.

It probably came from growing up with never having jack shit, Trask thought as he sat in his custom designed leather chair in his home office. The chair was built exclusively for him to provide maximum support and comfort for his large frame and was covered in the finest Italian leather. It was adjustable in every way conceivable, was heated and gave an unbelievable back massage. Now if it could only give head, he would have married it. It cost over $4000 and he insisted his other two offices each have one, so that wherever he chose to work that day, he would be comfortable.

He loved to sit in his chair at the end of the day and take a mental inventory of all his possessions. The beautiful mansions, the expensive cars, and even the people that all belonged to him. It was a ritual he enjoyed performing each and every night. He would head over to the bar, pour a glass of Chivas Regal, open up his handmade humidor and pick out a Cuban Cohiba and sit back at his desk.

Sipping scotch and puffing away on his cigar, he would begin to unwind. Once he was relaxed enough, and had gone over in his mind all the glorious assets he held, he would start planning what his next acquisition would be.

Tonight he decided it would be a new wife. Sure, he had had a mistress for years and never had a problem finding a date, but he was looking for a woman of a certain caliber. It would be better for business and for his image. Not that he gave a rat's ass what anyone thought about him, but business was business and it did look better to have a wife in the picture. He could keep his little fuck dummies on the side, but he needed an adoring woman at home to complete the picture. He wanted her to be gorgeous, intelligent and classy, someone who would not only look good on his arm, but could play the role of his wife well. Her job was to plan and host parties, handle the charity work, and be able to hold up her end of the conversation without getting too lippy.

He needed a modern, clever woman who would still stay under his thumb. He let that thought roll around his head for a few minutes. He would almost need to find the ideal woman he wanted, marry her, then find something to blackmail her with to keep her under control. Or threaten her with something dear. A smile spread across his face as a plan began to form.

He frowned as he thought of his first wife, Michaelene. Yes, that's the problem with the educated broads, he thought as he blew a ring of smoke up in the air, they are harder to control and they think too much.

Someone like that doctor lady, Davis's wife. She had been

a looker, though she dressed too plain for his tastes. For a minute he was almost sorry that she had been killed.

His private line rang and he picked up the receiver without looking at it.

"What is it?" Irritation gave an edge to his voice, though he knew no one called on this line without good reason.

"That missing plane has turned up," the unidentified voice said cautiously.

Haidyn was monetarily caught off guard. The cigar that was halfway to his mouth went back down to the ashtray. "Any souls on board?" he asked finally.

"Just one. The remains are being processed for identification right now by the FBI." And then anticipating his boss's next question, he knew he had to continue. The caller was glad to be phoning in the report instead of having to stand in front of him. "It is not clear who made the discovery, but someone stumbled upon the site and tipped off the FBI."

"Someone?"

"Yes. Our reports do not have a name yet, sir. It possibly could have been a man and a woman." He didn't have to add that part. It hadn't been confirmed anyway. But the caller was smart enough to know if the boss found out about it later and had not been informed, he was a dead man.

Haidyn Trask paused so long the caller might have thought he had hung up the phone and the prickly sensation of fear traveled down his spine as he waited patiently for him to continue. The caller had somehow hoped his employer would not recall whose job it had been to hide the aircraft.

"I'll need to see you tomorrow. Call me in the morning." Without another word, he disconnected the call.

The caller squeezed his eyes shut so tight they hurt as he planned his escape. But he knew he could never run fast enough. Trask would hunt him down and make him die a death a hundred times worse than he could ever fathom.

It would only be a matter of time now before it was discovered that for the right price, he looked the other way and let Greenly take over.

With his right hand shaking and his eyes closed tight, the caller reached into the top desk drawer, removed his faithful .45 and opened his mouth.

* * *

Dena awoke with a start and a scream in her throat that sent Nick flying out of the chair he had been sleeping in.

He rubbed his eyes and ran a hand through his hair as he stood in front of her. She was sitting up on the couch, her eyes wide and wet.

"You okay?" His own heart was pounding so loud, he could barely hear his voice. Maybe he ought to stick to writing and just use his imagination for the plot. He was getting too old for this shit.

She simply nodded and pulled the blankets up around her neck. She looked uncomfortable as he stood above her, waiting.

"Well, are you going to tell me why you were screaming or do I have to guess?" If he was going to get jolted out of sleep in the middle of the night and practically given a heart attack, he felt entitled to know why.

"I had a bad dream." She shrugged her shoulders to show it was no big deal and hoped he would drop the subject.

"Really?" was his only comment, his voice thick with sarcasm.

She realized he was not going to let it go, and who knows, maybe she would feel better if she told him. She wasn't going to be able to get back to sleep anyway. She rearranged the blankets around her and tried to get comfortable in her spot, while she stalled to find the right words.

"I was dreaming I was in a cellar. It was dark, cold and had a peculiar smell, like something musty and rotting. I hated that smell, couldn't stand it, but I was terrified to leave my spot. I was hiding from someone, frightened they would find me. So, I had to stay perfectly still and breathe carefully and as quietly as possible so I would not be discovered."

Dena inhaled deeply as panic rose in her at the memory.

"Then my grandmother was there at the top of the cellar steps calling out to me. She yelled down the steps, 'Dena honey, are you down there? Don't hide on your grandma.'

"Only I wasn't hiding from her, I wanted desperately to call out to her. I was just afraid if I spoke, the evil would know I was there. But when I heard the worry in her voice I could not keep quiet. I started to answer her when a big hand roughly covered my mouth. I could not answer her and finally, she went away and closed the cellar doors, leaving me with the monster in total blackness."

She stopped talking but didn't look at Nick. She had a film of sweat on her pale face and her pupils were dilated.

"Was that the end of your dream or was there more?"

"That was the end, but I know there was more."

Nick held her chin gently and turned her face to him. "Was that a dream or a memory?" he asked softly. He knew the answer, he just wondered if she did.

"It felt like it was a memory. Before I went to sleep, I was willing myself to remember. I need to know everything about myself and about those I used to care about."

"And who was the evil presence in your dream, Dena?" His voice was almost hypnotic, so peaceful and reassuring that she felt compelled to recall all the details. She realized then that the memories had been trying to resurface for a long time, that she had known they were there and always, as they started to come into the light, she would push them back down.

She must have drifted away for a second, because Nick was repeating the question to her.

"Who was the monster that held his hand over your mouth, Dena?"

"I don't..." she had started to say she didn't know. But she did. They both knew she did. "It was my father. He followed me down there, I think. I don't remember what happened next." She took in a deep breath and closed her eyes. "But I will."

Nick decided to spend the remaining evening down by the

206

fire. Unable to fall back to sleep, he worked while Dena slept. When he had caught up with everything at the office that he could do from here, he pulled out the first few chapters of his book. It was coming along nicely, although the feeling was surreal. Instead of sitting down at his laptop pulling a story out of his head, he was writing about the events as they unfolded daily. The emotions and feelings were real and neither character nor author knew the ending.

Occasionally his eyes would wander away from what he was doing and he would find himself watching her. He had given her another dose of aspirin and some soup and she seemed to be doing much better. Taking care of someone wasn't so hard after all. Maybe when he got home, he would buy a plant.

He worked throughout the night and must have fallen asleep sometime near morning, as he awoke when he heard the phone ring. It was Pete calling with an update, and since Nick knew his friend did not like to start his day until at least after 10:00 am if at all possible, he assumed it would not be good news.

The remains had positively been identified as Paul Davis and, worse, Greenly had made bail.

Not a nice a way to start the day.

Chapter Twenty-Two

Nick always thought it best to give news, good or bad, straight on. He also was a believer of delivering news on a need-to-know basis. She needed to know that it was her husband he found on the plane. She didn't need to know about Greenly. Not yet anyhow.

When he got off the phone he realized Dena was awake and was watching him. She appeared drained of color as she pushed her body to sit up on the couch. When she finally got situated and smoothed the covers on her lap, she folded her hands and waited for him to speak.

"The remains we found were confirmed to be Paul's."

She closed her eyes and nodded. Then she opened them and asked what else.

"The FBI used his dental records to make a positive identification. He had been shot. They did a thorough sweep of the grounds surrounding the barn and house and it all came up empty. No sign of Michaelene Trask."

Dena simply nodded again. She had been expecting them to say it was Paul. Other than wondering what happened to him and where the woman he supposedly ran off with disappeared to, she felt at peace. It's the not knowing in life that's hard.

"You okay?" Nick asked after she remained silent.

"I'm fine." She had already had the memorial service years ago. She had grieved as much as she was able. "I was merely wondering what happened to Michaelene. This could have given some closure to her sister if they had found her body as well."

"Yeah, I know." He had been hoping for the same thing. "But I don't think her body is even in this state." He wanted to be able to give Clarissa something. "I need a beer and a shower." He stood and went to the kitchen. Probably a little early for alcohol, but what the hell?

When Dena heard the water turn on upstairs, she picked up her purse and pulled out her cell phone. She hadn't checked her messages in days, nor had she called Brad to find out how her patients were doing under his care. Not that she could do that if she was supposed to be dead. Time was slipping away from her along with her responsibilities and it left her with a feeling of guilt and uselessness.

There were a few old messages, nothing important. One from Brad, pre-explosion obviously, telling her that all was well and not to worry. She smiled when she heard his reassurance. She dropped the phone back into her purse and went into the kitchen in search of something for lunch.

She pulled out the "fixings," as her grandmother would say, for a salad and began putting it together. She found the pantry to be well stocked and felt a bit of excitement over the various possibilities for meals. She settled on a cheese and tomato pie that was a favorite of hers, easy to put together and wonderful with a green salad.

Chopping, stirring and creating. It was the best therapy that she knew of and soon she found herself lost in the mundane task, humming and, God, almost relaxed. She paused to take a sip of the excellent Chardonnay she discovered in the refrigerator and rotated her neck from side to side to work out the kinks. It felt good to be able to unwind.

She was opening up the oven when she became aware of a distant ringing.

Frowning, she closed the oven door and went to answer the phone. It was then she realized it could not be the house phone, it was not loud enough. She thought of the fax phone and headed towards the office when suddenly she paused.

Turning her head slowly, she stared back at the purse she had left on the table.

She had left her cell phone on.

She thought of the few people who knew this number, Brad, Marcy and her answering service, though she had them direct all her calls to Brad. Then of course, there was Doug. Only none of them would be calling her now, would they? Not when they thought she was dead.

Dena felt suddenly chilled as she reached into her purse and pulled out her cell phone. The caller ID only told her it was an out of area call. She scolded herself for feeling so uneasy. After all, it was most likely just a wrong number.

She needed to simply ignore it and turn the phone off when it stopped ringing.

Only it did not stop, and before she could stop herself, she flipped it open.

"Hello?" Her voice came out in a whisper, promptly realizing what she had done.

"Good of you to finally turn your phone on, *Deanna,*" the male voice said.

"Doug," she stated quietly, as if she had been expecting his call. Perhaps she had.

"Miss me?"

"I don't even know you."

"Sure you do. I'm your childhood friend and your savior." He gave a sarcastic laugh.

"What did you save me from, Doug?"

"Oh, very good, Dena. You are using your psychologist voice with me. Let's see, what secrets will the good doctor get out of me?" He suddenly laughed hard, as if he had thought of something hilarious. It had a slightly muffled, odd sound to it and Dena wondered if his jaw was still wired shut. "You're no match for me. I've always been two steps ahead of you, waiting for you to catch up."

"Why don't you help me catch up, Doug?"

"What fun would that be?" Again the laugh. "Tell me, Dena, did the old house bring back memories?" Suddenly his tone became serious.

A slight intake of air showed her surprise. "What old house?"

"You're wasting time, Dena. The clock is ticking and I'm about to end this little chat; if you want answers you will need to do better than that. If you play stupid again, I will hang up."

She hesitated for a second then continued. "The house reminded me of my grandmother's."

"Very good!" He practically shouted. "I had to get rid of Paul anyway, and I thought, what a nice touch. His death would finally help poor, pathetic Dena put the pieces together. You see, he wasn't useless after all." He laughed again.

"How did you know I would find the house?"

"You never were that bright, but I knew you would eventually figure it out. But I must say, I am surprised it has taken this long. You even had meathead there to help you." He made a clucking sound. "Oh well, I have to go now. Maybe next time I call, you will have something intelligent to say."

"Wait Doug..."

"Don't worry. I'll be sure to check in again." Then his voice dropped real low, becoming almost unrecognizable. "Oh, and Dena...how did you like the cellar?" Then he started whistling, softly. The eerie sound came through the phone, making her head spin.

Her knees felt like rubber and the room became dark.

The whistling continued. Loud. Distinctive.

And so familiar.

Strong arms caught her before she hit the floor and took the phone out of her hands.

When she opened her eyes, Nick was hovering over her. Waiting. He watched her with a puzzled look as she checked her wristwatch.

He'd want an explanation as to why she had used her phone to begin with. He had made it pretty clear to not make any calls.

"I only checked my messages. I didn't call anyone, honest," she said weakly, realizing how lame that sounded. She obviously was having a conversation with someone.

"Who were you talking to?"

"Doug." She sat up and waited for the spinning to stop. "I forgot to turn my phone off. It was ringing, so I answered it."

Nick's face held no expression as he listened, but his eyes darkened with fury. He gave a small nod for her to continue.

"He said he planned all this and that he was my savior. He knew I was at that old house and said he left the body there on purpose." She hesitated for a second and took in a deep, shaky breath. "He wanted that old house to help me remember."

"Remember what, Dena?"

She shook her head. "I don't know. What he said about him being my savior, maybe he wanted me to remember all the times he used to patch me up, everything he used to do for me. Maybe he thought I was ungrateful."

"What else did he say?"

The words were stuck in her throat. It is just a place. Dark, cold and full of spiders. The very thought of it made her throat dry and her stomach churn. She tried to conjure up a memory of her grandma's cellar when her head was suddenly gripped in a vice. She grabbed her head as if it would stop the pain.

"Dena, are you all right?" *Jesus*, he thought, it's always something with her. She is going to give me a heart attack. He watched the color leave her face again and her eyes fill with pain and wondered if she was having a seizure.

"Get me my purse, please."

He stared at her like she had lost her mind. She was clearly having some type of stroke or medical problem and she wanted her handbag?

"*Please!*"

She sounded so desperate that he had to obey and went

quickly to retrieve her purse from the table. When he handed it to her she dove into it, and pulled out a plastic case. He watched speechless as she took out what appeared to be a small pen, stood up and pulled her pants down and jabbed herself in the leg with it.

Then she fell back on to the couch with her pants still around her ankles and one arm bent above her head and closed her eyes.

Nick had no idea what to make of this scene. Since he sincerely doubted she would jab herself with an ink pen, and he was sure she wasn't shooting up with something illegal, it had to be a medication. He bent down and picked up the plastic case she had taken out of her purse.

The outside of the case said Imitrex. He flipped the lid open on the case as he had seen Dena do and found a cartridge refill. He waited for her to open her eyes.

After ten long minutes, she did.

He held up the plastic case and raised his eyebrows in question.

"For migraines, which I have had since I was a teenager. And, being the brilliant doctor that I am, it only took me about twenty years to figure out why I get them," she said bitterly and closed her eyes again.

"Whenever I would think of the past, especially about what I did to my father, I would get a blinding headache. I accepted that. I mean, if you shot and killed your own father, it's bound to cause you some trouble. So, I learned to stay clear from reflecting on anything that had to do with the past unless I wanted to be down with a headache for a couple of days."

"That makes sense." Surely she must realize how dangerous to her mental health that sounded, even to him.

"But things are different in the migraine world these days. I have pills and the injection you saw me take works miracles. For years, I would lose days of my life to blinding pain; I could barely get out of bed." She shrugged her shoulders as if it was no big deal.

"I told myself the headaches were nature's way of keeping

me from having to relive those painful memories. But I lied."

Something in her tone made him leery. "What do you mean?"

"There are some memories I am choosing not to remember. Something dark and evil." She hesitated and looked him in the eye. "And Doug knows what it is."

* * *

Detective Thatcher stormed into his office before Margaret had a chance to announce her. Not that she actually tried. She had been typing a letter when the irritated detective had appeared in front of her and asked which way to GQ's office. Amused that anyone besides herself would give Pete a hard time, she waved her down the hall.

Pete looked up as Detective Thatcher marched in and he noticed she was dressed casually today and wore her favorite scowl. It made him chuckle.

"Capaldi. Nice of you to keep in touch," she barked at him as a greeting. "And why do you always have that stupid grin on your face?"

"You know, Thatcher, you might actually try some of the more common social graces to start a conversation and get rid of the frown that appears to be frozen on your face. It's giving you wrinkles on your forehead."

"Gee, your opinion means the world to me. And it has been a few years since I attended that finishing school in Europe, so if you would start moving that pretty boy ass of yours so we can wrap up this case, maybe I can go back for a refresher course."

"You really think I have a pretty ass?"

She made a quick move towards him, as if to pull out her gun, and Pete held his hands up in mock surrender.

"Okay, okay, just relax, Thatcher. Actually, I just left a message for you at the station." He swung his feet off his desk and waved for her to sit down. She shot him a look of impatience. "Paul gave Greenly flying lessons."

It was her nature to come back with a sarcastic reply, but he saw her hesitate and knew she was thinking.

"So, Greenly could have flown away with Paul, killed him, took over flying, and then hid the plane. He would have Paul out of the way plus all the money Paul was leaving town with. Not to mention any merchandise Paul might have had on board to deliver."

"Yep, it makes sense. We can prove he learned how to fly, Bob Denton will testify to that. I also sense he would have killed Paul no matter what, solely because he married Dena. It would be nice to find that gun though." A mix of sadness and anger flashed in his eyes. "I want to nail him for the murders of Bridgett Bonner and her roommate," he added, almost as if to himself, "So, is this enough to make it stick?"

"That's what I came to tell you. One of the names Marcy gave us checked out and he sang like a canary when we played the right tune for him. He named Greenly. Trask will be a hard one to get, though, no one is willing to say jack shit about him." She let out a big sigh. "Well, that's the feds' problem anyhow. I'll have Greenly picked up. I bet Trask and his people have washed their hands of him now and Greenly should be begging to be brought in, before they off him." Just then a pager beeped and Thatcher reached for her belt.

She picked up Pete's phone and punched in a number.

"Thatcher," she said in a toneless voice and ignored Pete's flip comment to help herself to his phone. She listened for a minute and hung up with fury registered on her face.

"Good news, Detective?" For some reason Pete enjoyed messing with her. She was like an older sister that you enjoy pissing off.

"Greenly is missing."

* * *

All the doors and windows had been checked and locked. The curtains and shades throughout the cabin were pulled tight. The only light came from the glow of the fireplace.

His gun was within arm's reach. He was ready for the enemy.

It wouldn't be long. Nick knew he would be coming.

Since Pete's call, he couldn't stop thinking how extensively Greenly was involved in Dena's life. The bastard called himself her savior. He picked up his laptop and sent an e-mail to Edward. It was clear Greenly thought Dena was indebted to him. Time to find out why.

Dena stepped out of the bathroom, immediately sensing something was different in the air. It was both tension and anticipation.

She peered down the steps at the darkness and started to reach for a light switch.

"Don't," Nick's voice warned as he shined the light from his flashlight at her feet so she could see her way.

She walked down in silence and he took her hand and led her to a spot in front of the fire. Her eyebrows went up when she saw the gun out on the coffee table. He indicated for her to sit.

"We have what we need to put Greenly away, for a while anyway. But before they could even pull him in, he took off."

She noticed he refrained from calling Doug her buddy or *friend*. Then she really took note of the drawn shades and the darkness. And the gun.

"You think he is coming here?" She found that hard to believe. Even if he could find this place, he would be on the run and would want to get as far away as possible. "Or are you thinking he might come to me for protection because of our friendship?"

"He is coming for you, but the reasons have nothing to do with friendship. I think he wants to settle a score with you."

"Settle what score? What are you talking about?" She was shaking her head in disbelief.

"He thinks he was your protector. You ran to him when you where a child, and when you became an adult, I think he took it upon himself to keep helping you. I believe he killed Paul for you; the money he got and the business he could take over were simply perks. But Paul was cheating on you and Greenly knew it, so Paul was punished. He wants you to know all he has done for you."

Dena wanted to argue his insane reasoning, but something was ringing true in what he was saying.

"So, for patching up a few cuts and scrapes when I was a child and for killing my husband, he what? Wants me to say thank you? Pledge my love to him?" Her voice was shaking as well as her hands.

"Yes. I think he has lived his whole life for you, every decision he ever made was based somehow on you. However, I think the drive for money may have been about something else. Now, he most likely sees you as ungrateful and undeserving. Especially now, shacked up here with me." Nick knew the thought of him being here with Dena would drive Greenly over the edge. Memories of being with her that night about did the same to him. "I think he is coming to punish you."

"What makes you the expert? Shouldn't I be the one analyzing him?" She shot him a look, angry at herself more than anything. But she had to admit, it sounded right. Even the part about Doug's obsession for money. That would be more about his mother, the housekeeper. He was always ashamed of being poor.

"No, you are too close to the situation. In fact, you are right in the middle of it. I've worked cases similar to this before and I did a good deal of research once for a book I wrote."

"Well, that's just great." She began pacing in front of the fire. She glanced down at her watch, not even noticing the time.

"Why do you do that? It can't actually matter what time it is, can it?" He had wanted to ask that question since the day he met her and had always assumed it was an amusing personality quirk.

She looked confused. "What?"

"You check your watch all the time. Why?"

She suddenly seemed panic stricken and he could see, she was about to deny it. Then she shrugged like it was no big deal and surprised him by telling the truth.

"I used to lose track of time. I check my watch now more out of habit, but I used to have to be sure I wasn't drifting away."

His eyebrows knit together to frame his intense eyes.

"How much time are we talking about?"

"Hours. Sometimes...an entire day." She issued him a challenging look. "It hasn't happened in a long time. But during times of extreme stress, I am afraid it will happen again. I'll just slip away and I won't even know it." Her voice became a whisper and he realized how much it cost her to confess that. She wanted to appear strong, confident and in charge and letting him know that piece of information made her vulnerable.

He realized he had wanted to help her and protect her from the minute she stepped through his office door. It wouldn't have mattered what she wanted, he would have helped. He saw that clearly now and wondered why. Perhaps he needed a little self-evaluation. Well, maybe when this was over....

He turned his attention to the laptop he left on the coffee table and reached over to check for e-mails.

He wasn't surprised when he saw Edward had something for him; the guy was a genius.

Nick read the e-mail twice, his hand rubbing the stubble on his chin that he had neglected to take care of when he showered.

"Dena," he slowly pulled his eyes from the computer screen to connect with hers. "It would seem we overlooked something Greenly wants to be thanked for." He took a deep breath in and exhaled. "Brace yourself, doctor, because I am about to drop a bomb on you."

Chapter Twenty-Three

She was fairly certain that whatever news Nick had for her, she did not want to hear, especially with the expression he had on his face. He looked like he might be ill or in pain.

She gave him a silent nod to continue and resisted the strong urge to check the time. She pulled the cream-colored afghan off the couch to lay it across her lap and let her fingers play with the fringe so they would have something to do.

"What do you remember about shooting your father?" He kept his voice steady. Calm. But the words made her jump all the same.

"My father? What does that have to do with anything that is going on now?" She dropped the afghan and starting massaging her temples.

"Where did you get the gun?"

She looked weary but decided to answer him. "It was my father's gun, part of his collection. He had several of them and never kept them locked. I don't remember taking it, but I must have." Even to her own ears, it sounded like a canned speech. It was. The same one she had given years ago. Funny how it slipped out this easily when she had tried so desperately to forget everything and anything associated with that day. She didn't want to have a conversation about her father and his gun collection. What difference could any of this make now? She wanted to run out the front door, into the night.

"The bullet that was taken from your late husband matches the one that killed your father." He stopped talking to let his words have time to move around in her head. He was surprised that they would have even kept the bullet they retrieved from her father, probably storing it more as a keepsake than for forensics. He could almost see the wheels turning in her mind and watched the inner turmoil. She was shaking her head no.

"That can't be, Nick. Unless you think I killed Paul as well. Is that it?" Shock registered on her face.

"No," he stated firmly and grabbed her hand to keep her from fleeing. "What do you remember about your father's death?"

She shook her head no and tried to pull away. His grip increased and he repeated his question, his voice a little more stern.

This time she would will it to come. It was past time. Bits and pieces had been trying to surface for a while now and as a therapist, she knew how unhealthy it was to keep them buried so deep.

Think of the new life that is waiting for you, Dena. Your new adventure. Starting over.

She took a deep breath and held it, releasing it slowly.

"I don't remember much about killing my father or even my childhood, only certain things stand out in my mind. I used to get flashes, images of things, but I am not sure if they are memories or something I was told or heard at the trial."

"Close your eyes and try to recall the day your father died. What do you see?" Nick held her hand gently now, unconsciously stroking her palm with his thumb.

"I can remember being cold and that I couldn't stop shivering." She could almost feel that bone-chilling cold now, and wrapped her arms tightly around herself. "I can see him sprawled out on the floor with a pool of blood around him."

"Did you ever use hypnosis to try to remember?"

"No. Why would I? I did not want to remember all the ugly details. The end result would still be the same. I shot and killed my father."

Again he was reminded of how different their childhoods were and all things considered, he thought she turned out okay. She had a few quirks, but other than that, she seemed well enough adjusted. At least she was not losing track of time anymore.

"You need to remember the details, Dena, because I think you have been punishing yourself unjustly all these years." He took his hands and placed them on her shoulders and pressed gently but firmly, trying to brace her. "I believe Greenly shot your father."

She heard the words, but they made no sense. As always, when she tried to recall the moment when she had pulled the trigger, no picture would form in her mind.

She squeezed her eyes shut and Doug's face was summoned. She saw him then, very clearly. Like a short clip from a movie she watched him turn and face her, a wry smile on his face as he took her hands in his. *"I will always be your savior, my dear Deanna,"* he had promised.

"Deanna? Who is Deanna?" Nick hated to interrupt if she was remembering something, but he wondered if she was getting off track.

His question surprised her. She wasn't aware that she had spoken out loud. *God, do I really want to go through all of this again?* The heart-wrenching pain of having no one believe you and making you stand all alone. The embarrassment and shame of killing your own father. The people in the very town she had grown up in and known all her life calling her a murderer and some, demanding the death sentence for her.

"That was my real name. Deanna." She even hated to say it out loud. Her mother used to pronounce it like it was two words, Dee Anna, and asked that others do the same. The only ones that ever did were friends of her parents and the hired help. The people in town called her Deanna.

She had chosen her new name with great care, a deliberate act of defiance, and hoped her mother was infuriated when she heard it. And to be sure her mother would know about it, Dena mailed her a copy of the court document stating her new name.

Death for Deanna. Deanna killed her daddy. Friends she grew up with and their parents had all turned on her. Wished her dead. She shook her head to get rid of the ghosts. "I had it changed legally when I turned eighteen. When I finished my sentence, I packed up and moved away. I never went back."

"What about your grandmother?"

Her eyes filled and she gave him a sad smile. "She died while I was doing my sentence. I never got to say good-bye."

"Do you remember where your father was killed?"

She shook her head no. "I always assumed it was at his home, but I really don't know for sure."

Nick leaned back against the couch and brought his hands together in front of his face, two of his fingers forming a steeple. He noticed she referred to the house she grew up in as his house, instead of their house.

"We could get the transcripts from the court. It could help trigger some details you are not remembering." Even though he was sure the trial was built on lies.

"I don't think there was much of a trial. Don't forget, this is a small town we are talking about, and it all happened a number of years ago. Everyone said I did it, I never said anything otherwise, so that was pretty much it."

Nick was about to say something else when he caught what she said. It was the way she said it. "What do you mean, you never said anything?"

"I did not speak for almost a year after the murder."

Fresh, raw anger washed over Nick. He was starting to form his own picture of what had happened all those years ago to a little girl named Deanna, and it made him want to drive to her hometown and pound the shit out of anyone still there.

She had a horrible childhood and when she did reach out for help, she was rejected. Though he suspected many knew of the abuse she suffered, not one person stepped forward on her behalf to help her. Then, when she supposedly killed her father in what had to be self defense, they quickly locked her up and threw away the key.

Only they locked up the wrong killer. He was sure of that. It all made sense now. The savior business. Wanting to be thanked.

He looked over at Dena's beautiful face and wondered how he could help ease the pain, watching as her expression changed.

A flicker of a memory came to her. She saw herself sitting in front of a window, in a chair, staring outside. She wondered what other memories would come, if she let them.

Nick's cell phone rang and he saw it was Pete. He answered as he walked out of the room.

"What's up?"

"I had Edward pull some news clippings and I made some calls to people in her old town that might remember her." He paused for a minute. "I got some interesting stuff. None of it very pleasant, I'm afraid."

"Whom did you talk to?" Sometimes small towns were protective of their own. Even if one of them was a murderer, they didn't like to give away secrets.

"The former mayor, a retired librarian and one of Dena's grade school teachers. Even got hold of the nurse that used to work for the town doctor. All much older now."

Nick was sure he did not want to hear this, but he knew it was necessary. After all, she lived through it; the least he could do was sit and listen. They needed to get the missing pieces she could not remember.

Greenly needed to be caught and punished. Dena needed to be set free.

"Go ahead," Nick said grimly.

"Well, some of this I believe you know. Like the fact that she was abused as a child. Of course, no one came out and said that. The former nurse told me of all the times little Deanna would come in with broken bones or cuts that needed stitches.

Oh, did you know her real name was Deanna?"

"Yes. Go on," Nick said, a little too sternly.

"Okay. Well, she said she suspected all her injuries were from more than playing and said as much to the doctor. She was told to shut up and mind her own business or she would be out of a job. She said she recalled once they took an x-ray of Deanna's arm and the doctor noticed the bone had been broken before and never set. He was upset about that, but never told anyone else. She suspected Deanna's parents were only bringing her in for the severe injuries they couldn't treat at home, like once when they brought her in unconscious. The parents had said it just happened, but they suspected she had been out for a good day at least. Another time she came in with a bad cut that had already been stitched up. They took their own needle and thread and did a real hack job. It got infected and they had to take out the stitches, clean it up and re-do it. The parents told the doctor that the neighbor's kid must have played doctor."

"That part was probably true."

"Really? What, you think Greenly stitched her up?" Pete was surprised. He couldn't see the greedy lawyer doing any good deed, even as a child, unless he got some pleasure out of her pain, then charged her a fee.

"Yeah, he patched her up on a regular basis," Nick said, venom in his voice. He wanted to punch something.

Pete felt a new wave of pity for that small girl that was so mistreated. He cleared his throat to continue. "Anyway, the mayor was a real ass, he didn't think there was any abuse and acted shocked to hear me ask. He said young people these days don't know how to properly discipline their children."

"Did he give you any details of the shooting?"

Nick could hear Pete shuffling papers on the other end.

"Yeah. He said it was an open and shut case. The mother heard her husband scolding Deanna and then a shot. She went downstairs and found her holding the gun and her husband dead. The mother testified her daughter had always been difficult and unstable and resisted all discipline."

"So they were at home when it happened?"

"No, they were visiting Dena's grandmother. That's what didn't make sense. The mayor didn't want to chat anymore, so I got the rest from old newspapers and the librarian."

"What part didn't make sense, that they were at the grandmother's?" Nick was trying to visualize what had happened.

"No. I find it hard to believe that with such controlling parents, Dena was able to sneak one of her father's guns out of the house and take it with her and neither parent noticed. Not to mention the father kept his guns locked in his study where he spent all his time when he was home."

"It would be helpful if Dena could remember what happened." Nick paused for a second. "So, was the shooting in the cellar?"

Pete was slightly taken back. "Yeah, as a matter of fact it was. Are you telepathic or was that something she remembered?"

"It's something she is trying not to remember."

* * *

Dena went about the task of going through the rest of the boxes they had abandoned the other day. The papers that she felt were of no value to anyone, she started to throw in the fire, one page at a time. She sat mesmerized as she watched each sheet ignite in flames, then she finally threw the rest of her pile in the flames.

Slight images began to play out for her and this time, she let them. She wanted to be able to recall just one or two incidents from her past to help her now, but she knew it didn't work that way. Her training had taught her that when you open that door, you cannot select what you want to come through. Unless, of course, she was hypnotized. With the right person guiding her, she could be more selective in what she pulled out. She never wanted Brad to try and he himself never brought it up. There was no reason for him to bring it up; he had no idea what tormented her. Well, she might submit to hypnosis now, but there wasn't anyone here to do it. She would have to do this on her own.

Her mind began to meander through time, not going in any particular order or focusing on any one event. Like watching a movie, she saw a young girl hiding in her room, trying to stay out of the way. Wishing she was invisible. And there was her mother, sitting in her favorite high back chair doing needlepoint. She always looked fresh and attractive and of course, wore a dress. Then she saw her father hovering over her as she cowered in a corner. He was yelling and took off his belt and she recalled how she had wished he would die. That thought didn't surprise her. She thought of the age-old advice, be careful what you wish for.

To her surprise, some pleasant moments drifted through as well.

Spending time at Grandma's house, sitting on the swing on her huge wraparound porch. In the evening, she would sit out there for hours and listen to the crickets and frogs sing their song. She would count the stars and Grandma would come out with popcorn and join her. She could almost smell the clean, country air. When bedtime came, she would tuck her in and kiss her head and never in her life had she felt so safe.

She tried to stay with this memory, but instead felt herself being pulled in a different direction. The scene that played out in her mind was replaced with a film of darkness and the room seemed to fill with cold air. She suddenly found it difficult to breathe. But it was the strangest thing, as she was still at her grandmother's house. A haven she only associated with pleasant memories. She wanted to run from this image but forced herself to stay with it.

She reminded herself she was an adult now, and whatever came her way she could handle. She didn't have to hide, she could face it.

She began to hear whistling so clear, she almost spun her head around expecting to see someone behind her. The haunting tune her mind was playing for her was familiar and sent chills down her spine. It filled her with a sense of loathing and dread.

And she knew why the melody was so recognizable. It was the same one Doug had whistled.

Chapter Twenty-Four

Nick raked his fingers through his hair and let out a frustrated growl. Greenly would find them. It was only a matter of time. And considering all the high tech surveillance equipment that was accessible to him, he was most likely on his way. He didn't want to give the guy too much credit, but the fact was he was dealing with an intelligent nut case. The most dangerous kind. They can almost read your mind and are always one step ahead of you.

He leaned back in the chair and picked up his pen, pushing the top of the pen down until the room was filled with the familiar clicking noise.

Silently he wondered how the hell he would ever stop recalling those images his brain had created of Dena as a child.

* * *

It was tempting to ask Nick to sleep with her. Have his warm body next to her, maybe even hold her. But there was no going back to that. As wonderful as that night had been, it was a mistake that had no future. Anyway, she was sure Nick wasn't interested in a long term relationship with her. A man with his looks doesn't stay unattached unless he chooses to. No, his interest was in seeing this case through and finishing his book.

Thinking about his book delivered a sick, sinking feeling in the pit of her stomach. That particular sensation, she told herself wryly, is from being used. God, how could she have been so blind?

She reminded herself that when this was finally over, she was leaving. It was a positive affirmation statement she gave herself, and she repeated it daily. She was going to give herself a fresh start. Even thinking about a new beginning in life filled her with a sense of peace and serenity, like taking in a deep breath and releasing it slowly. She thought of the sound of crashing waves that would someday play a lullaby to sing her to sleep.

But tonight it was just her, alone in this room, and she desperately wanted this whole episode to be over.

Fed up with not being in charge of her life, she decided to take action. Fragments of her past were starting to come forth, but it was taking too long. She needed someone to guide her through her memories. Someone who already knew the answers.

She threw back the covers, quietly got out of bed and untangled the nightgown that was wrapped around her legs from tossing and turning. For the life of her she couldn't figure out why she kept buying these contraptions when they always ended up spiraled around her torso. She would be better off sleeping in the buff, like she did the other night. She quickly pushed that thought from her mind and realized that sleep was never going to come anyway, so she might as well be productive.

She turned on a small brass lamp on the dresser, found her purse and pulled out her cell phone. The number she needed was saved in memory. It rang three times.

"Hello?" A women's alarmed voice answered. It's never good news when your phone rings at 1:00 am.

"Hi Marcy." Images of her lifelong friend skipped quickly through her mind. First the happy ones, then the betrayal.

She gasped loudly and her voice quivered. "Dena?" She said something that wasn't audible and seemed to have temporarily lost her voice.

"Marcy? Are you still there?"

"Oh my God! Dena?" She asked again, this time the words a little louder, but still filled with disbelief, then anger. "Who is this?"

"Yes, it's me. Look Marcy, I need some answers from you," Dena said in a voice that only could be hers and a tone her friend would recognize. She heard a muffled kind of noise coming through the phone and realized her friend was crying. It made her pause for a second.

"Are you crying because you are happy I am not dead or because you are sorry I'm not?"

Marcy let out a sob. "Oh God Deanna," she said again. "How can you even ask that?"

"Well, let's see. You slept with my husband. You lied to me about your job and may be involved in some serious criminal activity. One could see why I might doubt you."

She stopped crying now. "I am sorry to say you are right about the first two, Dena. I lied about the job because Doug wanted it that way and I really wanted the job more than I wanted to tell the truth. I wanted the money and all the freedom it gave me. It granted me a new life. But as for sleeping with Paul, there is nothing that I can say in my defense. I was young, unhappy and looking for someone to make me feel special. It was wrong and stupid and actually made me feel worse. I know you hate me for it, but you couldn't hate me anymore than I hate myself. But I didn't do anything criminal. Whatever Doug did, he did on his own. I thought Paul died in a plane crash just like everyone else did. And everything at the office is legit."

She didn't call to make peace with Marcy or to help her

clear her conscience. She could deal with that on her own.

When she held the photo that came over the fax machine, she noticed for the first time how Marcy was looking at Paul. She had no physical proof that Marcy had an affair with Paul, only a feeling, but she needed to know the truth. Dena was amazed that Marcy confessed so readily. Perhaps she was tired of carrying around that burden.

"I am surprised that Doug didn't tell you I was still alive. Must have slipped his mind."

There was a pause on Marcy's end that almost said the same thing, like-yeah, the bastard might have mentioned that when he called. "I am just so glad you are okay."

"I need your memories so I can fill in the pieces. Where were you, Marcy, when I killed my father?"

The silence was deafening, so much so that Dena wondered if Marcy had hung up. Finally she spoke. "I was at home, playing in my yard. I was alone, but Doug showed up at my house that day and he had blood splattered on him. He told me he was helping a wounded animal, and I believed him, but later on, like years later, I wondered."

"Why didn't you ever mention that to me or to the police?"

"Well, you never said anything about Doug being there. And you never denied shooting your father, so there wasn't anything really to tell."

"Tell me, Marcy, did that little recollection help you get that job with Doug?"

Marcy was determined to be honest. "It may have improved my chances. I did mention it to him once, not very long ago."

Dena was quiet for a second and decided to let that go. She wanted to remember everything. "Tell me everything you know, from the time you first heard I had killed my father."

She let her friend tell a tale that was heartbreaking and starting to sound familiar. Parts of the story she had heard before, but some of it, she was sure, she was hearing for the first time. Pictures began to form in her mind to match the words Marcy spoke.

"What did my mother ever say about what happened?" She

was afraid to ask and did not want to hear the answer. But she had come this far, she might as well finish.

"She said she was in the house with your grandmother when they heard the shot. When they got outside they saw the cellar door was open and your mother went down the cellar steps. She found you holding the gun and your father lying on the ground in a pool of blood. She told this story at the trial. She didn't try to defend you in anyway and I don't think she ever visited you afterwards."

"But you did." She had known most of this, but hearing it again, after so many years, was like a knife in her chest.

"I did what?" Marcy asked.

"You came to visit me. I remember that. I mean, I don't think I did until just now, but I recall us sitting outside talking under a tree. You came often, didn't you?"

"Yes," Marcy said softly. "I was glad your father was dead. He was a real bastard. But I missed you terribly." She breathed in deeply. "Like I do now."

Chapter Twenty-Five

Dena stepped over to the sliding glass door, unlocked it and opened it slightly. She knew the breeze that came through would be bitter but fresh and she needed to clear her head. After a few deep inhalations, she went over to the fireplace, dropped down in the recliner and stared out the window into the night. She closed her eyes and allowed her mind to run through time. It was like starting at the end of a novel and flipping through the pages to the beginning. Only then would it all make sense.

And it was all there. All the memories she buried were now being dragged out of storage. She needed to sort them, dust them and eventually re-file them all in a safer spot. She gave a slight laugh at how she'd allowed herself to get away with this all these years.

It was then she heard the whistling. Softly at first, then growing stronger and a little louder. She was sure it was coming from the darkness, and not from the corners of her mind.

Her heart stopped for a second and then proceeded to beat loudly, almost painfully, against her ribcage.

It scared her, but it didn't surprise her. After all, she had been waiting for him.

She watched as the sliding glass door opened slowly and a dark shadow filled the opening. Silently, the figure stepped into the unlit room.

"Hello Doug," she said quietly from across the room. She was momentarily pleased her voice did not betray her.

"Dena," he acknowledged her. "How thoughtful of you to wait up. Did you want to chat about old times?" His words came out a little slurred and she wondered at first if he had been drinking. Then she remembered his jaw. The wires had come out, but it must still be a little stiff and, she hoped, painful.

"Yes, I would like to do a little reminiscing. I think I have most of it figured out, but there are some areas I need your help with."

"Really?" He sounded genuinely intrigued with the idea.

"I don't need to go through each year of my life, just some of the highlights. After all, I am sure you're pressed for time."

He laughed at that. "Not really, Dena. You are my last stop, so please, by all means, take your time."

"Okay. How did you come to be in my grandmother's cellar that day?" She could smell Ralph Lauren's Romance for men that she had once mentioned she liked. It now came across too strong and overpowering and made her queasy.

"Finally, you want to thank me. Is that it? It's a little late to start showing your appreciation now, but what the hell." He moved slightly to his left, until he found the dresser, and turned on the small lamp. It unnerved her to realize he knew the exact layout of the room, even in the dark. He had been here before. She said nothing and waited for him to continue.

"I was always looking out for you, even then. Especially then. I knew you were visiting with your parents that day, so I rode my bike to your grandmother's house. I hid my bike in the barn when I arrived and just kind of hung around. I saw you go into the cellar and I started to follow you down when I saw your father go in next. As I got closer to the doors, I could hear what he was saying to you. He called you a worthless slut and said if you were going to dress like a whore, he would treat you as one. I heard what sounded like him hitting you across the face and you letting out a muffled cry, as if you were trying to hold it in." He had moved over to the edge of the bed now and sat down, a scene resembling that of two close friends having a chat. Well, they once were.

Dena nodded her head and spoke softly. "Yes, I remember the outfit. It was a bright pink halter top with pictures of black buttons on it. It was so cute and all the girls were wearing them. It was very modest and I never dreamed my father would not approve. I was crushed when he said he hated it..." She stopped as she tried to remember the rest, but the details were hazy. It was as though she were looking at a movie of herself through the fog. She blinked her eyes as if to get it into focus and to let the film continue. She looked over at the face she once thought handsome. She viewed him now with disgust and studied him as though seeing him for the first time.

"What's the matter, *Dea-nna*? Having a little trouble remembering the rest? I'm not surprised. It's not very pretty. When I came down the stairs, ever so quietly, I might add, he was ripping the top off you. You were trying to cover up your exquisite young breasts, but he was pulling your hands away. I must say, I was struck dumb for a moment or two. For such a young girl you had a remarkable chest. I always suspected your breasts were beautiful, but you wore such drab clothes, styles that were designed for a much younger girl. I think your mother wanted to keep her little girl from growing up, or maybe just keep your father at bay." He smiled at that and gave her a wink. "But that day he wasn't seeing a child. He wanted to get a look at that rack of yours almost as bad as I did." He shook his head and laughed a bit, like the two of them were sharing a treasured childhood memory instead of this sick, twisted nightmare.

Dena felt bile in the back of her throat. The pain behind her eyes was almost blinding and she felt she might pass out. Her injections were in her purse, across the room, but she couldn't risk moving. Instead she used all of her will to push it away, or at least back. She didn't know if she could survive reliving this and now understood why she had blocked it out for so long.

She didn't want to recall these memories, but God help her, she was going to, even with all the shame and humiliation.

"I was temporarily mesmerized by the sight of you. Images of me fondling you and mounting you clouded my brain. But I soon snapped out of it when I realized your father was having the same fantasies. I didn't want to share you with anyone. I was, and still am, possessive of you. Anyway, I came charging in and yelled for him to leave you alone. He was so surprised to be interrupted, he merely stared at me. Then he ordered me to turn around and go up the stairs and forget what I saw. He said this was a private family matter. When I told him I wasn't leaving, he gave me a hard push, knocking me to the ground. On the way down I fell against a shelf and cut my head on a sharp corner. Blood poured down my face, in front of my eyes. I heard you scream and the next thing I knew, you had a gun pointed at your father."

Dena let out a little moan and shook her head no. No, this could not be right. She brought the gun?

"He laughed at you and called you a stupid slut. He said you should be ashamed of yourself, showing your breasts to your own father and your friend. With one swift move, he took the gun from you and pointed it at me. He accused the two of us of doing unspeakable acts. He was going to shoot me and tell everyone he caught me raping you. He looked over at you with such lust in his eyes, I could read his mind. I knew what he would do to you after he shot me."

Dena didn't know if she could believe her father was capable of that. Violence, yes, but rape? The two go hand in hand, she understood that. And rape wasn't about sex, but power and control. Her head felt like it was in a vice now and about to explode. "Did he?" Her voice quivered. "Did he rape me?" Her stomach was churning now and she was sure she would be sick. And she didn't care.

He was smiling. She realized these were happy memories

for him and he was enjoying telling her the story. Thriving on her grief. He was also sexually aroused.

"He started moving towards you and you threw a jar of canned tomatoes at his head. Got him smack in the forehead. You probably don't remember the look on his face, but God, it was priceless! Well, anyway, he dropped the gun and I picked it up." He added this in a matter-of-fact tone and shrugged his shoulders.

It was almost all there. She could almost see it in her mind, but God, she had buried it so deep. And it was no wonder. Her father wanted to rape her. She still could not fully believe that and she was unsure if it was because it didn't ring true or she just didn't want to believe it. But never in her life prior to that date had he ever done anything sexual towards her. What if the attempted rape was all just a part of Doug's sick fantasy?

"So you shot him?" Her best friend shot her father. Now she could see it. Doug aiming the gun, his eyes wide, and a happy expression on his face, even then.

"Yes, I did," he replied proudly.

"You shot him and ran out the door, leaving me to take the blame."

"Yes."

"Why?" But more important, why did I let him?

"Because you asked me to. You told me to pull the trigger."

"I *asked* you to? So then you pulled the trigger six times?" That she remembered from the trial, or maybe it was the talk in town. Overkill, they called it.

"No. I only shot him once. And I did not run. I dropped the gun and walked up the cellar steps, got on my bike and left. I went to Marcy's."

"What?" Confusion mixed with fragments of memory was clouding her brain.

"You may have finished the job, but it was my bullet that stopped him from taking you. You were such a young sweet virgin, someone had to look out for you. I was your protector then and now. I've punished every man you've ever been with. Remember the man before Paul? The one that left town without saying good-bye? I always thought his body would wash up and there would be some kind of investigation, but it never did." He tapped his long fingers on his chin while thinking about a body decaying in the water. He had waited a long time to get credit for that.

Her mind was in complete chaos. Something wasn't right. When she allowed herself to think about what happened, she began to realize she did not kill her father. As a child, she couldn't explain it to anyone, but it was almost as if she sensed she did not do it, even then. And the more she learned about Doug, the more reasonable the explanation was. It was almost easy to see it had been Doug, acting as her protector even then. And perhaps the trauma of that event changed him forever, deeply scarring him emotionally. The therapist in her had it all figured out, or was it the little girl in her wishing for a happier ending. But would she have felt so indebted to him that she would give up five years of her life to be punished?

None of those rationalizations mattered now, she thought. Because if Doug was telling the truth, and he only shot him once, then she must have been the one that finished the job.

So lost was she in her puzzling drama, she did not realize Doug had gotten off the bed and was now standing in front of her. His closeness startled her and he reached a hand out to her hair and lifted a strand. "I like it better up," he declared, with his head cocked to the side. "You look beautiful, Dena, sitting by the fire in that long white gown. And as much as I would like to take you right here on the bed or even the floor, I would imagine we would be interrupted. So, let's go, darling." He pulled a baffled Dena up by the arms and started moving her towards the door.

"Doug!" She raised her voice loud enough to hopefully warn Nick but not piss off Doug.

And just like that, Doug's hand forcefully covered her mouth from behind while his other hand dug painfully into her neck. "Shut your fucking mouth," he said slowly and calmly. "I am going to take you out of here. I will claim what is mine and you will thank me for it. Do you understand, Dena? Just nod your stupid head if you understand."

She nodded yes for him and let her body relax into him so he would feel her surrender and relinquish the fight. The severe pain in her head mixed with Doug's overpowering cologne made her retch into his hand.

"What's the matter? Don't you like my cologne?" He spun her around so he could see her eyes when he spoke. "Maybe I should have borrowed Paul's again." He caught the small flicker of recollection in her eyes and that pleased him. "I put a splash on before breaking into your house to look for his planner. I wanted to mess with your mind." His raised his eyebrows and he laughed. "How did I do?" He didn't wait for an answer and began pushing her towards the door.

Apparently, he wasn't going to let her get changed or even put on a sweater. "Doug, can I at least put on some shoes?"

He didn't seem to hear her request as he dragged her out to the edge of the balcony. She could barely make out the tips of the ladder that went down the side of the house. She panicked when she realized she would have to climb down the steps with only the faint moonlight to guide her already frozen feet. She wondered where in the hell Nick was.

She took the cold metal steps cautiously, trying to concentrate only on easing one foot down, then the other. The arctic air was blowing up her nightgown and she was pleased Doug was still at the top of the ladder instead of at the bottom getting an eyeful. She had taken her underwear off before going to bed.

When she got to the bottom of the ladder she would make a run for it. She could make a fast sprint to the front door then pound and scream her head off for Nick. Dena looked up to be sure Doug was still on the balcony when she saw him wave to her. Her eye caught something shiny in his hand and she swore she saw his lips curve up. In the semi-darkness he looked like the devil himself. He made his meaning clear. If she ran he would shoot.

He dragged her out to the woods. He found the path easily that she and Nick had taken when they went to explore her newly discovered property. She recalled him saying how the road was hidden and unless you knew it was there, you would miss it. Well, it looked like he didn't have too much trouble finding it; his car was waiting down the road. He stuffed her wordlessly in the driver's side door and scooted in next to her. He hadn't said more than two words to her since they left the comfort of her cozy bedroom. His eyes were distant and glazed over and she wondered if he was playing out a fantasy in his mind. He started the car and drove slowly away from the cabin.

Dena shuddered with the vicious chills that shook her body. She reached over and turned up the heat full blast, not caring if that would make him angry. But he paid no attention when she did. The drive seemed to go on forever and she suspected he was taking her back to the city. In the darkness it was impossible to see where they were going, only the stretch of road directly in the beam of the headlights was visible. She wondered how he could see anything in this blackness and she remembered how Nick could see so clearly at night. Maybe it was just her that had horrible night vision.

Then she knew. They were going to her property. To Hert. She clamped her eyes shut so tight it was painful.

The old farm house and barn in the middle of nowhere with no neighbors within fifty miles. No one to hear her screams and certainly nowhere to run barefoot in five degrees below zero and snow past your knees. How ironic she should die in the same place they found Paul's body. They would most likely find her body sooner than later now that they knew of the property. For some reason, having someone find her corpse in a state of rot and decay bothered her.

It's amazing what your mind thinks of when you are sure you will be facing death in the near future.

It would be impossible to find the lane that led to the house. She remembered even in the daylight she and Nick had a tough time finding it. No sooner did she silently express her doubts than she saw a light up ahead on the right side of the road.

He had marked the spot with a lantern. Doug pulled up next to the glowing light and pulled it in through his open window.

He held the light close to his face and smiled at her. The effect was frightening. "Bet you thought I would miss the turnoff." With that he threw his head back and laughed devilishly.

They drove up to the house which was again marked with lights. Again he collected the lamps one by one, along with any hope she held of being rescued. There was no way in hell Nick would be able to find this place, even if he were to discover her missing before morning. And unless he planned to pay her a surprise visit here during the night, it was unlikely he would even discover her gone until the next day.

When Doug yanked her roughly through the front door, the light he held cast an eerie glow around the empty living room.

"Upstairs," he said as he nudged her forward.

Her feet felt welded to the ground. She couldn't move, even with the gun now poking her in the back.

"You will walk up the stairs. You will not spoil this for me, Dena. I have waited too long for this. If I have to shoot your foot to get you going, I will." He took aim at her right foot and she was certain he was not kidding.

She was going to die anyway, but she'd rather be given one fatal shot than to have individual limbs blown away one at a time. But God, she didn't know how she was going to stand him touching her.

He nudged her forcefully up the stairs and to what she had thought of before as being the master bedroom. When his lamp lit up the room, she saw with a sickening feeling he had made the room ready for her. His light cast an eerie glow over his well-planned fantasy.

A queen-size bed with an iron headboard sat in the center of the room. She could see the bed was made up with ivory satin sheets and a matching comforter. Unlit candles of various shapes and sizes surrounded it.

It wasn't as if she was not afraid, because she certainly was. But this was still after all Doug. Someone she had known her entire life. She tried to imagine how terrified she would be if she were walking into this scene with a total stranger.

Doug closed the door behind them and she heard the click

of a lock. She turned to see what he did with the key, but he was too quick with his actions.

Music began to play and she spun around to see a boom box in the far left corner. Some 'easy listening' love song was now filling the room and she saw Doug practically prancing around the room lighting the candles. Then it struck her what was truly bothering her about this whole scene. Not that it didn't greatly disturb her to be held at gunpoint and forced to participate in this charade. But what had been gnawing at her subconscious ever since Doug first announced he had wanted her was surprise. Genuine shock that he wanted her in a sexual way or noticed her as a woman. She had always assumed that Doug was gay.

They never talked about it, but she thought he would tell her when he was ready to come to terms with it. She felt a flash of shame at herself for stereotyping; as a professional she knew better. She thought back to see if she missed something. What she thought were the signs. He was always so...particular about things. His clothes, his apartment and even his coffee. And he never talked about other women unless it was to critique their choice of clothing or accessories. In fact, she often joked with Marcy that the three of them were like sisters.

So this announcement of his long burning desire for her did not even seem believable to her.

"Lie on the bed," he ordered, waving the gun in the direction he wanted her to go.

She wondered where he was going to put that gun when he started on her, but she did not have to wonder long. He grabbed one arm and put it above her head and she felt cold metal around her wrist then heard a click as the handcuff was attached to the iron frame. He did the same with the other arm. She closed her eyes as she realized there was no way out of this one.

She kept her voice steady. "I didn't realize you were into this, Doug."

"What man doesn't like a little bondage now and then?"

"No. I mean women."

His hands stopped moving and his body went still. She realized he was trying to hold back surprise as well as rage. "Does this look like a man who doesn't like women?" He thrust his hips forward to show his erection through his pants.

"Are you trying to convince me of that or yourself?"

"I've always burned for you, my dear. Ever since that day in the cellar." His frustration was coming out in his voice and she didn't want to push it too far, but something was becoming clear for her.

"Is it possible that seeing my breasts did excite you, but that you were and still are attracted to men?"

"Stop trying to stall me, Dena. I'm not one of your pitiful clients. There is no other outcome for you here, I am afraid. Relax, you might even enjoy it. I know I will."

"Are you sure?" She kept her voice soft and serene.

He was already standing to take down his pants. "Am I sure of what?"

"That you will enjoy this? My body? Or do you believe, Doug, that if you could have had me all those years ago, you would want women today? That somehow, that day scarred you, keeping you from wanting other women?"

He tried to put a wicked grin on his face that instead just came off as twisted. "It's true I feel cheated that I never got to play with those big tits of yours." Doug trying to use the macho phrase sounded almost funny to her.

"There is nothing wrong with being a homosexual, Doug. What is wrong is trying to go against what you in truth are." This time she knew she went too far.

She recoiled back but his hand was too fast. It cracked loudly against her cheek and her eyes automatically began to tear.

"I tried to set a mood here, Dena. To make this pleasurable for both of us. But you just can't keep your mouth shut." His voice was shaking. He started folding his clothes neatly and placed them on the floor while yelling at her. "Next you will try to blame it all on my mother! Try to brainwash me into thinking she did improper things to me."

"Did she?" she asked bravely, even though she knew the consequences. This blow split her lip open.

"Do not ever say anything so disgusting about my mother again," he warned her. "You are not here as my friend or my doctor, but merely as my wench." He stood naked in front of her now and she kept her eyes on his face. He lowered his voice and snarled, "So, did you figure it out yet?"

She was unsure what he meant. "What?" She shook her head. "Did I figure out what, Doug?" She wanted to keep him talking and continue saying his name to keep this personal.

"Who shot daddy?"

The air suddenly felt much colder. She had been trying not to think of that now and instead focus on getting out of here. But she could see he wanted her to know. By his own admittance, he said he shot him once, but only in the leg to stop him.

"Well, if you only pulled the trigger once, I guess that leaves me." Which, unless someone was hiding in the dark corners of the cellar, was true. But she tried to consider why she would block out Doug's presence at the scene. The only obvious reason was to protect him.

His eyes narrowed darkly and he put his hands on either side of her head, lowering his face to hers. "Guess again, *Deanna.*" He raised his voice in a mockingly sweet tone when he said her name.

He saw the confusion on her face and laughed, clearly enjoying himself. He reached back to find the hem of her nightgown and tugged it up high under her chin, so she lay naked and exposed to him.

"Deanna honey, I have windmill cookies for you in the pantry. Why don't you run and get some for you and your friend?"

She instantly knew he quoted her grandmother. God, he even sounded like her. She could see Doug with her on her porch on the swing. An image of her running in to get them cookies. Carefree, easy days when they had nothing more pressing on their minds than collecting fireflies after dinner.

Doug laughed again, throwing his head back while Dena stared blankly at him. "Oh, Dena darling, you are precious!"

"You're talking about Grandma, but I don't get the connection, other than it was at her house." What was it he was getting at?

He said nothing. Staring at her, he waited patiently for her to remember.

His silent, intense gaze on her face was making her uncomfortable, and she wondered what he was after.

Her mind went in several different directions and she wanted to ask him questions but could not seem to form one in her mind. He was waiting and studying her face.

Why was he watching her so? What was he hoping to see? No sooner did she think these words than she suddenly understood.

He was waiting to see the pain. Anguish and suffering would obviously show on her face when she remembered and he wanted front row seating.

Without her mind even understanding yet, her body knew. Every ounce of blood drained from her face and a cold, clammy sweat blanketed her body. Tremors she thought were from the cold racked her body.

The only reason she would allow the humiliation of taking the blame was to protect someone she loved. And it would not have been Doug. As good a friend as he had been back then, it would not have caused her to stop speaking for one year and agree to be locked up for five.

"Oh God!" She whimpered. "Oh God." She knew on some level he was basking in her agony but she didn't care. Pictures were flashing before her eyes at such a speed she could barely catch them. Only they were coming in no particular order and not yet in focus.

Doug had left the cellar after he shot her father. She ran up for help. She crashed into her grandmother's arms screaming, barely aware her mother had moved past her. Grandma had sent her into the house to phone for help and as she went to hang up the phone, she had heard more shots.

The phone fell from her fingers and she ran to the back of the house and out the backdoor, praying her grandmother was okay.

She took the cellar steps too fast and tripped on the bottom two and when she pulled her head up, relief filled her as she saw her grandma was fine. She didn't know how she would survive if anything had happened to her. Only then did she allow herself to look down at the hard, dirt floor.

She looked in horror at the bloody, disfigured mass she could only assume was her father and she began to gag. His face was, for all practical purposes, gone. Grandma put her strong, loving arms tightly around her and ushered her up the stairs and into the house. She took her to the bedroom she always used when she was visiting and had her lie on the bed, covering her with a handmade quilt that had always been Dena's favorite.

She awoke to voices outside her bedroom window.

When the sheriff got there she listened with disbelief as her own mother told the law that her daughter shot and killed her husband. She had always suspected her daughter was not quite right, but she never thought she was capable of something like this.

She screamed and cried that she never even touched the gun but they still took her away. No one believed that the respected Mava Landell would not be telling the truth about this terrible situation, and to help her through her grief, they rushed the trial and sent Deanna away to a juvenile home. There the young girl could be watched and perhaps obtain the treatment she so desperately needed.

When Dena repeatedly told counselors and anyone else who would listen she was innocent, her mother finally paid her a visit. Mrs. Landell, dressed sharply head-to-toe in widow black, told her daughter the awful truth. She told her to stop making all this fuss or she would end up killing her grandmother. As Dena stood with her mouth hanging open in surprise, she listened to her mother tell the tale of how it was in truth Grandmother she needed to protect. And, if she kept this up, they might take her away and throw away the key. At Grandma's age, she would never make it. They would be extremely cruel to an old woman in prison and she would surely rot there.

Her mother stood up and adjusted her stylish black hat and gave a glance back at her daughter. "Just shut up and finish your sentence, Dee-anna, or you really will be a killer." And with that she strode out the door.

Chapter Twenty-Six

How ironic that she should get her life back just as it was about to end. Images began bursting into her head, one after the other. Various scenes started to play out for her, some long forgotten and sweet. She saw the little girl she once was, mending a bird with a broken wing, feeding and nursing it until it was well enough to fly away. She had always felt she wasn't the nurturing kind, but now she could see she was wrong. She did not think of Paul, but instead it was Nick's face that came sharply into focus along with a heated memory of them making love. She saw his easy smile and those incredible blue eyes.

Doug hovered over her and she felt his hot breath on her face. "I have another surprise for you."

He was waiting for her to open her eyes so he could continue his torture.

"Well, don't you want to know what it is?" He sounded irritated at her lack of cooperation.

No, I've had enough surprises today, thanks. "Sure. What is the other surprise, Doug?" She tried her best to sound interested.

He put his mouth on her ear and whispered, "I was there when your dear grandmother died." He felt her entire body tense up and he paused so he could cherish her alarm and fear. He wasn't disappointed. "I stood over her and waved bye-bye as she left this world." He threw his head back and laughed joyously. "God, Dena, the look on your face is even better than my best fantasy."

He placed a kiss on her forehead that made her want to vomit.

"Thank you," he whispered.

"She died of a heart attack." She was unaware of the panic in her voice.

"True. True." He nodded in agreement. "She just dropped to the ground. Here we were having this nice little heart-to-heart about all the fun things I was going to do to you one day and the more I talked, the tighter she grabbed onto her chest. And the rest, shall we say, is history."

The voice that came out of her was unrecognizable. "You killed her."

"Well, technically, no. Bad ticker. But I didn't do anything to help her, you're right. And perhaps my graphic, elaborate description of my plans for you might have been the trigger for her unfortunate heart failure." He shrugged his shoulders as he stared off into space. "I was always envious of you growing up. I mean sure, your dad used to beat the stuffing out of you, but at least you had a dad. And your mother didn't have to work herself to the point of exhaustion every day. She was the perfect, proper lady and always looked fresh as a daisy. Your father was respected and loved by all the members of the community and you had one of those sweet old grandmothers to boot." He loosened the tight hold he had on her arm and let his hand roam freely to her abdomen, his fingers doing a seductive dance.

As he became aware of her again, he gazed into her eyes like they were two long-lost lovers finally able to come together again.

"God, I have wanted to do this for so long. I can't even remember a time when I didn't. And now that this time is finally here, I don't know where to begin." His hand moved up to her breast and began lightly tracing her nipple.

He had given her so much to think about that, for a moment, she forgot where she was. Until, that is, he put his hand on her breast. He gave her nipple a hard pinch and her entire body tensed up, bracing herself against the unwanted touch. She looked up at her wrist cuffed to the bedpost but then remembered she had taken her watch off when she undressed for bed.

"Wondering if you're lost in time again, Dena?" His voice sounded lower and now husky as his hand moved on to the other breast.

It took her by surprise that he knew her secret.

"Look behind me." He ducked his head out of the way so she could see. "See, I am not entirely heartless."

Behind him, mounted on the wall, was a large clock.

Her migraine was becoming increasingly worse and without her medication, there was no chance she would feel better soon. Her head felt like it would explode. She almost wished that if he was going to kill her, he would hurry up. She felt weak and very tired, so she didn't think she could muster up the energy to fight him off even if her hands weren't tied. He was larger, stronger and practically lying on top of her. What would be the point? Talking would be her only chance, that is, if he didn't bust her chops for speaking.

Her musing was interrupted by what sounded like some primitive animal sound. It took a minute for her to comprehend that it was Doug groaning.

He was hard and pressing against her thigh. So much for her homosexual theory. In fact, the hell with most of her theories and observations.

She felt Doug's hands wrap tightly around her throat, making it impossible for her to speak even if she could think of something useful to say. His grip tightened and his groaning increased.

The choking sensation in her throat was overwhelming.

Bursts of light like stars were going off behind her eyes and she tried to keep her lids clamped tight for fear the evil on his face would be the last thing she ever saw.

Then she felt him parting her legs with his knees and she knew what was next. Bile rose bitterly in the back of her throat.

She was aware he was saying something and it took a while for it to become clear.

"You'll have to forgive me, Dena. I've never been one for foreplay."

* * *

Nick was having an experience that every writer dreams of. Out of boredom, frustration and a reminder from his agent, he decided to get to work. He expected he would find himself staring at the blank screen of his laptop and thought he might be able to choke out a paragraph or two before calling it quits.

But to his astonishment, the minute his fingers hit the keys he was off and running. The story poured out so fast he could hardly type fast enough to keep up. And it was good. At least he thought it was a work of art and hoped it was not the ravings of a tired, horny, half-crazed man writing well after midnight. He would read it over in the morning just to be sure, but he felt he was on the right path.

His fingers flew over the keys and the roof could have fallen down around him before he would notice. Eventually, he would. He would stop to think about a word or try to remember a phrase he wanted to use and then he would slowly resurface. It was almost like coming out of a trance. He would check out his surroundings and notice for the first time things like the answering machine light blinking or that it had grown dark outside and he needed to put another light on.

Gradually Nick became aware that something like that was happening now. His fingers started to slow down until they finally stopped and rested on his keyboard. He looked around the room and waited to acknowledge whatever it was that broke his concentration. The house was dead silent and Dena was probably fast asleep.

That is when it hit him. Somewhere in the back of his mind he recalled hearing noises upstairs and thought she might be coming downstairs. He hadn't wanted to be interrupted and hoped she'd go back to bed.

That was most likely what she did and was now fast asleep. But the house just seemed...too quiet. He couldn't even say for sure how much time had passed since he heard the sounds above.

He knew now he would not be able to write another word until he checked it out. The former cop in him overruled the writer as he pressed a key to save his work then stood up to stretch out the kinks of sitting too long.

As he approached the stairs he felt the cold air and suddenly bolted up the stairs two to three steps at a time and when he reached her door, he threw it open with such force it bounced off the wall and came back and hit him. His eyes registered it all in seconds that seemed like an eternity.

The dying fire in the hearth. The book she had been reading fallen to the floor. Then there was the sliding glass door left open a few inches.

Shit. The scene played out quickly in his mind and a film of rage started to cloud his vision. He gave his head a hard shake to clear his disbelief. Then he got moving.

He ran around the room like an Olympic hopeful and grabbed her boots, socks, robe and a blanket as fresh fury filled him when he discovered she'd been dragged out in the cold with probably no more than a nightgown on. She's just not made for the cold, he thought angrily. And once again, damn it, not dressed for it.

As he started to sprint out the bedroom door something caught his eye. On the chair Dena had used to sit and enjoy the fire sat the book she had been reading. He recognized the cover. It was a current bestseller and he felt a flash of irritation that she hadn't been reading one of his.

Nick grabbed a coat for himself and his keys on the way out the door all the while mentally kicking his own ass for being so absorbed in his work he did not hear what he should have. Hell, knowing how he got when he was writing, he should not have even tried to complete a sentence, let alone several chapters.

Now he was trying to race to find Dena in the dead of night, tearing down the blackened road with only his headlights to lead the way. With no streetlights to guide his path and the roads covered in fresh snow, it made the journey almost impossible. But he would make it, he swore to himself. He would find her. After that, he wouldn't be responsible for his actions.

"Greenly," he said out loud as his hands gripped the steering wheel tightly, "you're a fucking dead man."

The drive took longer than forever and Nick wondered how he would ever live with himself if he was too late.

It wouldn't be the fact that he screwed up, which he did. But he was starting to realize how much he cared about Dena.

He did not want to care, and the knowledge that he did was not making him too happy. However, at the moment, he had more pressing things to think about.

Like snuffing the life out of Greenly. The sun was starting to rise as he yanked his cell phone out of his pocket and punched in Pete's number. With the agency's current workload, Nick knew Pete would be in the office early.

Pete's ever present, famous grin faded fast when he heard the tone of his friend's voice.

"He took her." His teeth were clenched so tight he was having trouble getting the words out. "I think I know where they are and I am on my way."

"OK. You armed?" Pete asked as he stood up, ready to take action.

"Yeah." Nick glanced down at his hand clenched into a fist. "Yeah, I'm armed."

"Tell me where you are headed and I'll call for the locals," Pete asked calmly, but was waving frantically for Margaret to come over to his desk. Taking in the look on Pete's face, she ran over and took the paper out of his hand.

"Let this be a lesson for us, Pete. Next time you really feel the need to kill someone, don't hesitate." With that, he hung up and concentrated at the job at hand. Driving.

* * *

Pain was everywhere. It filled and consumed her entire body, making it impossible to distinguish the exact source. Her head was ready to explode, her wrists were cut and bruised and the weight of his body was crushing her. She knew her bottom lip was bleeding and puffed out. He loosened his grip slightly on her neck, which she felt was only because he was not yet ready to end his fantasy. Her throat was on fire. The raw, burning sensation was so intense that she barely even noticed her feet were suffering the effects of the long walk barefoot through the snow.

Then he lowered his mouth and bit her nipple hard enough to draw blood, then did the same to her other breast. Dena screamed. First out of severe pain and then another, longer and born of sheer frustration. It was deep and soulful. It was a death wish.

Nick heard the scream just as he opened the back door. Unsure exactly where on the property Greenly would drag her, he had checked the cellar first. Knowing what a deranged idiot the man was, he would get off on the irony of taking her there.

But the rusted padlock was still clamped tightly on the old cellar doors so he moved on to the house over the barn and prayed he made the right call.

Her scream told him he had and to his credit, he faltered only for a second when he took in the sound. It almost brought him to his knees, but he kept on moving and followed the cry.

He exploded through the bedroom door much like he did back at the cabin. He stood silently as he took in the scene in front of him.

Greenly was naked and kneeling between her open legs, pushing them farther apart. He did not seem to hear the door crash open and made no move to stop.

This was a picture he was sure he would never get out of

his head or his nightmares. Dena's hands shackled to the bed-post and Greenly on top of her. He could see that her breasts were bleeding and felt his stomach turn.

He reached his enemy in two steps and wrapped his hands around Greenly's neck. He had wanted to break each bone in-dividually, to do a thorough and painful job of killing him, but he did not want to risk any delay in getting medical attention for Dena.

So instead, in one quick move, he reached down and got hold of Greenly's neck and rammed him into the wall. The force was so great that Nick was, after all, rewarded with the sound of breaking and crunching bones as Greenly dropped to the ground.

He didn't need to check for a pulse. He had felt the bone in his neck snap under his strength and if that had not done the trick, he was sure the bone fragments lodged now in the man's brain would finish the job.

He turned his attention to Dena, speaking calming, reassur-ing words while searching for the key. Knowing how anal Greenly was, he would have made sure it was left out in a con-venient place. He found it next to the boom box on the floor, which still played out love songs. He quickly shut it off, resist-ing the urge to smash it into a thousand pieces.

He freed her hands, covered her up with the thin blanket on the bed and reached for his cell phone. She was in shock and needed to get to a hospital. He was unsure of all her injuries and did not want to move her himself.

Frantically, he patted down his pockets and let out a stream of foul words when he realized he had left his phone in the car along with a warmer blanket and her clothes. He would have to leave her alone while he ran down to retrieve them. He hated to leave her side but he had no other choice.

All of a sudden, what sounded like a chopper very close by broke into his thoughts. He ran to the bedroom window and looked out to see if he was correct in guessing who it was.

A sleek, shiny black helicopter was landing on the yard next to the house and it was clearly not your standard police-issued model.

Shit. In his anger and arrogance to take care of this himself, he had not only neglected to arm himself or inform his partner where he was headed, but he also skipped notifying the police. He was so focused on Greenly that he temporarily forgot who the man was associated with. He remembered the house blowing up and ran back over to Dena.

Well, he was done. He would not leave Dena behind and there was no point in running with her. How far could he get with a wounded woman in his arms? He could hear the door crashing open downstairs and heavy footsteps now.

Nick's eyes swept the room quickly for a weapon or some means by which to suddenly save them. He swore at his own stupidity as he tore the room apart in search of a firearm. Dena would not have left with Greenly unless he had held a gun to her head.

He found what he was looking for under a blanket that had fallen on the floor, took the safety off and quickly checked for bullets.

He looked down at Dena and whispered an apology and placed a gentle kiss on her forehead.

He counted at least two different footsteps in the hall that were slowly approaching the door and there would most likely be more men behind them. He would be greatly outnumbered but he would not go down without a fight.

The first man through the door wore a grim expression and held a gun in his hand, which he pointed directly at Nick's head. He was huge and solid with hands like meat cleavers.

There was another man directly behind him, and though Nick could not see him, he was reasonably sure he would be sporting a weapon as well. The second man made his way cautiously around the first and quickly took in the sight of the bloody corpse on the floor, the woman on the bed and then finally Nick.

Their eyes met briefly but neither spoke nor moved.

"Nick, you're a lucky bastard to have me for a friend," the man said with an easy smile.

"Don't I know it. I have to say, Pete, I am sincerely impressed that you figured out where we were and managed to get a transport here so fast." He hadn't a clue how Pete had pulled this off.

"Nick, meet Kurt Kaven, police pilot and rescuer."

The two men shook hands and Nick gave him his genuine thanks. The man looked more like a professional wrestler or a bodyguard than a pilot but obviously Pete trusted him.

Pete crouched low on the floor to get a better look at Dena. "How's she doing?" he asked tentatively and gently moved the blanket away that was partially blocking her face to get a better look. "Jesus..." was all he could say and the disgust showed on his face.

"We need to get her out of here. I brought some warmer blankets and clothes for her; they are down in my car."

With that, Kurt turned around and ran out the door, yelling over his shoulder that he would meet them at the front door.

The sound of sirens was getting closer and Nick glanced over at Pete while carrying Dena out of the bedroom.

"I called the local sheriff just before we landed. Took them long enough. Listen, I'll stay here and square things away, you go with Kurt. He will get you to a hospital."

The sheriff came running over just as Nick was lifting Dena into the chopper. The older man's pot belly jiggling as he sprinted over was almost comical. Nick paused long enough to show him and his deputy that she was okay, but needed medical attention as soon as possible. He had no intention of sticking around chatting with the locals when Dena needed help.

Pete took charge of the situation and pushed Nick into the chopper, told the locals to move back and duck and gave Kurt the thumbs up to take off. With that, he turned his attention back to the men.

"Thank you for getting here so quickly, gentleman." He flashed them his professional, courteous smile and both men simply stared at him. He could tell the sheriff was a tad put out and was getting ready to give him a lecture on jurisdiction so he started directing them to the house. "I'll be happy to help you in any way I can. Oh, and you might want to grab your evidence kit and camera. We have a homicide inside," Pete said in a matter-of-fact tone once the helicopter was on its way. He hid his legendary smile when he saw the young deputy turn a sickly shade of green and walked them upstairs. Ah, the many perks of his job.

Epilogue

"Finding her proved a little more difficult than I thought."

"Well, I did offer my expertise," Pete said as he stopped typing, leaned back into the chair and lifted a memo off the desk.

"I know. I had to do it alone."

"Does she know about the book yet?"

"No. I don't know." Then he added, "I haven't actually talked to her yet." Nick walked with his cell phone over to the large bay window and stared out at the water.

That got his attention. Pete put the piece of paper he was half reading down and frowned. "I thought you said you were calling from inside her living room?"

"I am. But she's not here at the moment. I'm just having a look around," Nick answered absently, his eyes drinking in the spectacular view.

If Pete was concerned that his best friend had turned into a stalker and a burglar, he didn't say so.

Pete said after a pause, "Do you plan on making contact with her anytime soon? 'Cause I gotta tell you, the suspense is killing Margaret." He laughed. He had never heard his friend behave like this before and found it unnerving, but amusing.

Nick stiffened as a figure down by the water started to come slowly into focus. In the distance, a stunning blonde in a white bikini made her way leisurely up the brick path to the waterfront condo. The ocean breeze was doing something wonderful with her hair and it reminded him of a shampoo commercial.

"I'll talk to you later," Nick mumbled as he disconnected the call and slid the phone into his pocket, his eyes never losing sight of the vision in front of him. His mouth had turned dry as the desert.

Mesmerized, he stood still and watched her bend over and pick up a flower, smell it and then tuck it behind her ear. And then...she smiled.

Her face was ingrained forever in his memory and he was sure he would have recognized her at first glance no matter what the distance. He also thought, with his background, it should have been a cinch to find her. But instead, he had spent almost a week on a stakeout to be sure it was indeed her and almost three months before that to locate her.

He shook his head as he watched her and thought if he hadn't wasted an entire week confirming it was her, he would certainly have a few doubts now.

Her hair was a little longer, bleached by the sun and worn simply around her shoulders. She was trim, tan and could snag a job easily for Playboy if she wanted to.

But it was her eyes that held the greatest change. The windows of the soul told of a different Dena. Gone was that protective, hurt look.

They were now mirrors of a carefree, happy person who seemed to be holding a magnificent secret. She appeared to truly be enjoying life, hidden away here in her new environment.

She had done an astounding disappearing act, as promised. She had said when she was well enough to travel, she would be gone. And one day, well over a year ago, she walked away. It was almost like she had vanished into thin air.

And she had been damn near impossible to find. She had tucked herself away in a remote area of Costa Rica, which was the last place he thought to look.

He had given them both time to heal. About seven months' worth. He finished his book and made a few casual attempts to find her along the way, thinking that when he was ready he would pick up the phone and locate her. But when he felt that they both had had enough space and it was time to continue their relationship, he discovered she was long gone.

He had used every resource, called in each and every favor and even broken a few laws. He became a desperate man. He wanted to see her. Hell, he would be happy just being able to talk to her.

And finally, there she was walking towards him. He knew she could not see him yet, or she would not still be smiling.

She had made it very clear she wanted to vanish. Reinvent herself. Forget about this life and put as many miles as possible between the two of them. She wanted a clean, fresh start. *Alone.*

Suddenly, he felt a little tense as he watched her get closer. He did not think she would be too pleased to see that he had broken into her condo and was hanging out in her living room. He was not even sure what the hell he would say now that he was here other than yell out, 'surprise.'

But he hadn't moved heaven and earth to find her and not have his say.

She stopped on the brick patio where she must have been sunning herself before she took her walk. A chaise lounge had a big yellow towel draped across the back and a round white table next to it held a bottle of water, sunscreen and a book.

His eyes stayed on the book and he recognized the cover immediately, of course. If he flipped the book over he would be staring at a picture of himself.

His first book with the name of Nick O'Neal on the front cover instead of his pen name.

It was also his first piece of non-fiction. And it was a bestseller, exactly as Dena had once sarcastically predicted. Inside the dedication read: "To Dena...wherever you may be. I hope you find what you are searching for."

He had wanted to say more. Needed to, actually. But he could not bring his fingers to keep typing. The rest, he knew, had to be said in person.

He had been half hoping she would not have read the book yet. What he had written was all truth and extremely fair to her; in fact, he had made her the hero of the story. Which, of course, she was.

But it was also tremendously personal and divulged a lifetime of secrets that he did not have permission to tell. Even though the newspapers had a field day when the police broke the story, it was different having your entire life story, things you recently just discovered yourself, put all into one tell-all book.

He realized he was procrastinating. After all, he had been over this before with himself and anyone else who would listen a half a dozen times.

* * *

Dena took in a deep breath of the intoxicating ocean air and sat down in her lounge chair. She did not think she could ever get bored with this amazing view. She loved the solitude of living out here. She could not get enough of the peace and quiet.

She had spent countless hours when she first arrived out on the beach, staring at the water or walking along the shore. She enjoyed watching the sun set and rise and cherished the rhythms of nature. Her new atmosphere was most tranquil and with all of that, came great healing, understanding and eventually, forgiveness. She felt simply wonderful and, finally, at peace.

The euphoria was not instant, however. She had made a few plans while recovering in the hospital and then the day she was released, she went to work setting up her new life. She was beaten up, bruised and hurt from head to toe, but all she had wanted to do was to pack up and get out.

It took some time, but she did it. She sold all that she had left, which consisted of the home and property in the small town of Hert and her car. That, along with the insurance money from her house and a fairly generous savings account, bought her a new life.

Dena knew that Brad would take excellent care of her former patients and she said as much when she called to say good-bye.

She had chosen Costa Rica after reading about it a travel magazine and called up a real estate agent to find the perfect spot.

Packing was easy. Everything in her home had been destroyed so that only left the clothes on her back and a few things she purchased to tide her over until she moved.

She absently reached behind her back and undid the clasp of her bikini top, took it off and let it drop to the ground. She gave a slight laugh at how free she felt to do whatever she liked and reflected back to how she was when she first arrived at her new retreat.

It had taken her a week to venture outside. The first few days she had been afraid to close her eyes. She kept her ear bent, expecting to hear something like the phone ringing or worse, the door being forced open. Terrified that if she closed her eyes, someone would drag her off in the middle of the night. Finally, she had a security system installed and broke down and took a sleeping pill. She slept for two days.

Each day she felt a little better. Stronger. The rest, exercise, fresh air and time alone eventually healed her. She had started a journal to record her progress and soon found herself writing a book of her own. A self-help book for victims of violent crime. It was like a continuation of her previous practice and it made her feel good.

Each day she woke, made coffee and went over to the one piece of furniture she had shipped to her new home. It had been Paul's desk, the one she had left in storage. When she got rid of the storage unit, she had gone through and pitched or donated everything. But when she came across the desk, she remembered what Nick had said about her giving away something with such history. He was right; it was a beautiful desk after all. And though Paul had done some pretty shitty things, she did have a few fond memories of him. But to be truthful, when she looked at the desk, she was thinking more of Nick than her late husband.

Nick's mouth had gone beyond dry when she took off her top. He stood silently inside the patio door and simply watched. He knew if he spoke the spell would be broken. Not to mention he would scare the daylights out of her, which was not exactly the way he wanted to start this reunion.

But he was utterly aroused and felt a bit like a peeping Tom standing there in the shadows spying on her. Hell, he had once arrested a man for doing something like this.

"Dena," Nick said softly.

Her eyes flew open wide to find Nick standing in front of her. She blinked several times, but his image was still there.

Their eyes locked together and neither said anything. Nick wondered if she remembered she had taken her top off and though he warned them not to, his eyes traveled on their own down for a peek.

She saw his eyes roaming down to her breasts and she flushed. She quickly reached behind the chair for her beach towel to cover up.

"Don't bother on my account," he said with a grin. His mouth had gone from dry to drooling.

She was speechless. First, she was in shock to find him, or for that matter, anyone standing on her patio. And second, she was not used to talking. Other than exchanging a few pleasantries when she went into town to shop, she saw or spoke to no one.

When she felt well enough, she had allowed herself to think about him. She had done a great job of convincing herself that what they had was a byproduct of having been lonely and thrown into a dangerous situation together. Besides, he was so good looking, who in their right mind could resist?

She no longer allowed herself to fantasize during the day, after all, what good could come out of it? But at night it was a different story. She tried not to recall her dreams the next day, but they somehow would find their way into her thoughts. In fact, she had a rather interesting dream of a sexual nature last night and now seeing him stand in front of her made her blood rush to her face. Her hands would have flown to her face if they were not covering up her breasts.

Why did he have to come here and spoil everything?

Her face was turning red, which he did not take to be a good sign. She looked like she was going to let loose and let him have it so he should probably speak his peace first. He had rehearsed his speech a thousand times on the way here.

Only now he could not remember one damn word of it, so he bent down and picked the sexy white bathing suit top up off the ground and held it out to her.

"Here. Put this on." He turned his back to her and shoved his hands in his pockets and waited. "It wasn't easy finding you, Dena," he said after a few seconds.

"It wasn't supposed to be." She tested out her voice and it seemed to be working; it was merely a little raspy.

Nick had turned back around and raised his eyebrow at her as if to question the new sound coming from her. God, she looked...striking. She even sounded sexy. "You look incredible."

She heard the sincerity in his voice and she was surprised. She never put on make-up anymore or did a thing with her hair; after all, who would acknowledge her efforts? She hardly glanced in the mirror when she was brushing her teeth.

He pulled a straight-back chair over by her and sat down and for the first time, she got a good look at him. His eyes, though they still possessed that remarkable shade of blue, looked tired. It occurred to her he probably was and felt her heart soften a little.

"What do you think of it so far?" He nodded towards the hardcover he had sweated blood and tears over.

She hesitated briefly before replying. "It's actually very

good, Nick." Her eyes met his and held them. "I was prepared to hate it and its author. But, I am finding it accurate and sensitive. It is almost as if I am reading about someone else's life. I have to remind myself it is about me. Strangely, though, I am finding it therapeutic." Then she smiled at him. "You were very thorough with your research."

He almost fell off his chair. He was expecting anger. He did not anticipate praise and gratitude.

"You look shocked, Nick," she said when she noticed the look on his face. "Didn't you think it was any good?"

"I just wasn't prepared for you to like it. I am glad you do, of course. I thought you would hate me for writing it."

"Oh, I did, trust me." She seemed puzzled for a minute. "If you were so sure I wouldn't like it, why did you send it to me?"

Confused, he answered, "I didn't."

Her eyebrows arched and she reached over to the table and picked up the book, opening the front cover. She held it open for Nick to read.

Dear Dena,

As you know, without you this book would not be possible. Thank you for your bravery and inspiration. You are the hero in this story.

Love always,

Nick

Nick stared at the book a second longer then looked up to meet her eyes. "When did you get this?"

"It arrived in the mail over a month ago. I'll confess it took me a while to start reading it, I was afraid it would be too painful." She had actually been livid when the book came, her temper cooling slightly after she read the inscription inside. After that she had been too frightened to even peek at the first chapter. Then one day, out of the blue, she wanted to read it. She was ready. And now she was on the last chapter.

"I wish it had been me that sent it to you and who signed it over to you. But the truth is, I only found out a couple of weeks ago where you were."

She looked skeptical. "Who could have known where I was before you?"

He laughed. "Someone who is a better detective than I am."

She had not wanted to be found; she enjoyed the solitude and tranquility she had discovered with her new life. But now that he was sitting here, next to her, she realized how lonely she was. And that she had desperately missed him.

"How long can you stay, Nick?"

"Is that an invitation?" He wore that playful grin that made her want to jump on his lap.

She laughed. "I guess it is. You can stay as long as you want." She was stunned to hear herself saying that and she could tell Nick was surprised as well.

"It just so happens that my schedule is very flexible at the moment." His expression turned a little more serious. "I put my condo up for sale and Pete has been running the office in my absence. I think he wants me out of his hair. He offered to buy me out with the promise to feed me story lines if I should ever get writers block. I can do my writing from here if that sounds okay to you."

It took a second for her to be sure he was not teasing.

"That sounds okay to me." Actually, it sounded more than okay to her. She did not want to make any plans for the future just yet, but only enjoy each new day. She did want to finish the book she was writing, not only because it was good therapy for her, but also because it might help others.

She stood up slowly and walked over to him and sat on his lap so they were facing each other, her legs straddling his chair. "Are you sure you won't miss the big city life back home?"

He responded by kissing her passionately. One hand went up to get a handful of that thick blonde hair while the other masterfully undid her little bikini top one-handed, like the trained professional that he was.

Printed in the United States
138783LV00002B/1/P